A DEATH IN VALENCIA

A DEATH IN VALENCIA

Jason Webster

Chatto & Windus
LONDON

Published by Chatto & Windus 2012

2 4 6 8 10 9 7 5 3 1

First published in Great Britain in 2012 by
Chatto & Windus
Random House, 20 Vauxhall Bridge Road,
London SW1V 2SA
www.randomhouse.co.uk

Addresses for companies within The Random House Group Limited can be found at:
www.randomhouse.co.uk/offices.htm

The Random House Group Limited Reg. No. 954009

A CIP catalogue record for this book
is available from the British Library

ISBN 9780701185084

The Random House Group Limited supports The Forest Stewardship Council (FSC®), the leading
international forest certification organisation. Our books carrying the FSC label are printed on
FSC® certified paper. FSC is the only forest certification scheme endorsed by the leading
environmental organisations, including Greenpeace. Our paper procurement
policy can be found at www.randomhouse.co.uk/environment

Typeset in Garamond by Palimpsest Book Production Limited,
Falkirk, Stirlingshire
Printed and bound by
CPI Group (UK) Ltd, Croydon, CR0 4YY

For Ollie, Nikki, Lena and Maddie
y en memoria de Javier Botella

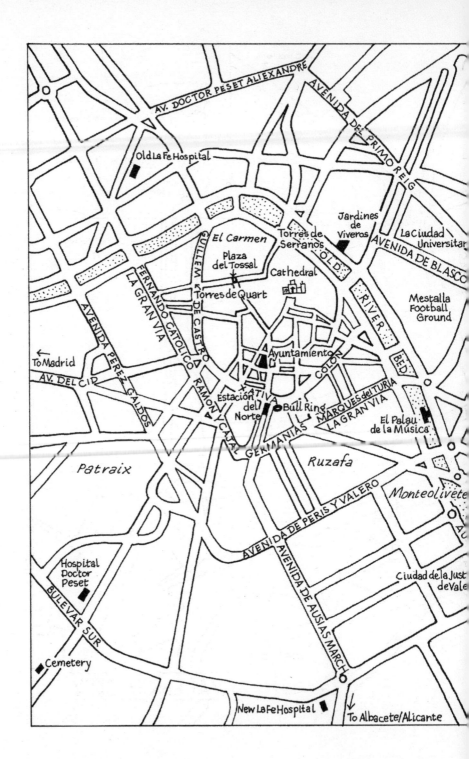

To Barcelona

SPAIN

Barcelona

Madrid

VALENCIA

Albacete

Seville

La Universidad
Politécnica

AVENIDA DE NARANJOS

La Universidad
Politécnica

Malverrosa
Beach

IBAÑEZ

El Cabanyál

AVENIDA DEL PUERTO

AVENIDA DE FRANCIA

Ciudad de las
Artes y las Ciencias

The Port

DEL SALER

Natzaret

VALENCIA CITY

You are a little soul, carrying a corpse.

Epictetus

Note

There are several police forces in Spain. Chief Inspector Max Cámara works for the *Cuerpo Nacional de Policía*, or *Policía Nacional*, which deals with major crimes in the larger towns and cities. The *Guardia Civil* is largely a rural police force, or gendarmerie, covering the countryside and smaller towns and villages, although it also carries out border duties and sea patrols, takes part in operations abroad, and has city-based headquarters. Both the *Policía Nacional* and *Guardia Civil* report to the Interior Ministry, although the *Guardia Civil* is paramilitary and has links with the Defence Ministry.

In addition to these national forces, towns and cities tend to have a local police force – the *Policía Local*, also known as the *Policía Municipal*. This deals with smaller crimes, official engagements and traffic duties, and is under the control of each respective Town Hall. A member of the *Policía Local* may sometimes be referred to as a '*Municipal*'.

ONE

Sunday 5th July

The green-and-white *Guardia Civil* patrol boat looked out of place so close to the shoreline. Its sharp-cut lines and metallic sheen spoke of thrust and speed in a place where people sought the softening embrace of sand, the gentle peal of waves and the caress of the sun. Sitting there motionless, an invasive presence, it was unclear what was causing the greater disturbance: its own arrival, or what it had come for.

A couple of *Policías Nacionales* from the squad car accompanied him as he found an alleyway cutting through the row of cafés and paella restaurants and headed towards the beach. Along the promenade a few heads turned towards the sea trying to make out what was going on, but the terraces were filled mostly with early-evening drinkers, children eating ice cream, and overheated waitresses carrying heavy, laden trays through a tide of discarded straws and paper serviettes. Above their heads, palm trees arched into the humid blue sky, while yellow-and-white flags from the lamp posts rippled as they caught an unlikely breeze.

Ignoring the main entrance to the beach a few yards away, he skipped over the low wall and on to the sand. The presence of uniformed policemen among the bystanders seemed to confirm to most that whatever was going on was serious, and needed to be witnessed. Yet already different types were discernible, like competing currents of water: those moving away, not wanting to see; others flowing in. From underneath their mirror sunglasses, he saw the eyes of the officers with him darting over the array of exposed flesh as they grimly maintained their expressions of serious business-at-hand. He, too, was conscious of rounded forms, of browning skin and wet black hair streaking over naked shoulders. But there was only ever one body for him.

A second group of *Policías Nacionales* was standing on the shoreline. He felt sand seeping into his shoes as the officer in charge saluted and held out a hand to shake.

'Been there at least half an hour,' he said, nodding in the direction of the *Guardia Civil* boat.

On the deck, he could make out the captain standing with his legs wide apart, a green cap on his head and his eyes shaded by the black binoculars he was holding up with both hands. They were so close that the two groups of law officers could almost talk to one another without needing to shout, but he knew that so far there had been no communication. A stand-off. Whoever was first to breach the silence would later get the paperwork load describing every step of protocol, every detail of what happened next.

And all the responsibility if things went wrong.

The police officer handed him a pair of binoculars, the same Interior Ministry standard issue that was being trained on him at that moment. He'd already seen the body as he'd walked over the wide expanse of the beach, already sensed in his guts who it was, but nonetheless he focused the glasses on the floating, bloated form as it lay still in the tranquil Mediterranean waters, exactly halfway between the *Guardia Civil* boat and the *Policía Nacional* officers lining the shore, with a thousand sunbathers at their backs.

Half an hour, and still no one had made a move. The *Guardia Civil* captain would be wondering what would happen now that this more senior policeman had showed up. He'd be weighing him up, concluding, quite correctly, that being out of uniform he was a *Judicial*, an investigating cop. And from the way the others in his group deferred to him, he was almost certainly an inspector, perhaps even chief inspector, although on the young side. Still, superior enough to make a call on this, to break the impasse.

So whose was it? A body out at sea was *Guardia Civil* property. On land, here in the city, a stiff belonged to the *Nacionales*. And this one just couldn't decide which way it wanted to go. Caught between earth and water, floating in a legal grey area in the unmoving, shimmering blue. He glanced down at his feet: other detritus from the Mediterranean appeared to have less of a problem finding its way ashore. The usual collection of driftwood, scraps of plastic, seaweed and used contraceptives had found refuge on the pale brown sand, discarded rubbish and waste from the ships in the port just a few metres away.

He trained the binoculars again on the body. A light westerly *poniente* breeze was blowing across from the plains and flattening the sea, which stretched out ahead like a sheet of glass. No waves, no currents to push the body in either one direction or the other.

For a moment he became aware of the crowds behind them. There were the usual groups for a weekend in early July: couples, families, professional sunbathers, elderly men with their lives in plastic carrier bags and nowhere else to go, teenagers still feeling their way around their changing bodies, students pretending to revise for the September retakes. He saw that a large number of them had yellow-and-white rucksacks, the same colours as the flags further back: free gifts from the Church preparing for the Pope's visit later in the week to head the World Families Conference.

There was another sound, though, another group among all these: the sound of light giggling mixed in with the occasional cry. There were children on this beach, dozens of them. Some with their parents, others in a small group from the El Cabanyal district just behind them. For half an hour police officers had been standing here watching a dead body breaking the surface while kids were still splashing in the water only yards away.

He took one last look at the floater, then up at the *Guardia Civil* captain, a rage willing itself into life inside him. Strictly, this was a *Guardia Civil* job. The man should have sent a dinghy out there and pulled the body back out to the boat. But something about his posture, something about his appearance, made Cámara relent. There was a look about him he had seen before, something he'd caught sight of in his colleagues, and in himself on occasion, something that, at times at least, seemed to be growing more frequent: the frozen, almost death-like expression that came when real decisions had to be made, and responsibility taken. This wasn't bloody-mindedness on the captain's part, it was inertia brought on by the bureaucratic labyrinth he could see himself getting caught in if he took just one step.

Handing the binoculars back to the officer at his side, he slipped off his shoes and pulled the belt from around his waistband, folding his jacket and laying it on the sand.

'I'm going in,' he said. 'Send two others to come with me.'

A foreign backpacking couple were sitting up and watching from nearby. He walked over to them and through sign language and a few words of English, made them understand he wanted some toothpaste. Reluctantly, a white tube was handed over; Cámara checked the writing on the side, then slapped a thick amount just under his nose to create a protruding blue Hitler moustache. After ordering the two officers volunteered for the job to do the same, he gave the tube back to the bemused tourists.

Bodies fished from water stank. Most people simply couldn't cope with the putrid, rotten stench. Those with strong stomachs only managed to do so by disguising it with the one thing that worked: menthol.

By the time they'd reached the body and brought it closer to the shore, a first group of crime scene officers from the *Policía Científica* had arrived and were putting up screens to form an area of relative privacy. Meanwhile, the uniformed officers were moving people on, trying to empty the beach as best they could. Cámara and the two volunteers waited in the water for a couple of minutes for plastic sheets to be laid on the sand before finally the order was given for the body to be hauled out. As soon as it was clear what was happening, the *Guardia Civil* boat powered away in a white arc, heading towards the port.

Confirmation would come later, but it was already clear who they'd found, despite the effects of being in warm seawater for over a week. Pep Roures's distinctive ginger hair looked brighter than usual against the green-black marbling of his skin. Any doubt that it wasn't the fifty-year-old had been removed in Cámara's own mind by the sight of the tattoo still visible on the corpse's left shoulder: a paella dish, complete with green beans and bright yellow rice. Few artists, he imagined, were asked to scratch out one of those.

He stood to one side for a moment, feeling the salt water dry on his skin as he tried to forget the stench of decay that seemed to have penetrated his brain. First the *científicos*, then the *médico forense* and

4

the investigating judge and his team from the City of Justice, would be showing up. The usual circus surrounding the dead – at least while they still mattered to people. Then they would all be gone and he'd be left alone.

With his murder.

His before the body had even been spotted here off the Malvarrosa beach. Pep Roures had disappeared from his home and restaurant in El Cabanyal seven days before, and from the start Cámara had known it was more than a simple missing persons case. Something about the man, something about what he'd seen of his place, told him Roures had never intended to vanish. Besides, La Mar was his life. They all knew him, they'd all eaten there at some point. The restaurant was virtually an institution among Valencians. Or a certain kind of Valencian. Where would Roures go to? No one had seen him. No one really knew if he had anywhere else to go. He was dead. An accident? Perhaps. They'd just needed to find the body.

Back up at the promenade, he spotted a green uniform breaking through the dark blue line of the *Nacionales*. The face was almost familiar now. Rubbing his hand through his hair a last time to shake off the water, and wiping the remains of the toothpaste from his top lip, he strode barefoot and shirtless over the sand. Others might have waited, let the bastard come all the way, but they'd be better off speaking out of earshot of their respective colleagues.

The *Guardia Civil* captain stopped a few yards short and saluted.

'Captain Herrero, of the *Servicio Marítimo*,' he said sharply.

'Cámara. *Homicidios*.' There was a pause while the other man waited for him to fill in the missing information. 'Er, chief inspector.'

Cámara held out a hand to shake before the captain could begin his prepared spiel excusing himself over what had happened.

'It's ours,' Cámara said as he sniffed at the salt water dripping from the end of his nose. 'I know the guy. Went missing a while back. I was already looking into it.'

Captain Herrero stood motionless, his brow glistening in the heat trapped under his cap. He was taller than Cámara, with a sinewy strength in his limbs. Late twenties, perhaps early thirties. Still young enough to care.

'He was practically on the beach already.'

'What's that?' Herrero said, seeming to come to life of a sudden.

'I said it's ours. You won't be hearing from me. Or from anyone in *Homicidios*.'

The captain let out a sigh.

'Half our lot are off sick,' he said, shaking his head. 'Depression. Can't cope with the new hours they've given us. Arse of a new general has come in changing all our rotas. *Estamos jodidos*.' We're fucked.

Cámara forced a sympathetic smile.

'We're not even treading water with the drug runs along the coast. The last thing we needed was—'

'It's OK,' Cámara said. 'Really. If you can fix things at your end, no one's going to hear from us about you spotting the body. Understood?'

Herrero looked him in the eye. Yes, something told him he could trust this half-naked police chief inspector.

'I owe you one.'

'Forget it,' Cámara said. 'Besides, *el muerto es del mar cuando la tierra lejos está.*'

'*¿Qué?*'

'One of my grandfather's old proverbs: A dead man only belongs to the sea if land is far away.'

TWO

The entrance-hall light was still on when he got back to his block of flats in Ruzafa, and he found his downstairs neighbour, Susana, struggling with a buggy as her one-year-old did his best to scatter toys over the stairs.

'Here, let me help.'

'Could you just grab Tomás for me?' she said with a sigh. 'He's in an exploring phase at the moment. Boxes, cupboards, bags – he absolutely has to know what's inside them all.'

Cámara leaned down to pick the baby up.

'Come on, *chiquitín*.'

Tomás gave a whine as he was dragged away from his brightly coloured plastic keys, then stared up into Cámara's face and giggled.

'You're growing pretty fast.' Cámara stroked his head. 'And a nice crop of hair growing up here as well, I can see. Unlike some of us.'

Susana smiled as she picked up the buggy and started climbing the stairs.

'I'm glad we're only on the first floor,' she said. 'I can't imagine having to carry him all the way to the top every day.'

'There was talk of putting in a lift once,' Cámara said. 'Years back. But the landlady refuses to spend any money on the place.' He shrugged.

Tomás had rested his head on Cámara's shoulder and was now chewing at his neck.

'He's teething,' Susana said. 'I'm sorry. Probably kept you awake last night with his crying.'

'Didn't hear a thing. I'm a heavy sleeper.'

Susana placed the buggy down in front of her door.

'Here, let me take him.'

Tomás allowed himself to be prised away and slid into his mother's grip.

'I'll just run down and get your bags,' Cámara said.

'Oh, really. I can get them later.'

But he was already halfway down the stairs.

'So, you ready for His Holiness coming next week?' she said with a raised eyebrow as he returned. 'They're talking about a million people descending on the city.'

'I'd happily leave town,' Cámara said. 'But they've cancelled all leave. Security. Just in case someone takes a potshot at him, or something.'

'I bet there are plenty in this city that wouldn't mind having a try.'

'Yeah, that's why I'd like to get out. Resist the temptation.'

It was only when she giggled that she really looked as young as she was. Having a baby, and then being left to look after it on her own, seemed to have put extra years on her. But laughter exposed the twenty-five-year-old she actually was. She'd moved in just a few months before giving birth to Tomás. Cámara had only bumped into the father a couple of times before he'd vanished.

'Have you seen the flag Esperanza's hung from her balcony?'

Cámara rolled his eyes.

'No, I haven't. Let me guess, another Vatican banner?'

'You'd kind of expect it from her, I suppose. Someone of her age. But they're everywhere. I never knew we were surrounded by so many fans of the Pope. It's like they're all coming out of the woodwork, or something.'

They heard the click of the main door in the hall beneath them, and stopped talking. Looking over the staircase railings, Cámara spotted the shape of a young man in an orange T-shirt.

'*Propaganda*,' the man called.

'Just delivering junk mail,' Cámara explained.

'It's like we're having to talk in secret,' Susana said. 'In case anyone overhears. I'm thinking of putting up one of those anti-Pope banners on my balcony. They're spending millions of public money on this, but I certainly didn't invite him.'

'He's not scheduled to come round this part of town. Not with the metro works.'

Susana rolled her eyes. For over a year life in their normally quiet street had been disrupted by the extension of the number 2 metro line: the road had been torn up and traffic diverted. Pneumatic drills hammered incessantly at the tarmac during the day, while lorries wheeled tonnes of sodden earth away through the night, keeping the local people awake with the rumbling of engines and their high-pitched safety wail when they reversed. Sleeping in summer with the windows closed was impossible, so there was nothing to filter out the racket. Complaints had been made to Valconsa, the construction company carrying out the work for the Town Hall, but the noise never abated.

'They'll only show him the pretty bits,' Susana said.

Tomás had grown bored of sitting in his mother's arms by now, and was exploring the top of her chest with his hands and mouth in search of sustenance.

'I'd better take him inside and give him a feed,' she said, pushing the buggy and her bags through the open door with her foot. 'He's getting hungry.'

'OK. Just give me a shout if you need anything.'

Cámara walked up the next flight of stairs to his own flat, and unlocked the door. In the silence he could hear Susana cooing to Tomás from the floor below. These buildings had been put up on the cheap in the decades after the Civil War, when sound insulation had only been for the wealthier parts of the city. Here you were forced into a very intimate cohabitation with your neighbours, whether you liked them or not.

In the tiny kitchen he found a two-day-old piece of bread, cut it in half lengthways and placed it face down in a small dry frying pan. The familiar smell, like burnt chicken feathers, rose up when he lit the gas with an old cigarette lighter, catching the hairs on his fingers as the blue flame whooshed into life. He waited until smoke began to waft up from the bread, then flicked it on to the marble counter, cutting a piece of Manchego cheese to place on top, with a leathery slice of *jamón serrano*, showing the beginnings of a greenish sheen, to finish off his impromptu toasted sandwich. Grabbing a can of Mahou beer from the fridge, he sat down on the sofa and started to eat.

A cheap print of Klimt's *The Kiss* hung on the opposite wall, and he found himself concentrating on it as he chewed, the bright gold, the power of the man's embracing shoulders, the pale skin of the woman's arm and face. He forced his eyes to stare at it, to absorb its details, willing away the visions of Roures's rotting corpse shuddering though his mind, and the sound of the baby in the flat below. It had meant something to him once, this print, when the woman who had given it to him was still a presence in his life, and ideas of having a little Tomás of their own scuttling around their feet had been a shared hope, however briefly.

He put the unfinished sandwich down on the sofa beside him and stood up. He wasn't hungry. He should go out, have a drink. Or something. Vicent, the guy who ran the bar on the corner, was friendly enough. At least to exchange a few words with, chat about the news. Sometimes Cámara relied on him to find out what was going on in the world – or in the city anyway. Commissioner Pardo could never quite forgive Cámara for his aversion to newspapers.

His hand reached down to the bookcase where he kept his special wooden box. Just a small one, he thought to himself. Take the edge off. No point going anywhere given the way I am right now.

His fingers found the paper, the crispy leaves and spare cigarette, and began their work, breaking, rubbing, moulding and rolling, before lifting the joint up to his tongue so he could lick it tight. It had been a few days since the last one. He deserved this. Needed it.

The smoke bit into his lungs as he reached for another chair and slumped down. The sandwich looked back at him from the sofa across the room. It would stay there for a couple more days until the sight of its desiccating form would finally force him to throw it in the bin. Why didn't he reach out now and dispose of it? Later. It would mean getting up, and getting up required energy, something he seemed to be lacking recently.

He shifted his chair round and looked back up at the print on the wall. A kiss. Memories told him he had kissed like that, that moments of merging with someone else had once formed part of his life, but it was intellectual knowledge only, like opening a drawer in high summer and finding woollen winter clothes, struggling to remember what it felt like to put them on.

His eyes twitched to one side as he spotted something out of place. A line running almost vertically up the wall on the far side of the print.

Taking another drag on the joint, he hauled himself up to have a look. The light from the lamp wasn't very bright, but as he ran his fingers over the mottled plaster he could feel the crack. Had it been there before? He couldn't remember. It might have been there for a while, perhaps even since he moved in. But the fact that it had caught his attention now made him doubt that. The building was rotting from the ground up. Only a couple of weeks before, workmen had had to come round to connect them to the main sewerage system. It turned out all the waste had been seeping into the ground for years. Which was why there was so much damp. Susana downstairs had complained of it a couple of times: the paint job they'd given the flat just before Tomás was born had barely lasted six months before it started peeling off. They'd only found out the truth thanks to the work on the metro line. Digging down five or six metres in such watery earth had brought a few surprises, setting back the construction timetable by months.

And now this. A crack running up his wall. He'd keep an eye on it. Perhaps even measure it just to be sure. But later. Tomorrow perhaps.

The joint had gone out and he reached over for the lighter, falling back into his chair. The tiredness seemed to have got worse in the past few days. Was it the Roures case? They hadn't come up with much since he'd gone missing, and now the body had finally floated to the surface; he'd get confirmation from the forensic doctor in the morning, but he was certain that Roures had been violently attacked.

But it wasn't that, not the sense of making little progress. Something else? In the past just the mystery itself, the need to repair – in however messy a fashion – the tear in the fabric that each murder signified for him gave him the drive to carry on. Now he seemed to be losing that. Why? He asked himself every day. And though he felt he should know the answer, expecting it to be as close to him as the pulse in his throat, he could never say.

As it often did in these moments, the phone on the table seemed to signal to him. And as ever he ran Alicia's Madrid phone number through his mind, the one he had thought about calling so many evenings. He couldn't remember the last time he'd actually memorised a number: they were all stored inside mobile phones these days. And the truth was he hadn't really made an effort to learn it. At least not consciously. But it had stuck, almost from the moment he had seen it in an email months back.

Call me some time.

And he never had.

He picked up the receiver and held it to his ear, then pushed down with his fingers. He could hear the phone at the other end singing out. Once. Twice . . . There was a click as it was picked up.

'*¿Sí?* came a gruff voice.

Not Madrid tonight. Not Madrid ever.

An Albacete number. The only other one he knew by heart.

THREE

'You usually wait at least a month.'

'What's that?'

'You were here only a fortnight ago. You usually wait at least a month since your last visit before calling.'

'Oh.'

'On your own?'

'Yes. Well, of course. Would I be ringing you if I weren't?'

'That's the point, then.'

'What?'

'You're on your own. Calling me.'

Cámara was silent for a moment.

'All right. Take your point. What am I doing calling my grandfather at eleven at night when I should be out with someone else.'

'I didn't say you should be out with them. You could be in the sack. Probably should be in the sack. But you need someone else to talk to. I'm not going to be around for ever.'

Cámara frowned. Hilario had never been one for talking about his own death, despite his advanced years.

'Well, I've called you now. It's a bit late to go out and pick someone up.'

'Eleven o'clock? In Valencia? It's a bit early, I'd say.'

'The city's changing. Not so much of a fiesta atmosphere these days. At least on a Sunday night.'

'Or you're changing, more like. Getting old before your time. Don't expect me to come to your funeral.'

'Hey, why are you talking about death all of a sudden? I'm the one who has to deal with dead people.'

'Oh, like that, is it? If you're feeling sorry for yourself it's probably because you've got a new one on your hands. Well, I didn't tell you to be a policeman, remember? Your decision. Sullied the name of Cámara for ever.'

'Give it a rest.'

'So who is it this time?'

'Remember that paella place in El Cabanyal? I took you there once.'

'La Mar. Best paella I ever had. And I've had a few.'

'Yeah, well, it's the guy who ran it.'

'Pep Roures?'

'You remember his name?'

'I wasn't going to forget a genius like him. Red hair, well fed but tough looking.'

'That's him.'

'What happened?'

'Went missing a week ago.'

'The place is under threat, isn't it? La Mar, I mean. One of the places the Town Hall wants to tear down for this redevelopment plan of theirs.'

'Looks like it.'

'One less person in their way, then. I take it you've found the body now.'

'Came floating up on to the Malvarrosa beach.'

'Wish I'd been there myself.'

'It wasn't pretty.'

'Wasn't thinking about your corpse. More the other kinds of bodies lying on the beach at this time of year.'

'Oh, for fuck's sake.'

'Calm down. I'm only kidding. You think you're the only person who's ever dealt with dead people? Some have had it far worse, but they still come through smiling.'

Cámara gritted his teeth and sighed.

'You're out of sorts,' Hilario said. 'Have been for a while.'

'I know. And before you ask, no, it's not woman trouble. I don't know. Perhaps it's the job. I don't know if I should . . .' He paused.

'Pack it in?'

It was as if he could see Hilario grinning at the other end of the line. Hadn't this been what his grandfather had always wanted? For Cámara to admit that becoming a policeman was a mistake? He should cut links with the State and rejoin the anarchist fold of his family. Or at least what was left of it.

'Maybe.'

He expected laughter, perhaps even a cheer. Instead, there was silence.

'How long have you been a policeman?' Hilario said eventually.

'Since I finished my law degree. Almost twenty years. You know this,' he added.

'So after twenty years you think you might just give it up.'

'I don't know. I'm wondering.'

'What would Pep Roures think?'

'What are you talking about? Pep Roures is dead.'

'Pep Roures was a good man. You could tell by eating his food. No one can cook like that and not be a decent person. You ate at his restaurant.'

'Hardly every day.'

'You're talking like a child. Stop feeling sorry for yourself and sort this out. Do it for Pep Roures. Do it for the man who made the best paellas in all of Valencia. You owe it to him. You owe it to all of us. Whoever murdered him needs to be found. That's your job. That's what you do.'

Cámara rubbed his fist over his forehead.

'All right.'

'I can tell you what Pep Roures himself would be saying right now. *Hecha la paella . . .*'

'*. . . Buena o mala, hay que comella,*' Cámara finished the proverb for him. Once the paella's made, whether it's good or bad, it's got to be eaten.

'That's right. You listen to your grandfather.'

Monday 6th July

The streets in El Cabanyal and the neighbouring Canyamelar district ran parallel to the sea. Once a fishermen's settlement, separate and distinct from the city set on the River Turia a couple of miles further inland, it had been swallowed up by an expanding Valencia during the nineteenth century, and the traditional thatched *barraca* huts had given way to colourful Art Nouveau and eclectic town houses with brightly tiled facades. A few unsightly tower blocks had been placed among these in more recent decades, but the area maintained a strong, village-like identity. It was the only *barrio* in Valencia to celebrate Holy Week in traditional Spanish style – with long parades complete with worshippers in conical hats and face masks – while no one in the area supported Valencia Football Club, preferring the less successful Levante U.D., which had started life there.

Since the conflict had begun over the Town Hall's redevelopment plan almost a decade earlier, however, decline had set in. Buildings that were due to be bulldozed fell empty, litter filled the streets. And then the drug dealers had arrived. But the remaining residents hung on, struggling to maintain the traditional culture of the area in the face of official neglect by opening bars, restaurants, theatres, even their own homes on occasion when the rest of the city was invited to visit this unique neighbourhood, and understand what exactly was under threat. Would they really allow these historic structures to be flattened to make way for more characterless apartment blocks, like the tens of thousands that grew like fungi up and down the coastline?

Inspector Paco Torres was already at the Montblanc bar on the Calle de la Reina when Cámara arrived, smoke sifting into his thick black beard as he read through his notebook. After Roures's body had been found, Cámara had arranged to meet his usual partner there to spend the morning having a look around. Knowing they had a dead body on their hands might change not only their own perspective of a district they had visited regularly over the past few days, but the perspective of those they talked to as well.

'Coffee's on its way,' Torres said as Cámara sat down on a shiny metal chair opposite him. From here they both had a view out over the street, and the traffic coming in and out from the nearby port area.

'Oh, and these,' Torres added, reaching into his pocket and pulling out a packet of Ducados cigarettes. 'You've never got any cash on you these days,' he explained. 'Saves you having to cadge one of mine.'

Cámara tore the plastic off the top, ripped open the packet and pulled out a perfect white tube of tightly packed black tobacco. Before he could find his own, Torres had pulled out his lighter and ignited it in front of Cámara's face.

'So how did shooting go?' Torres asked.

A couple of months earlier some pen-pusher in the Ministry in Madrid had decided that all ranks up to and including chief inspector would have obligatory firing practice once a week. Guns had never been one of Cámara's passions; he preferred to use his own hands, feet, elbows, knees and head as more reliable weapons. But somewhere inside him he knew that having a better working knowledge of his standard-issue Star 28 PK pistol – the one he'd been given back at the national police academy in Ávila – was going to be necessary.

'All to do with having the right stance and a high, hard grip on the handle, they tell me,' he said with a shrug. 'Best way to shoot straight.'

'Shooting straight is simple, but not easy,' Torres said with a grin, repeating the gun-handling trainer's oft-repeated motto.

'Yes,' Cámara mumbled. 'I'm still trying to work that one out.'

They smoked in silence for a moment.

'Call came through,' Torres said eventually. 'Another restaurant in the area's had a break-in. One of the ones down near the beach. No violence as far as we can tell. Just looking for cash.'

'Did they find any?'

'Just a few hundred euros. Took some of the booze as well.'

'All right,' Cámara said. 'We'll check it out later. But first,' he added as the barman placed their *cafés con leche* on the table in front of them, 'let's run through what we've already got on Roures. Today is Monday the sixth of July. Roures was reported missing on . . .'

'Monday the twenty-ninth of June,' Torres filled in.

'But we think the murder may have taken place on the Sunday, probably in the early hours.'

'It's not a bad assumption. Dumping the body at sea under the cover of darkness.'

'The sun rises at around six thirty at this time of year, so we're looking at some time before around five thirty. Six at the very latest if you want some degree of darkness.'

'Alarm was raised by kitchen assistant Santiago del Pozo,' Torres continued, checking his notes. 'Arrived just after ten thirty on Monday morning. Door open, no sign of forced entry, and no sign of Roures. Called him on his mobile, but no answer. Very unusual for Roures. Waited just under an hour before calling the police.'

'During which time . . .?'

'During which time he says he carried out his usual preparatory tasks in the kitchen. While waiting to see if Roures showed up.'

Torres stubbed out his cigarette and took a sip of coffee.

'Keep going,' Cámara said.

'Del Pozo is thirty-three years old and has been at La Mar for four and a half years. Left work at one o'clock on Sunday morning. The restaurant didn't open on a Sunday, so it was his day off. Spent it mostly in bed with his girlfriend, according to his statement. Went out to see a film Sunday night, then back home, before coming to work on the Monday.'

'Which is when he called us.'

'Right. The other employee there was Victoria Luna Pérez, a waitress, twenty-six. The Saturday was her last day at La Mar. According to what we've got, she went back to her flat, then caught the train the following morning to Zaragoza, before moving on to Logroño to stay with her family. Had been at La Mar for two months, but left because she couldn't stand the atmosphere there, according to the statement she gave to the La Rioja police. Del Pozo confirmed there had been tensions between her and Roures, but claimed it was just because of the intensity of the work, and Roures's attention to detail. Weak motive for an attack on her boss, although we're waiting for the Logroño *científicos* to analyse her clothes for any signs of Roures's blood.'

Cámara stared down at the coffee swirling around in his cup, part of his mind trying to decide if he wanted a brandy this early in the morning to wash it down with.

'Fine,' he said. 'So much for that. Let's concentrate on Roures himself.'

'Fifty years old, well-known owner of an El Cabanyal paella and fish restaurant,' Torres said. 'Opened La Mar twenty-five years ago. Small, highly respected, award-winning place, popular with artists and musicians and El Cabanyal locals.'

'And certain, more discerning policemen.'

'I didn't know you'd eaten there.'

'A few times.'

'As good as they say?'

18

Cámara nodded. 'And I'm not just speaking from nostalgia. There was something about those paellas.'

'Speaking as a native of Albacete, or a long-term resident of Valencia?'

'All right, you bastard. I may not have paella running through my veins like you, but I know a good one when I taste one.'

'It takes a true Valencian to tell.'

'Bollocks. Come on, let's keep going. Roures set La Mar up with his ex-wife, right?'

'Lucía Bautista Sánchez. From El Cabanyal, like Roures. Divorced thirteen years ago. Still lives in the area. I spoke to her a couple of days ago: good alibi – she was out all night at a friend's birthday party at a house in the mountains – and no obvious motive if you think they've been apart for so long.'

Cámara shrugged.

'Since the split there's been no sign of any other woman in Roures's life,' Torres said. 'Appears to have dedicated himself entirely to the restaurant.'

'Long, unsociable hours. Bloody hard work.'

'Yeah,' Torres hissed. 'Sounds familiar.'

'Anyone else in the ex-wife's life?'

Torres sucked his teeth.

'Don't know. I'll check.'

'Don't worry about it. I'll look into it.'

'Then there's this fishing business. It seems everyone knew that Roures used to put out some *palangre* fishing lines after dusk each evening, then pulled them in before dawn from his little rubber dinghy. It's illegal. Normally if a proper fisherman catches you doing that they tear up your lines. But he'd been doing it so long everyone turned a blind eye. God knows how he managed to keep the *Guardia Civil* patrols off his back.'

'They've got problems of their own, I hear,' Cámara said. 'Understaffed. OK, the dinghy.'

'Used to keep it in one of the abandoned boatyards next to the restaurant. Found floating near the industrial port two days later. With human bloodstains still on it.'

'Roures's?'

'Huerta refuses to say. The samples are too degraded, what with the heat and humidity from the sea.'

Their colleague from the *Policía Científica*, Chief Inspector Huerta, had done the tests himself. He was extremely proud of his record for getting things right, which meant there was no room for 'possibles' or 'probables'.

Cámara placed his fingertips together as he thought it through.

'So the fresh fish he's pulling up each morning he then offers to a select group of trusted clients. As well as putting some of it in his rice dishes, I suppose. I'm beginning to think this was the closest thing he had to a proper social life – a bit of a chat with some of the regulars, and then into the kitchen again.'

He thought back to the times he'd eaten there himself. It had been something of a habit of his to take girls to the restaurant, years before, when the city was still relatively new to him. Inviting them to La Mar had been a kind of private ritual: if they were still seeing each other after twenty-one days, he celebrated the event with paella in El Cabanyal. It acted as a sort of signal to himself that things were moving from a brief fling to something else, shifting into more dangerous terrain. None of the women had ever known the truth behind the pleasant rice-lunch; some had been enchanted by the place, others couldn't quite understand the charm. These ones hadn't lasted much longer: if someone focused more on the slighty grimy surroundings than on the authenticity of the place, they weren't worth hanging on to. Almudena had liked it, and he hadn't expected her to, which was perhaps one of the reasons why they had stayed together for over two years.

Then there was Alicia . . . He'd never even got the chance to bring her.

'Yes,' he said, his mind turning back to their conversation. 'That would fit. I didn't go often enough to be a regular there, but he was chatty. It certainly appeared that he enjoyed playing the host.'

Torres glanced down at his notes again.

'That's pretty much it. Other restaurateurs in the area respected him, but none of them seems to have known him that well.'

'They're all too busy. What about this local pressure group that's challenging the Town Hall over the development plan?'

'*El Cabanyal, Sí*. Roures used to go to their meetings. Active member, by all accounts. Provided free food once for a fund-raising event. Not surprising when you think his place was lined up for demolition.'

'People have been talking about this redevelopment project for years.'

'*El Cabanyal, Sí* have been fighting it in the courts since the late nineties. But they've just lost an appeal with the Valencian High Tribunal, and the bulldozers have already started work in some places. And now there's a new councillor in charge of pushing the plan through. Rafael Mezquita – youngish, good-looking guy. Very churchy. They reckon he might take over from the mayoress one day.'

'Any compensation for the people having their houses pulled down?'

'The Town Hall's been buying up affected properties and then leaving them empty. That's why the area's gone downhill so much. People who are holding out just get offered a token amount.'

'How much?'

'According to *El Cabanyal, Sí*, Roures would have got just over twenty thousand euro.'

'They take your house and livelihood and in return you get *veinte mil*?'

'And a new place to live. A flat somewhere. A low rent until you die, and then it reverts to the Town Hall.'

'So nothing for your children? The family property is just lost?'

'Yes. Although in Roures's case that wouldn't have been such a problem. No kids.'

'Is there a will?'

'No. And I'm not sure who he would have left anything to in the first place. Parents died long ago. There used to be a sister, but she died a couple of years back as well. Liver cancer.'

They both fell silent for a moment.

'No family. Virtually no friends,' Torres said. 'If it didn't sound so stupid I'd say he practically lived for his paellas.'

'Well, at least it might explain the tattoo,' Cámara said.

Who was it for, though?

FOUR

It was still too early for the cooling *levante* wind to come in off the sea, and the air was gaining the blanket heaviness of high summer, a white, humid haze blanching the azure dome of the sky. The Valencia city coastline was flat and featureless, and while at other times of the year the mountains to the north and south were visible, giving a kind of picture-frame to the sea view, now they would remain rubbed out until the rains of late September, leaving just beach and wide expanse of motionless sea, and the brightly painted cranes of the docks.

Already there were hundreds, perhaps thousands, lying out on the sands, but they were mostly packed close to the sea, leaving open, empty spaces nearer the esplanade. He cast an eye out to the mass of exposed, bronzing skin, watching for any spasm of desire to ignite within him. There were slim, dark Gypsy girls from El Cabanyal, in tightly packed groups with their brothers and male cousins like a wall protecting against their precocious eroticism. Groups of lighter-skinned twenty-year-olds, the boys with tight stomachs, the girls showing off their 100-euro bikinis bought in the spring from El Corte Inglés. Mothers, like Susana, with young children, using the free space of the beach to compensate for their cramped homes. Women in their fifties and sixties, hard-core beach hags, often in groups of two or three, sitting on deckchairs under a sun umbrella, playing cards, their lunch waiting in iceboxes underneath fold-up tables while their husbands walked up and down the shoreline with white hats and blackened, beaten flesh like the five-thousand-year-old bodies they found in glaciers and showed in television documentaries.

How many topless women could he see from where he stood? They were always a minority on a mainstream city beach like this; the real nudists had their own places to go, outside of town. But he liked to use it as his own unscientific social barometer: the lower the nipple count, the more conservative the mood. Only a few more days and the Pope himself was coming, and newspaper kiosks were being ordered to hide their pornographic magazines in a display of piety, while the Town Hall was closing down any public acts by gay rights activists or pro-abortion campaigners. For some the papal visit would be cause to cover up more than usual, but for others it would probably push them to strip off even more, invoking a particularly Spanish stubbornness. He counted: one, two, three topless women. No more. Clearly the powers of darkness were in the ascendancy today.

And no. He sighed: nothing in him beyond an anthropological interest.

Wooden decking led from the entrances to the beach, creating pathways towards the sea and giving the barefooted protection from the burning sand and from the broken glass that often nestled beneath the surface. He strolled out a few paces, looking over to where Roures's body had floated the previous afternoon. There was no sign of him or his dead presence now: everything back to normal.

Stepping off the boards, his feet sank into the sand. It was dense up here, away from the shoreline, and footprints left behind were quite visible. He could see dozens of them scattering around him, trails and clues that formed no pattern, made no sense, crossed over one another, and were lost, erased or smothered by a breeze bringing drier sand from further down the beach. Children playing football? A father playing catch with his little boy? A couple arguing? It was chaos. A chaos of smudged impressions and remains. How could one recreate and tell the stories of what had happened here based on such poor evidence?

Nothing. The truth was they had nothing on this case. No witnesses, no DNA samples they could point to, not even a clear idea of how the murder had taken place. And unless the Logroño police lab results showed positive for Roures's blood, they were without a clear suspect or even a motive. Roures ran a paella restaurant, a restaurant held in high esteem. He had a good relationship with his clients, his suppliers, and even the local fishermen, if the stories about his illegal fishing lines were true. Cámara was in the dark, and his usual method of waiting for something to show up or come along had only brought him Roures's corpse until now. He was blinkered somehow, but couldn't say by what.

Torres found him sitting on the wall, staring out to sea.

'Enjoying the view?' he grinned.

'What did they tell you?' said Cámara.

'Break-in last night. Pretty much what we already knew – took some petty cash and a few bottles of booze. The owner's new – only had the place since the spring. Previous owners went bust with *la crisis*. New guy's had a big new renovation done. Private investors – no bank's going to hand out that kind of money at the moment. But they've been having problems with the alarm system. Something to do with the humidity interfering with the electrics. Hence no one discovering it till early this morning. Reckons it was just some drunks or drug addicts.'

'Why?'

'One of them had a shit on the floor next to the bar. Quite common, I've heard. Marking territory, or something.'

'A calling card.'

Torres gave him a look.

'Anyone see anything?' Cámara asked.

'There are plenty of late-nighters out round here in the summer months, but most would have been too pissed or stoned to notice anything. The *Policía Local* took a statement from an elderly couple who were out for a stroll at dawn with their dog. Said they saw two men lurking around nearby. Long hair. One had a black shirt, the other wore no shirt at all. Couldn't get a good look at them as they were running away at the time.'

'Anything else?'

'There are some bloodstains near the window. One of them probably cut himself. I've passed it on to the *científicos*. See if it matches anything we've got from Roures.'

'All right,' Cámara said. 'Did La Mar have an alarm system?'

Torres shrugged.

'It's just round the corner,' Cámara said. 'Let's walk over. I want to have another look.'

Blue-and-white police tape trailed in an L-shape from the window bars on one side of the corner building, out to a lamp post and back to the main facade, where a dark green canopy still shaded a couple of pavement chairs and a shiny metal table. They both looked up at the outside walls, but there was no sign of any alarm.

'Perhaps he didn't feel he needed one,' Torres said.

The restaurant was on the corner of a large rectangular brick structure, two storeys high and about a hundred metres long, which took up an entire block on the street. This was the old Lonja de los Pescadores – the fishermen's lodge, where the original El Cabanyal working men had kept their equipment. Cámara looked up at an imposing, if understated, *modernista* structure, the date 1909 in brick relief visible above the main entrance.

'Became a hospital back in the twenties,' Torres said. 'Then people started moving in and living here after the war.'

'How many live here now?'

'One old woman who's virtually deaf, and some photographer guy. But he's away at the moment. The rest is empty. Hard to live somewhere where you don't know if the bulldozers are going to come from one day to the next, I suppose.'

'Did we . . .?'

'Yes,' Torres said. 'We spoke to the woman and the neighbours from across the road. None of them heard or saw anything. Although they all knew him, and about his dinghy and all that. So even if they did hear something, they may have assumed it was Roures going out fishing as usual.'

Cámara looked down the row of houses: some were in the original sand-coloured brick, others had painted their facades in pale yellows and pinks. La Mar itself had been painted a bright sea blue, for obvious reasons, he thought.

'You know,' Cámara said, 'people often used to call it La Mare, instead of La Mar. The joke was that when you came here you ate "the mother of all paellas".'

Before going inside he caught sight of a large blue-and-yellow sundial on the wall of a building across the road, the date 1895 painted near the top.

'The old Casa dels Bous,' he explained to Torres. 'Where they kept the bulls and oxen for dragging the fishing boats out of the sea and on to the beach. You know – Sorolla painted it a few times, along with all those naked boys splashing in the waves.'

Cámara pulled out the key and they stepped inside the restaurant. There were half a dozen dark wooden tables crammed into a small space, the chairs neatly pushed underneath, with cutlery laid out waiting expectantly for the next customers. The walls were painted a light shade of ochre, while the floor had scuffed terracotta tiles. Framed images of sea views decorated the walls – some original paintings, while a couple of reproductions of Sorolla's work were nearer the back, towards the kitchen. A large palm-like pot plant near the window already looked as though it could do with watering.

Cámara sat down in a chair looking out at the street, while Torres allowed his eyes to scan the room, picking up one of the menus and reading down the list. He was comfortable enough with Cámara's technique by now, having worked with him for over a couple of years: sometimes just being in a place, not seemingly doing anything at all, could bring answers of a kind – perhaps even to questions you hadn't yet asked.

'I'm surprised they had a menu here,' Torres said.

'Probably just for show,' Cámara said. 'You often had to book days or weeks ahead, and give your order over the phone at least the day before coming. Small place like this couldn't cope with people wandering in and ordering off a menu. Still, it wasn't just the paella that was good. Some of the starters were amazing, too. The *esgarraet* was the best in the city.'

The thought of strips of roasted red pepper with dried cod, bathed in olive oil and parsley, gave them both a mid-morning surge of hunger.

'*Paella, arròs a banda,*' Torres read from the menu. '*Arròs negre, arròs amb fesols i naps.* Not just the touristy stuff, then.'

'Oh, no.'

'And he did wet rice dishes as well. *Arròs melòs con bogavante.* With fresh lobster. God, I'm getting hungry.'

Cámara stood up and went to look in the kitchen.

'Checking to see if there's anything to eat?'

Cámara gave him a look.

'All right. You started it.'

The kitchen was almost as large as the dining area, with an over-sized hob to accommodate cooking four or five paellas at once. Steel paella dishes with scuffed green or red handles hung from the back wall, while an array of other pans and implements was stored on shelves above the cooker. Bright orange butane gas bottles were lined up under one of the counters, their presence only partially hidden by a greasy piece of brown cloth strung across the opening. The strip lighting on the ceiling brought out the harsh, metallic feel of a professional kitchen.

Torres opened a wooden door leading to a steep flight of stairs. They walked up and came out into Roures's first-floor flat. There was one bedroom, a small living room, bathroom and tiny kitchen. From the living-room window you could just make out the sea down a side street, palm trees swaying gently in the nascent breeze.

If the decor downstairs was minimal, almost functional, here it simply didn't exist at all. A grubby sofa had been pushed against one wall, and there was a table and chair by the window, with a couple of newspapers folded and placed in a corner. Above the sofa a cork board hung from a bent nail hammered into the brickwork, with a few cuttings about *El Cabanyal, Sí*, and the Town Hall's development plan. The bedroom was a mess; the bathroom and kitchen had nothing but the basic furniture. A small bookcase contained barely a dozen titles. Cámara leaned down, picking up a couple of works on the history of El Cabanyal, as well as one or two studies on 'the art of eating', and the role of paella in Valencian culture.

The bed was unmade. On the other side stood a small cabinet. Cámara squeezed his way round and opened the drawers to find a box of tissues, some painkillers, pills for high blood pressure, and the remote control for the small TV resting on a chair at the foot of the bed.

'Something about this place reminds me of flats I lived in when I was younger,' he said as he sifted through the shirts and trousers in the wardrobe.

'What do you mean?' Torres called through from the living room.

Cámara walked back to join him, staring out of the window at the tram that had just pulled up outside.

'It's a place to sleep, get washed – the basics, like student digs or something.'

He looked over at the sofa, its cushions set and rounded like stones.
'No one's sat on that thing for years, by the looks of it.'
He turned to leave.
'There's nothing here. No sign of life.'

FIVE

They walked out of the restaurant and crossed the road to a dusty abandoned building on the other side. Torres leaned on a wooden gate until it gave way, and they passed through. The roof had mostly gone, except for one corner where it offered partial protection from the elements.

'Del Pozo told us this was where Roures kept his dinghy,' Torres said.

A pair of oars was leaning up against one of the walls. Cámara knelt down and started rummaging through some old orange boxes full of *palangre* fishing lines, spare hooks and extra cord for repairs. A fishing rod in pieces was lying on top of some shelves, with a heavy layer of fine dust covering it.

'Perhaps he started out doing ordinary line fishing from the shore,' he said.

'You're allowed to start at dusk,' Torres said. 'So as not to get in the way of swimmers and sunbathers. Two rods per fisherman.'

'You know a lot about it.'

'My dad taught me. Used to do quite a bit when I was a teenager. Before I got married.'

A strong, rotting smell was coming from one corner of the den. Cámara hesitantly approached a blue icebox perched on the edge of a worktable.

'Whatever it is, it's in here.'

He lifted the lid and almost stumbled backwards as the putrid stench overwhelmed him.

'That'll be the calamari,' Torres laughed. 'For the bait.'

'Let's get out of here.' Cámara's eyes were streaming as he tried not to retch. 'I've seen enough.'

Instinctively they turned down the side street and walked in the direction of the beach, each one imagining the route Roures would have taken every night as he dragged his dinghy out to the sea for a spot of illegal fishing. Crossing an empty boulevard, they passed under the shade of the palms and out on to the sand. A cluster of traditional wooden fishing boats was parked there, painted in white, blue, green and red.

'I can get the owners' names from the marine authority,' Torres said in answer to Cámara's silent question. 'I'm not sure if they keep them there as a kind of tourist attraction as well.'

He took out a notebook and jotted down the licence numbers.

Wordlessly, they walked the rest of the width of the beach until they came to the shore, tiptoeing their way past a score of bodies. The sea had more life to it today, and children were playing in the waves while couples stood further out where the water covered their waists, draping glistening arms around each other and kissing as the sea rocked them to and fro.

'A small rubber dinghy isn't that heavy, but still, it's quite a way to drag it out each night.'

'Roures was a strong man,' Cámara said. 'Or at least he gave that impression.'

'And I suppose that if I wanted to attack him, out here would be my choice.'

Cámara asked him to continue.

'As far away as possible from the street lights, no bars or restaurants near this section of the beach, some amount of noise from the sea to cover the sound of any struggle, and he's already brought the boat out here so you can dump the body inside, row it out, throw it overboard and then come back ashore.'

Cámara looked down at his feet, at the crushed white shells and damp brown sand. A dog being chased by a little boy ran past them, splashing their faces with salt water as it skipped in the foamy wavelets.

Torres was right: this place, now full of joy, of fun and life, was almost certainly the scene of Roures's murder.

*

They walked back into the heart of El Cabanyal along the Calle de la Reina. This was traditionally the wealthiest street in the neighbour-hood, wider and with trees along the pavement, but the houses were still built in the El Cabanyal style, with carved wooden double-front doors designed to let the cooling sea breezes flow through in summer.

Passing a baker's shop, Cámara heard someone calling after him.

'Max!'

He turned to find a stubbly, friendly face beaming at him.

'Enrique.'

The two men embraced.

'¿Cómo estás, chaval?' How're you doing, kid?

Enrique slapped Cámara on the shoulders with powerful, bear-like arms, then saw Torres standing nearby.

'What? Working?' he asked.

'The Roures case,' Cámara said. 'This is Inspector Torres.'

'Paco,' Torres said, and stretched out a hand to shake.

'Enrique is a flamenco singer,' Cámara explained. 'He lives in the area.'

'Just in the next street,' Enrique grinned. 'Buying some bread for lunch. Do you want to come? Maite's roasting some fresh John Dory.'

'Love to,' Cámara said. 'But we've got to keep going.'

'Suit yourself. Sad business, the Roures thing.'

'Did you know him?' Torres asked.

'We all knew him. Everyone in the *barrio*. He was a local institu-tion. You'd see him at the market. Or at *El Cabanyal, Sí* meetings. We used to chat sometimes. He did the food for a fund-raising gig I did here once. Nice enough guy. Why the hell anyone'd want to do him in is beyond me.'

Despite his having lived in Valencia for almost thirty years, there was still a slight Andalusian lilt in the way Enrique spoke, a mark of his native Seville that he was proud of never losing.

Cámara made to move.

'Sure I can't tempt you for lunch? You're welcome to come along as well, Paco.'

'Really, we can't,' Cámara said. Strangely, he felt uncomfortable being with Torres in this purely social situation: the sudden use of first names clashed with the surname-mateyness of the police.

'All right,' Enrique said. 'But don't forget, Max. It's Carlos's baptism next Saturday. And you're the godfather.'

He turned to Torres.

'You know, sometimes I think I'm the only friend he's got.'

The headquarters of *El Cabanyal, Sí* were set further away from the beach on the Calle Escalante in an old two-storey building with graffiti-sprayed death threats on the front door.

'We don't bother trying to scrub them off any more,' Mikel Roig said when Cámara nodded at them. 'The *Municipales* are working for the Town Hall, so why would they bother trying to catch whoever's responsible?'

The house was run-down and drab in comparison to the brightly tiled facades of some of the neighbouring buildings, decked out in maritime shades of blue, green and turquoise. The sun reflected from their shiny glaze and Cámara found himself squinting against the glare. An elderly woman on a floor above was rolling out a wooden shutter over the edge of her cast-iron balcony, keeping the direct light out while leaving the glass doors behind open in preparation for the cooler sea breezes of the afternoon. Above her head, the face of a sea god peered out from a mosaic design below the eaves of her roof.

Mikel Roig was the spokesman for the pressure group. Torres leaned over and shook his hand.

'We talked on the phone,' he said.

'I'm not here all the time,' Roig explained. 'I have a job at the university library. But now in the summer months I can come down more often.'

He was a slightly built man, with a closely shaved dome-like head and a broad straight nose like an ox.

They went inside, seeking shelter from the sun, but the heat was even more intense. Cámara could feel sweat bulging from the back of his head and streaming through the hairs at the top of his shoulders.

'It's all we've got,' Roig said apologetically. 'We can't afford anywhere better. We're just a neighbourhood organisation, getting by on people's goodwill, mostly. Someone had this place in the family and wasn't using it, so they lent it to us. But we can't afford to do it up or anything. That's not what we're about, anyway. So we freeze in winter and fry in summer. As you can see. Here, have some water.'

He passed over a plastic bottle and Cámara took a gulp.

'That Valconsa lot, they're pretty well set up, though. You should see their place.'

'The construction company?' Torres asked.

'They're spearheading the whole project here for pulling houses down and extending Blasco Ibáñez Avenue through to the sea. You know, Emilia's big plan.'

'Yes, we've heard about what the mayoress is trying to do here,' Cámara said.

'It's some sort of personal thing with her,' Roig went on, happy, it seemed, to have someone to talk about the cause with. 'Wants to put her stamp on the city, and this old working-class district is getting in her way. I reckon she sees it like some kind of wall that she has to break down so she can link the city centre with the beach.'

Cámara took another gulp from the bottle, sensing the water as it trickled down his gullet and into his stomach, then passed it over to Torres.

'Then there's Cuevas, the head of Valconsa.'

'You mean José Manuel Cuevas,' Torres said.

'Yeah. This is just one big business opportunity for him. A chance to build some cheap apartment blocks and make even more millions. With all the right kickbacks to the politicians along the way, obviously.'

'Are you making a formal accusation?' Torres said.

'Nah. Come on. But you know how these things work.'

'That's not why we're here.'

'Yeah, all right.'

Roig looked away.

Cámara got up and went to the door to check the street outside while Torres leaned his chair in towards Roig's desk to glance over the leaflets and campaign material. An old man in a vest and a straw hat was walking his Alsatian dog at the edge of the pavement, staying as close as he could to the sliver of shade.

Roig got up and stood next to Cámara, greeting the man with the dog.

'I've got to take him to the vet,' the man said, pointing to his pet. 'He's got a sore behind his ear. Hasn't been himself since we moved.'

'I'm sure he'll be all right,' Roig said. '*Ánimo.*' Keep your chin up.

'It gets harder to say that as you get older,' the man mumbled, and he allowed himself to be dragged along by the dog.

'Jaume,' Roig explained to Cámara. 'Just got out of hospital. The whole stress thing of losing his home. They pulled it down last winter. He couldn't hold out in the end.'

He leaned over and opened a window on the other side of the doorway.

'Here,' he said. 'We might get a bit of breeze.'

'Tell me about Pep Roures, about his involvement with you,' Cámara said.

'One of our most valued members,' Roig said. 'Big loss. We're all gutted. Can't see Valconsa and the Town Hall being too upset, though.'

'How much time did he put into the organisation?'

'A lot. Attended all the weekly meetings,' Roig said. 'Let us use the restaurant for cultural events a couple of times. We put on concerts, art exhibitions, that kind of thing, to help raise awareness about what's going on here.'

'So everyone would have known about Roures being part of this.'

'He was one of the last people holding out – and one of the most visible,' Roig said. 'Lots of others here have been tempted to sell, or have made signals to Valconsa that they might sell. Not Roures. And what with most people in the city knowing his restaurant, he was a bit of an annoyance, if you see what I mean. We're just a residents' group trying to do what we can, but Roures counted for something.'

'There must be rivalries, tensions among the residents here.'

'We're not trying to cause any problems. We just want to save—'

'But still,' Cámara interrupted him. 'Not everyone's against the Town Hall plan. I've seen some banners around in favour of it.'

'Yeah, they're new. Emilia's paying for those,' Roig said. 'Look, of course something like this can get people upset. It's obvious. Arguments, people not talking to each other.'

'Was Roures involved in any of it?'

Roig hesitated.

'I didn't see or hear any of this myself. I don't want to give you dodgy info.'

'It's all right. Go on. Even if it's just a rumour, it might give us a lead.'

Roig crossed his arms.

'People said Roures was having problems with one of the fishermen who had a house down near La Mar. Sold up a few months ago.

Apparently he was annoyed that Roures was campaigning against the Town Hall plan, and was threatening to report him for his midnight fishing. Wasn't entirely legal, or something. I don't know the details, but I heard it was getting a bit heated.'

'Do you know the name of this fisherman?'

'Ramón. Everyone called him that. Don't know his surname.'

'Do you know where we might find him?'

'Ask around. He's usually knocking about somewhere.'

Torres joined them at the door, holding a clutch of *El Cabanyal, Sí* pamphlets.

'I'll take these,' he said. Roig nodded.

'Thank you,' Cámara said. 'Call us if you hear anything more.'

Cámara hadn't seen Dario Quintero for over a year, since they'd worked on the Jorge Blanco case together. The *médico forense* was staring down at some papers in reception as Cámara stubbed his cigarette out on the ground outside and walked through the doors of the *Instituto de Medicina Legal.*

'Chief Inspector,' Quintero said, looking up with a smile half-buried in his full grey beard. 'Always a pleasure.'

'Likewise, *doctor.*'

'I imagine you've come to visit *el pobre* Roures?'

Despite being able to poke, probe and cut bodies open with clinical efficiency, Quintero always treated the dead with an old-fashioned decency while they were in his care.

'I'm afraid this city won't be quite the same without him,' Quintero said as they pushed through a swing door and headed to the deposit. 'Or at least from a culinary standpoint.'

'I take it you were a regular.'

'Oh, perhaps not a regular. But like so many I'd been to La Mare enough times to know you couldn't find a better paella.'

Cámara smiled at Quintero's use of the restaurant's unofficial name.

'Not even La Pepica, with its photos of Hemingway on the walls, could improve on what Señor Roures was capable of doing,' Quintero added.

If there was anywhere as famous as La Mar for rice dishes by the sea, it was La Pepica, a large, almost warehouse-like establishment on the beach, where Papa often ate with his matador friends after a bullfight. But where La Pepica reeked of power and the Valencian establishment, there was something more intimate, counter-cultural, and more authentically 'El Cabanyal' about La Mar.

They entered the deposit. Quintero walked to a locker but hesitated before opening.

'We may all have appreciated his art,' he said, 'but we're not dealing with another famous murder victim here. Not another Blanco. Señor Roures was a *pez pequeño* – a little fish. He didn't have contacts or power. Which is why, I suppose, they were bent on pulling his house down, along with all the other buildings lined up for demolition. But it wouldn't have been under threat if he'd had strings to pull. That's the way things work in this city.'

He raised his eyebrows as if to ask whether Cámara was ready to see the body, and then pulled out the bench.

The decomposition had been halted temporarily, and the body had been cleaned up, but he was still a long way away from appearing like the chef whose paellas they had so enjoyed.

'I heard you were the one who brought him ashore,' Quintero said. Without looking up, Cámara gave a nod.

'You know, he drowned in the end.'

Cámara gave a look of surprise

'But you were right – he was attacked. From behind,' Quintero went on. 'Look.'

Walking round to his side of the body, Cámara leaned in and saw the wounds in Roures's upper waist.

'Three stab wounds,' said Quintero. 'The first two caught on the floating rib, but the third one went in. That would have stunned him. But the renal artery is intact. Often it's cut in attacks of this kind, and the victim bleeds to death in a matter of seconds. But not Roures.'

'Stabbed in the kidneys?'

'Perhaps a hand over the mouth – there's some light bruising just visible around the chin – and then, yes, a classic kidney stab, I'd say. Except that it didn't kill him. Being dumped in the sea did that. The lungs were full of water. Five litres of it.'

Cámara closed his eyes.

'He wouldn't have lasted long. No more than a minute or two at most. The stab wound would have debilitated him enormously.'

He closed the drawer and took off his gloves.

'Might still have been in the water at any other time of year,' he said.

'We were lucky that the sea is relatively warm now. Makes the body float to the surface faster, what with the gases from decomposition.'

'Any thoughts on the murderer, from what you've seen?' Cámara asked.

'Right-handed, from the position of the wounds. Stabbing from behind like this is often thought of as the mark of a professional.'

Quintero rubbed his hand through his beard and looked down at the floor.

'But there's something amateurish about this. We've got two attempts to stab him before the third finally penetrates. Even then it's not as deep as one might expect, and leaves the artery intact, as I mentioned.'

He paused.

'In my mind's eye I can almost see someone who's read up on how to stab someone from behind, but hasn't been able to practise. That's to say, not a true professional at all. Although appearing to be so may have been part of the plan.'

'Male?'

'A female could explain the lack of depth to the final stab wound. It takes a not inconsiderable amount of strength. But there's something quite masculine about the nature of the attack. Soldierly, almost.'

They walked back out into the corridor and headed towards reception again.

'And then . . .' Quintero began. Cámara urged him to continue.

'This is beyond my technical know-how, but there's one other thing.'

'What's that?'

'It seems quite clear to me that the murderer didn't row out very far to dump the body. The currents generally move from north to south along the coast. In ordinary circumstances, Roures could have been found anywhere from El Saler to Gandía. But leaving him so close to the shore, the harbour wall prevented him from being pushed southwards; there was nowhere else he could go.'

'Perhaps the idea was for him simply to disappear out at sea, make it look like an accident. Everyone knew about his fishing lines, it seems.'

'Perhaps,' Quintero said. 'But for that harbour wall you might be wondering if this really was a murder on your hands, or a case for Missing Persons.'

*

Cámara's phone rang as he stepped outside into the heat, and he could already feel his skin prickling from his shirt clinging to his back with the humidity.

He didn't recognise the number, but answered anyway.

'Maximiliano Cámara Reyes?' came an official-sounding voice.

'Yes.'

'Resident of number 6 Calle Luis Santángel?'

'Who is this?'

'I'm calling from the *Policía Local*,' said the voice.

Cámara cursed under his breath. Another parking fine? Someone had broken into his car?

'You have to come immediately to the Ruzafa office.'

'Look, what the hell's going on?' He was about to tell the official who he was: a chief inspector in the *Policía Nacional*, with a murder case on his hands. But the voice interrupted him.

'There's been an incident. It's urgent . . . Your block of flats has collapsed.'

SIX

Pulsating orange lights were reflecting off the shiny metal crane towers soaring high above the gaping holes of the new metro line. Approaching from a side alley, Cámara could sense a wailing, billowing crowd of people at the far end, on the corner of his street. Heavy, pale grey brick dust wrapped itself around him, clinging to the sweat on his arms and chest, and sticking at the back of his throat. In the fog, people pushed backwards and forwards like shadows, many with their hands over their faces, others with dirty streaks lashing their cheeks where the tears had stained.

He edged closer, feeling his way along by leaning on the parked cars, his eyes fixed on the steady rhythm of the flashing sirens. The crowd around him grew tighter, but rather than holding him back, it seemed to push him forwards, as though aware of who he was, that he should be allowed to see this.

Eventually he reached the front of the throng. A police tape had been strung across the top end of his street and a couple of *Policías Locales* were keeping watch. Behind them, blocking most of the view, were a couple of fire engines and an ambulance. He could just see the crushed back end of a car, its tail crumpled by lumps of misshapen masonry.

But he couldn't see his building – there were too many things in the way, too many men in suits shouting at their walkie-talkies, too many uniforms. The crowd itself shunted him a few feet to one side. Only then did the emptiness come into view, the space where once his block of flats had stood. The place where he had slept that night, had slept almost every night for the last decade or so. The world that had taken him in, given him refuge, a shelter, a place to wash, rest, and forget – if only for a short time – had vanished for ever.

For a moment he tried to imagine what it might feel like to be someone who had lost their home like this, to show up suddenly one day and discover the place you lived had gone, had simply ceased to exist while you were out. Perhaps only then could he connect with what was happening in front of him. Right now it was as if all this was taking place in another world, to someone other than himself.

He heard a name coming from his mouth, as though issuing from some other being: 'Tomás.'

He felt something on his shoulders: a warm, paw-like hand. Turning, he looked into a fleshy, perplexed face.

'I knew you'd get here soon enough.' It was Vicent, the owner of the bar on the corner. 'Here, you'll need this.'

A brandy glass was thrust into Cámara's hand and Vicent began to pour from a bottle of Carlos III.

'Do you want to sit down?'

Cámara didn't answer. Vicent finished pouring, then linked his hand into Cámara's arm and led him through to a stool inside the bar.

'Sit there. I'll get you a wet towel to wipe your face.'

The brandy slid through him like lava.

'Happened just after lunch, about half four.'

Vicent pulled up a stool next to him and left the damp cloth on the counter beside his glass. Other people were sprawled on chairs by the window, heads in their hands or with pale, empty expressions of shock in their eyes. Behind the bar, a girl was busying herself frantically with washing up plates, as though trying to block out the tragedy that had forced its way into her world. Through the open windows, Cámara recognised people he saw around here almost every day, neighbours he had greeted and chatted with hundreds, perhaps thousands of times, like an informal extended family.

'They've evacuated the buildings on either side,' Vicent said. 'The kids from the school across the road have been told to go home, so they're putting some up there. Camp beds and stuff. We'll be making some sandwiches and bits and pieces with what we've got here. There's not much, but at least we can do something.'

Cámara sipped on his brandy. The drink seemed to be injecting some kind of life into him, but he was uncertain if he preferred the dulled, half-death state of shock which had so quickly overcome him.

'It was just one almighty crash,' Vicent went on. 'We were cleaning up, just a few people still here. And then . . .' He tailed off. 'Never heard anything like it. Thought the world was crashing in on us. We all ran out into the street, sharpish. Didn't know what was happening. Could have been our building coming down on top of us. But all there was was dust. Then silence.'

He reached out and poured himself a brandy from the bottle at Cámara's side.

'Then the screaming started.'

Cámara's eyes darted towards the metro works just a few feet away.

'Yeah,' Vicent frowned. 'That lot didn't stick around for long. Reckon they've been expecting something like this to happen ever since they started. What with all these old buildings everywhere. This is Ruzafa, working-class area. They didn't build them as well as the ones on the other side of the avenue. Bound to happen. Remember that time in Barcelona with the metro line there? Same thing. Start digging underneath one of these places and sooner or later it'll come toppling down.'

'What about the others?' Cámara asked. It had been the only question on his mind since he'd arrived, but until now he'd been unable to speak.

'Well, I knew you'd be all right, 'cause you're hardly ever here,' Vicent said.

'What about the others?'

'*La Señora* Esperanza is fine – she was out shopping when it happened. Bit shocked, obviously. Her heart and all that. Then Antonio and Carmela were out at work . . .'

Vicent went through a list of Cámara's neighbours, ticking them off as having escaped the collapse of the building. But there was only one name he wanted to hear, one that Vicent refused to mention.

'What about little Tomás?' With a sudden jerk he grabbed Vicent by the shirt. 'Where are Tomás and Susana?'

Vicent looked him in the eye, but his expression had taken on the same emptiness as the others'.

'They're looking for them now.'

*

Night had fallen, and although the street lights on one side were no longer working, there was enough of a pink glow from the remaining lamps to illuminate the scene, while powerful white beams were being shone on the rubble itself to aid the rescue workers.

Cámara sat on the pavement opposite, his arms wrapped around his knees, waiting. The earlier crowds had gone, but still a core of neighbours and other locals stayed behind, staring at the destroyed block of flats, watching the firemen coming and going, the trail of Town Hall officials slipping under the police cordon, and leaving again with loosened ties and anguished looks on their faces. Already calculations were being made about the flows of responsibility from an event like this – where they were headed, and how they could be diverted.

The only noise came from the cars passing along the avenue at the top of the street. Many slowed to catch a glimpse of what they had already seen on the television news before speeding away. Here, in front of it, no one dared break the silent, hopeful vigil.

Above them, painted walls where the building had abutted the neighbouring houses stared out in shock. Pictures still hung in a couple of places from dusty hooks, while a bathroom sink was perched on the first floor on a lip of masonry, with a bright red-and-yellow child's towel draped over the edge next to the taps.

Below, smashed, destroyed brickwork was heaped in front of them. The pile was, Cámara thought, about a storey high. Take away the space, the lives that had filled this once, and that was all you were left with – a formless heap of mortar, plaster and splintered furniture measuring about three metres when compressed into this concentrated, if irregular, shape.

Someone had towed away the cars that had been crushed in the building collapse. On average he managed to park right in front of his block of flats about five or six times a year, what with all the cars cramped into the narrow streets. The previous Wednesday had been one of those occasions, and he'd almost leapt for joy at the time. But his old Seat had been the worst hit by the falling masonry, smashed into a dense little parcel. The insurance didn't cover events like this. Right now he didn't care.

He sat, silently smoking cigarette after cigarette as the sounds of people bedding down and preparing to sleep in the school behind him echoed out through the open windows. Ahead, a dog from the rescue team was scuttling about on top of the rubble, trying to find a scent. Most of them were local men – a team on permanent standby for flying out to disaster zones around the world in search of earthquake survivors. No one had thought they would have work to do so close to home.

Some had remained hopeful for a while. Susana had often taken Tomás out for walks down in the old river-bed-turned-park in the afternoons, playing in the shade of the mulberry trees, or in the spray of a fountain. Either that or to the beach, where the cooler breeze took the sting out of the burning sun. But they would have returned home by now; it was too late. Still, even if they had been caught by the collapse, there was hope that they might be alive. They'd seen the images on the television, when someone was dragged out from under an earthquake-hit house, shaken, dirty, but smiling. The same could happen here, couldn't it? Certainly the small group of women holding candles at the far end of the street thought so.

A piece of paper was fluttering towards him, caught in the light wind that had blown up, momentarily cooling their overheated, grimy bodies. Cámara watched as it skipped along the tarmac. It seemed familiar, somehow. As it drew nearer, he realised it was the sleeve notes from one of his flamenco CDs – *Omega*, by Enrique Morente. It was one of his favourite albums, and the black, white and red lettering seemed to call up to him, appealing for him to reclaim it, to say it was his.

With a frown, he quickly thought through what he had lost that afternoon: clothes, some books, a TV, music centre, pieces of furniture he wasn't too bothered about. The car. Perhaps, yes, the only thing he might really miss was his flamenco CD collection. It had taken a few years to build that up – there were recordings there he wasn't sure he'd ever be able to replace. But with this slight pang of loss, he realised there wasn't much he'd pine for. Had this flat really meant so little to him? No, despite being rented, it had felt like his – his bolt-hole, his retreat. Yet it wasn't the objects there that mattered to him; it was the memories. Memories of when he'd first arrived, back in the late 1990s. A couple of parties he'd had back then. The girls who had been and gone. Not that many, but this had been the first place he'd made love to Almudena. And she'd complained even then how messy it was.

It was over a year since they'd split, but whenever something brought her to mind, he was always glad they were no longer together, and even found himself wondering how they had ever managed to get together in the first place, so incompatible were they. A *poli* and an interior designer . . .

And then there was Susana. He'd never felt anything more than a friend and neighbour, and if it hadn't been for little Tomás, he might never have chatted with her so much. Something about her being left on her own by Tomás's father made him feel protective towards her.

Another push of wind, and the CD cover slipped past, and away down the street, unnoticed by anyone but him.

The dog barked. One of the firemen hissed for complete silence. Cámara stood up as the group collectively held its breath. He saw one of the rescue workers begin to clear away with his hands at the spot indicated by the animal, slowly, so as not to disturb the delicate structure created by the rubble. Piece by piece lumps of masonry were pulled up and placed to one side as the man tried to delve into the broken mass. Then he stopped. A torch was passed to him. He leaned in, pushing his hand through the remaining inches of debris before stopping and shining the torch down once again. He paused, checked once more with his hand, then stopped. After a couple of breaths, he stood up, shoulders tight and hunched.

The worst had been confirmed.

Whether minutes or hours had passed, he couldn't say, but he had the feeling of not having moved for a long time when he heard footsteps close behind. Gradually he became aware of someone crouching down beside him, placing small hands under his arms and pulling him up. After a moment, he obeyed, and began to lift himself on to his feet.

'Come on,' a voice said in his ear. 'You're coming home with me.'

SEVEN

Tuesday 7th July

The room was familiar, but in a distant, oblique sort of way, as though he'd slept so deeply he'd forgotten where he was. Yet he was certain he hadn't slept here the previous night. Nor for many nights before that.

The sound of a pneumatic drill down in the street buzzed through the open windows as a breeze blew in and played with the hairs on his exposed skin. Light reflected off the pale yellow walls, while the white cotton sheet felt soft and comforting. His fingers stretched out to find the edge, and he lifted it up to his eyes; the same thick yellow bordering as always. To match the walls.

Raising his head slightly from the pillow, he saw a bunch of white chrysanthemums in a vase on the bedside table. The sunlight was shining on them, casting a grey, hazy shadow on the parquet floor.

Yes, he thought as his head flopped down again, this room was all too familiar. As clean, neat, carefully arranged . . . and dead as it always had been.

But even then, comprehension was slow in coming. It was not until he heard a sound outside, a voice, that he fully realised not only where he was, but how he'd got there. And more importantly – why. He glanced quickly at the other side of the bed as the door opened. Someone else had slept there with him.

Almudena looked at him with a forced smile of concern as she placed the breakfast tray down by his knees. He hadn't seen her for over a year. There was something harder about her face than he remembered. Was that the time that had passed? Or the fact that now he could barely recall what it had felt like to be in love with her.

'I've put your phone on silent. It's been ringing all morning, but I thought you'd want to sleep. After last night.'

Cámara placed a hand on the bed beside him where the shape of her body was still imprinted on the sheet and pillow.

'We didn't . . . Did we?'

She smiled.

'Come on, Max. Have some coffee.'

She leaned over to the breakfast tray and poured him a thick, black *café solo*. His eyes strayed over the skin of her waist, exposed from under her T-shirt as she stretched out across his legs.

'You pretty much collapsed when you got inside,' she said, handing him the cup. 'I was hardly going to put you on the sofa. But I wasn't going to sleep there myself, either.'

Cámara took a sip – it was bitter and burnt, as it always had been.

'So, er, where's what's-his-name?'

'Esteban? Oh, he's away. On business. In Paris.'

'Are you two still . . .'

'Business partners? Yes, that's all going fine, thanks.'

'And what about bed partners?'

She looked him hard in the eye.

'I think your toast will be getting cold.'

He tried eating, but nothing would go down.

Torres was pouring brandy into a plastic cup for him almost before his backside hit the seat.

'I know you're not into that Yankee I-love-my-job crap, but even I'm amazed to see you here.'

Cámara drank it down in one, closed his eyes, then placed the cup back down on the desk, with a nod for Torres to pour some more.

'I'm as good here as anywhere else.'

'You want to go out for a smoke? You should take it easy.'

'I've done little more than smoke since yesterday. My lungs need a break.'

'As you wish. You know, if you need somewhere to stay we can always put you up at our place.'

Cámara had seen Torres's home once – a cramped, low-ceilinged flat in the Mislata district, just off the Madrid road heading out of the city. One of the blocks that had been put up in the seventies, with sliding aluminium windows and no balcony. There was barely room there for him, his wife and their little boy, let alone a guest.

'I'm fine. Thanks. Appreciate it.'

Torres sat down opposite him, rubbing his hand through his beard.

'The Town Hall should probably be fixing something up for you.'

'They put people up in the school last night. But that can't last long.'

'The landlady?'

Torres had heard plenty of Cámara's stories about his landlady, about how the tight old widow refused ever to carry out any improvements on the building, about how her husband had won the block of flats years back in a game of poker and added it to his property portfolio. The chances were, Cámara thought, that some of her other flats were empty, and she could put him and the other neighbours up somewhere – probably even for free, if they pressed her hard enough. But the thought of having to deal with her, just the grubbiness of having to ask her for charity, no matter what her responsibility was in the collapse of the building, made him queasy. He'd lost a large part of himself the previous day.

'Something will come up,' he said.

Last night it already had. He'd left Almudena's without clearing up on what basis exactly he'd spent the night there with her. Or if she was expecting him again that night.

'And I'm really sorry about your neighbour,' Torres said, looking down. 'The woman and her little baby. They, er, mentioned it on the TV.'

'Yeah,' Cámara said. 'So am I.'

He finished off his second cup of brandy, and reached forward for the hip flask they kept in their shared office as an emergency supply. It had been Cámara's turn to refill it, though, and there was barely a drop left.

'I can go out and get some more,' Torres said. 'You look like you need it.'

'I'm all right,' Cámara said, raising a hand. 'Thanks. I'll pick something up myself later on.'

He crinkled the plastic cup in between his fingers, his gaze unfocused.

'They'll be wrangling over the responsibility now,' he said, gritting his teeth. 'The Town Hall trying to claim it was nothing to do with them. The landlady saying it was all their fault. She's well connected – it won't be easy to lay it on her.'

He threw his head back and sighed.

'What I'm wondering is if there's a case for manslaughter here.'

Torres gave a low whistle.

'The building was falling apart. I saw some cracks in the wall myself, but . . .'

He covered his face with his hands.

'You couldn't have done anything,' Torres said. 'You couldn't have saved her. The building could have come down at any time. Just because you didn't mention some cracks in the wall? How long do you think it would have taken the Town Hall to send the inspectors round?'

'They're building the bloody new metro line right outside. They must have been on the alert.'

Torres pursed his lips.

'Come on. You know they don't work like that. That's far too proactive for this lot. Wait for the disaster to happen and then blame it on someone else – that's how they operate. You know that. Trying to fix things before they occur takes up far too much time. And money.'

'A young woman and her baby died.'

'I know. It's the kind of thing we deal with every week.'

Cámara shot him a look.

'I'm not trying to say it's not horrible, that it's not awful and disgusting,' Torres said. 'But who's your manslaughterer here? Your landlady? She'll just say the Town Hall failed in their responsibility to inspect all buildings over fifty years old. And then they're building the metro line – well, that's not her fault, either.

'Then who? The Town Hall? They'll say that they did carry out inspections, that their technicians did all they had to do, but it's not their fault if the cracks were invisible, or in flats they couldn't get inside because no one was at home when they called. They'll have records of all their visits, and everything they saw. And it will prove that they did the minimum, and that they can't be held responsible either.'

Cámara tapped his fingertips together as Torres continued.

'So where do you go from there? The original builders? That place went up, when? In the fifties?'

'About that.'

'Right, well, you try and find the architect now. Might be difficult to press charges. Know what I mean?'

Cámara was shaking his head.

'What I'm trying to say is that this is a political case. Yes, a woman and her little son have died. That's the human side of it. But we both know that that will soon be drowned out by the sound of politicos and civil servants scrabbling to save themselves while they're busy putting the boot into their opponents. The opposition are already using this to make waves. Emilia's even appeared to make a statement about how everyone's homes are safe, and there's nothing to worry about.'

Silently, Cámara wondered if Mayoress Emilia Delgado, or her ill-dressed sidekick Javier Flores, knew that he lived at the now collapsed block of flats. The three of them had a history from the Blanco case the previous year, when the murder of Spain's leading matador in the Valencia bullring coincided with a Town Hall plan to outlaw *los toros* within the city limits. The bulls and bullfighters were still there, and Emilia and Flores were still in power, but that was largely in spite of Cámara's successful conclusion of the investigation, not because of it. If Emilia and Flores had a list of their favourite policemen, Cámara wasn't on it.

'There'll be an official inquiry, the Valencian High Tribunal will get involved, it will drag on for years, and meanwhile memories will begin to fade, until finally there'll be a decision absolving everyone except a couple of minor officials who'd already been blacklisted for some misdemeanour, and the whole thing will be forgotten.'

Cámara stretched out his hands, as though trying to grab Torres by the neck.

'I can't just give in like that.'

'It's not about giving in. It's about staying alive. You know what I'm saying is true. You'd just get yourself in a mess, with no justice for your neighbour or anyone in the end.'

'Susana,' Cámara said. 'Susana and Tomás.'

'You'd never get the case in the first place,' Torres said. 'You're compromised by the whole thing – you lived there. Just forget it. Forget it.'

'*Si buscas la venganza, prepara dos tumbas – una de ellas será tuya.*'

Cámara nodded. If you seek revenge, prepare two graves – one of them will be yours.

He let his head drop.

'Come on,' Torres said. 'Let's go out. It's nearly lunchtime. You need some food inside you, a glass of wine. It'll do you good.'

'What have you been working on?' Cámara asked as they headed out into the corridor.

'Roures,' Torres said. 'Got the breakdown of calls on his mobile.'

'And?'

'Mostly to his suppliers. A couple to the office of *El Cabanyal, Sí*. One to the department of *Urbanismo* at the Town Hall. Probably to complain about something to do with the development plan.'

'Anything else?'

'Haven't had a chance to find Ramón the fisherman yet, but the tests from the break-in at the other bar came in. No link.'

The doors at the end of the corridor flew open before they could reach them.

'I've just heard something utterly fucking stupid!'

Commissioner Pardo's tie was pulled to one side, and sweat-patch stains were visible under his arms – a side effect of the underwhelming air conditioning inside the Jefatura building.

'Some idiot just told me that Chief Inspector Cámara was here. That he'd reported for work. "Fuck off," I said. "The bastard's house just fell down. He's not going to come in on a day like this. Hasn't even got anywhere to fucking sleep." "Oh, no," my informant insisted. "He's here all right." So I thought I'd better come and have a look for myself. And you know what? It looks as though the cunt was right. 'Cause here you are standing right in fucking front of me.'

'Morning, Commissioner,' Cámara said.

'Fuck off!' Pardo shouted. 'Now. That's a fucking order. You can't be here. Go where you have to go, sort your life out, get shagged, do whatever you have to do. But don't come in here. You're on compassionate fucking leave.'

He pushed his way back through the swinging doors.

'You've got twenty-four hours.'

They'd opened up the street again to traffic, and a stream of cars was rolling past, pausing so the occupants could glance up at the sight of the 'tragedy' that filled the news. A row of skips lined the pavement, filled with rubble and personal effects. An effort was being made, at least, to salvage something, but peering in he saw nothing but smashed household items, bits of broken wood from chairs and table legs, smashed crockery, clothes covered so thickly in brick dust you could hardly see what colour they were. It was all of the past now, all gone, finished. Yet still he'd found himself walking here to take another look, as though part of him was still struggling to absorb what had happened, that his body no longer slept, ate, shat or washed in the parcel of space that had once been his, there, about seven or eight metres up from where he was now standing. Now it was just a gap, emptiness. Was there any memory there of his emotions and experiences? If he were to float up and occupy the space that had been his home, would he feel anything, any echo?

A horn blew, loud and long. He turned to see a truck inching its way down the street, annoyed at the cars setting off too slowly from the traffic light ahead. From the shape of it, and the name of the company on the side, he could see it was coming to pick up one of the skips and take it away. Already the lives of those who had lived here had become rubbish to be dumped in some hole in the ground.

From the other direction he heard a voice calling his name. It was Vicent, from the bar. They shook hands and stood in silence for a moment, staring at the rubble.

'They'll be burying Susana and Tomás in a few hours' time,' Vicent said at last. 'We had a whip-round at the bar, sending some flowers.'

Cámara pulled out his packet of Ducados and gave one to Vicent.

'Put your name on it as well,' Vicent said.

'Thanks.'

Instinctively, Cámara reached into his pocket to feel for some money.

'No, come on,' Vicent said, putting his hand on his arm to stop him. 'You've got enough to be thinking about.'

They turned away from the destroyed block of flats and started strolling down towards the bar. Some of the neighbours walking past greeted Cámara with sad, sympathetic smiles.

'There's a meeting this evening at ten o'clock,' Vicent said. 'Local residents – to talk about the situation. There's a couple of lawyers involved. Trying to nail down who's responsible for all this, and what they're going to do about the other buildings here. I mean, if it can happen to one, it could happen to some of the others. Probably even more likely now – structural damage. Not just from the metro work, but from the collapse of your place. Must have weakened the buildings next door.'

Cámara nodded silently as they walked along, stepping to one side every now and again to let people pass along the narrow, uneven pavement.

'And then there's the problem with the sewerage – not connecting the street up properly,' Vicent went on. 'The paper says the construction company got paid for the job years back, but never actually did it. So we've all been floating on our own shit for years. That's got to have something to do with it. Places rotting from the bottom up. Someone's got to take the blame for that. They've stopped the metro work for the time being, but they'll be wanting to start again as soon as possible. Working through the night again. All those vibrations can't be good. We won't know what's keeping us from sleeping – the noise from the machinery or wondering if we'll wake up with a ton of masonry on our heads.'

They stopped at the corner, hovering around the door to the bar. A television crew had arrived, with a handful of men in light summer suits. At the centre of the group stood a woman with a heavily made-up leathery face, her hair shaped into a black bouffant, and oversized shoulder pads in her lime green jacket. Emilia Delgado, the mayoress herself, had come to inspect.

'Looks like the cavalry's arrived,' Vicent said. 'Oh, and they've announced the Pope is swinging round when he's here – to bless the rubble.'

'Thoughtful of him.'

Cámara scanned the faces, looking for Javier Flores, Emilia's right-hand man. He was usually easy to spot, with his clashing dress sense, but he seemed to be absent. Cámara gave a sigh of relief; he could do without Flores's sneering grin on a day like this.

'That's the new one,' Vicent said, nodding at the group of journal-ists and politicians.

Cámara saw that the TV crew was focusing on a second politician hovering next to Emilia as the group looked for the best place to do a piece to camera. The man's dress style was clearly one up from Flores; he'd opted for a well-cut grey suit with a black tie. He was tall and well built, and although he was a few years older than Cámara, perhaps close to fifty, his face was smooth and shiny, as though he'd just shaved. He was looking down at Emilia over a crooked nose with slightly dreamy, glassy eyes. Emilia appeared to be briefing him for the interview he was about to give the local TV station, Canal 9.

'New one?' Cámara asked.

'New councillor in charge of building projects,' Vicent explained. 'Mezquita. Only been in the job for a couple of months. And now he's got to wriggle his way out of this mess. But there's something non-stick about him. Can't see it making him sweat too much.'

'What happened to his predecessor?'

'You really don't follow the news, do you?' Vicent said, rubbing the grey stubble on his cheek. 'García Ramos. Big scandal. The guy was fucking the wife of the Valencia goalkeeper. I tell you – they can steal as much as they like, this lot, and no one bats an eyelid. But start messing with the wife of a football player and you're finished. No matter how powerful your friends are.'

Mezquita had started the interview by this point, and they could hear him talking in a slow but assured fashion about all the measures they were taking to ensure nothing like this ever happened again, and that every effort was being made to rehouse those who had lost their homes.

'Will there be any legal action taken over what has happened?' the interviewer asked tamely.

'An inquest will be held in due course and in the proper way,' Mezquita purred.

Cámara's eyes wandered back to Emilia: she rarely gave interviews herself, preferring her team of men to do them for her. It was all part of an image she liked to project of herself as a sort of high priestess overseeing the affairs of the city – an icon or a goddess. All the more reason why the former cabaret singer had never got married.

Emilia caught sight of the two of them watching her from the other side of the street, and gave them a professional smile. Then she did a double take: there was something familiar about one of them. Yes, it was Cámara, the policeman who had caused them so much trouble with the Blanco case.

The smile dropped as she turned away. Cámara shrugged and ducked into the bar. Vicent followed after him, walked over to the beer tap and started pouring them a couple of *cañas*.

'*Salud*,' he said as he raised his glass.

'Cheers.'

EIGHT

The offices of the department of *Urbanismo* were about to close for lunch by the time he arrived, wondering about finding someone who could fill him in on rehousing possibilities, and whether he could make a claim for compensation. Eventually, after queuing twice for the wrong desk, he was hurriedly told that they were aware of the problem and were working on a solution for the remaining residents of his former block of flats. They took his name and mobile phone number, and promised to call when they had news. But in the meantime, if he had friends or family who could put him up . . .

Back outside the heat was sticky and intense. He'd have to get some new clothes; all he had was what he was standing in, and his shirt was feeling stale and limp.

His phone rang: it was Almudena.

'Have you eaten yet?'

'No.'

'Good. I'm taking you out. And then we'll go shopping. You're going to need a whole new wardrobe.'

They met outside the post office, and she took him to a salad buffet bar, filled with office workers trying to eat themselves into better health by piling their plates high with lettuce leaves and rocket doused in creamy dressings. Cámara fancied a hamburger, something heavy and greasy to soak up the brandy and create a sense of weight in him as a counter to the light-headedness he had felt since that morning. But they didn't have anything like that, so he settled for chicken pasta and some wholegrain rice, washed down with peach juice.

It felt odd being with her like this, having slept in her bed, and acting as though nothing had happened over the previous year, as though they had still been lovers all this while. Yet the last time he had seen her before this she had been gripped tightly in the arms of a killer pressing a gun to her head and threatening to shoot. Had she ever got over that? Was the shock still coursing through her in some hidden, more secret parts? He wanted to ask, but his own current state barely allowed room to discuss another's anguish.

So much had remained unsaid between them. The relationship had ended in part because she was having problems conceiving. At the time she had hinted the fault was his, yet he had discovered subsequently with another woman that he wasn't infertile at all. He shuddered at the thought of telling her now; she wasn't part of his life. Or at least hadn't been until she'd scooped him up from the pavement. And what about the new guy? Was she trying to have a baby with him?

'We can start at El Corte Inglés,' she said. 'It's just round the corner.'

Of course, being told by a woman you felt on the brink of falling in love with that she'd aborted your child wasn't the best way to discover you were, in fact, capable of having children. He still felt a smoking anger about it even now, a year later. But that had been between him and Alicia, nothing to do with Almudena.

For the time being he should remain silent, and do what he did best: watch and see what happened.

On Almudena's advice, at the department store he bought a sponge bag with essentials, two triple packs of stripy boxer shorts, some thin summer socks, spare shoes, leather sandals and flip-flops. A couple of short-sleeved white shirts were on special offer. At Zara, he picked up some light cotton trousers – one pair blue, the other grey. He would have bought linen ones, but he was thinking more about work clothes than anything else, and tempting though it was in the summer heat to buy only shorts and T-shirts, part of him knew that he had to put some effort into appearing like a chief inspector. At least for now.

Here he was, he thought to himself, a man whose house had fallen down, taking most of his possessions with it, his neighbour and her little son – a boy he had felt closer to than he had cared to admit – dead. And yet he sensed a curious, if slightly unreal, calm. No shaking, no panic, no short, shallow breathing. Yes, he felt tired, and would happily have given up the mundane task of finding new clothes to wear in favour of sitting down somewhere, lying back, perhaps helping himself to another brandy. But the crash, the stress, the sense of loss and lack of direction had come before the disaster of his house falling down. Now that he was facing a real crisis, he might possibly start to get on with things again.

He grabbed another couple of shirts from the rack without trying them on, and went to the cash register to pay. He checked the time from the watch on the checkout man's wrist: there were probably still a few minutes before Susana and Tomás's funeral, and he could make it if he rushed. But the weight of Almudena's presence, combined with a growing leaden sensation in his body, was temporarily depriving him of the energy and decisiveness needed to get there. At that moment he felt like a dead leaf being blown about by a cold, cutting wind, a man no longer in charge of his own movements. Almudena stepped outside to wait for him in the dying evening light.

'You can stay at my place again tonight,' she said when he emerged on to the street. 'Don't tell me you've already arranged to go some-where else. I know you too well.'

'Are you sure that won't be a problem?'

She ignored the question, and pushed her hand down into her handbag, before bringing out a package for him.

'Here,' she said. 'A present.'

He unwrapped the paper to find an iPod underneath.

'For your new flamenco collection,' she said. 'To start again. You'll need a computer for it as well, to download songs. But we can use my one at home for now.'

Cámara smiled.

'You'll have to show me how it works,' he said.

'You're not an old man yet,' she said. 'No matter how much you tell yourself you are.'

Back at her flat, he had a long, cold shower, taking advantage of the momentary coolness to try on some of the new clothes before the humidity stuck them to his skin. She walked in as he was pulling on a pair of trousers.

'They suit you,' she said. 'The boxers, I mean. Colourful. More fun. Make you look younger.'

He stopped.

'Look, Almudena.'

She reached over and placed her hand on his cheek, then let it fall slowly, drawing her fingers over his exposed neck, till it rested on his chest, circling her thumb in the hairs around his nipple.

'I've been making some margaritas while you were in the shower. Come into the living room. We can drink them there.'

Wednesday 8th July

He woke up on the sofa. It was already hot, and he felt the blood pulsing in his thighs, a sheen of sweat on his upper lip. He placed his hand down between his legs and felt the frustrated stiffness of his erection. No, this time he had to allow his head and heart to make the decisions. He had done the right thing.

It was curiously quiet outside. In the absence of traffic he could even hear birdsong coming from the acacia trees. Should he get up now? Perhaps he could wash and dress before she'd even woken up. He checked the time on his phone, and sighed. Past eight o'clock. Her regular morning routine would have already kicked off. At least, though, he'd got somewhere to sleep for another night. Even if he'd refused to pay the price that she'd been asking. The margaritas had slipped down easily enough. Things had only got more complicated after she started kissing him. Or at least five or ten minutes after she'd started kissing him, when she'd moved on to taking off their clothes.

The door opened and Almudena stood there with her hair in a towel, wearing a thin white cotton dressing gown through which the shadow of her sex was partially visible. The hardness in her eyes, with which he had once been so familiar, had returned, as if to reproach him for what he had turned down the night before. This could have been yours again, they said.

'The shower's free,' she said out loud. 'There's still some hot water. I've got to leave in five minutes.'

He waited for her to go before getting up. There was no point displaying the weakness in his resolve.

She was already standing by the door with the key in her hand, as if about to walk out, when he emerged, drying his hair with the hand towel she'd left for him by the sink.

'Esteban's coming back today,' she said.

He nodded.

'He called. Catching a different flight. Says he doesn't want to miss the Pope's visit.'

Cámara tried, but failed, to stifle a laugh.

'You mean he's . . .'

'You'll have to go,' she said.

Trying to stop just made it worse.

'Did you hear me?' she yelled over his guffaws.

'Yes, yes.' Cámara wiped away the tears from his eyes. 'Of course. Didn't realise he was a believer.'

She swung the door open out on to the stairwell.

'Fuck you.'

The laughing stopped.

'Yes,' he said, more seriously. 'Fuck me.'

Now he was a homeless policeman investigating the murder of a man who had been in danger of losing his own home. There was a curious symmetry to it, one that he wasn't sure he appreciated.

He placed his bags down in a corner of the office and stared out of the window at the brick facades of the tower blocks opposite. That was all he had: a few shopping bags with a couple of changes of clothes, and some dirty washing. He'd forgotten to buy a new charger for his phone the previous day, and the battery had gone dead. Perhaps he'd pop out before lunch to get a new one. With that, his wallet and his police badge, he'd be pretty complete. At least to survive for the next few days.

He wondered about digging out an old camp bed he'd used to sleep here a couple of times, when they'd had to work through the night, catching a couple of hours before dawn. It had made his back ache, he remembered. But it might do for a few days. A week if necessary. He'd have to ask Torres if he knew where they'd put it.

But Torres wasn't there. Nor was anyone by the looks of it. Other offices along the corridor were empty.

Cámara pottered around for a few minutes, pouring himself some bitter, frothy coffee from the new machine that had finally been installed, reading notices on the walls. There'd been a shoot-out at an immigrants' house on the Avenida Burjasot. Two black Africans had been killed and another had died of his injuries after jumping out of the fourth-floor window. Survivors of the attack talked of white men bursting through the door, shouting at them in what might have been Russian accents. But they weren't sure.

Then there was a new wife-murder. A former soldier this time, who had managed to hang on to his service weapon, and then used it on his wife and their two children before making a dash for it. For some reason he hadn't used the pistol on himself afterwards – which was the more common pattern, especially when military men were involved. Eventually the soldier had been located at the house of his brother, who had also been armed. The two of them held out for over five hours before handing themselves in. Not that they would have had a chance if they'd insisted on fighting it out, Cámara thought to himself, especially when he saw that his old mate Enric Beltrán, a sharpshooter now back in the GEO special forces, was part of the emergency team that surrounded the flat. In tight circumstances you could rely on Beltrán's sharp eye and steady trigger finger, as he'd learned himself.

So this was his life. Sorting out the mess, trying to pick a line, to find a meaning – a coherence – in the chaos. Other people's chaos.

It was time to find Ramón the fisherman.

There was a shout – a gruff, familiar, if unexpected voice.

'We've been calling you all fucking morning.'

He couldn't remember the last time he'd seen Pardo without a suit.

'The battery's dead,' he said. 'I still haven't—'

'Get into the conference room, like all the others,' Pardo barked. 'Now. The whole of *Homicidios* has been ordered to report. Emergency meeting.'

'What's it about?'

'You'll find out soon enough.'

NINE

The air-conditioning unit in the conference room had broken completely, so the windows giving out on to the street had been opened in an attempt to keep the temperature down. But the collective heat radiating from a score of men and women of the *Policía Nacional* punched him like a greasy fist. Unhindered by the glass, the noise from the cars and buses racing along the avenue outside filled the room like an echo chamber, and Cámara noticed that Chief Inspector Maldonado, recently promoted to head of the organised crime squad, was having to use a microphone to make himself heard.

'Nice of you to join us.'

Spotting a seat at the back near the window, he eased himself down behind Torres, who sat bolt upright, ignoring him. Perhaps it was his position at the back of the room, or the fact that his old bugbear Maldonado appeared to be in charge of things, with a seriousness on his face that spoke of ambition and lust for power, but Cámara was seized by a schoolboy urge to lean over and pull on Torres's hair. Pardo, however, had taken a seat on the dais next to Maldonado, and was watching them all like a headmaster.

He leaned back, trying to make himself comfortable on the hard plastic chair. No breeze came from outside, and the yellow-and-white flags strewn across the street hung like dead animals being left to dry in the sun. From the front, Maldonado began his talk, revelling in his new-found importance.

'As I was about to say,' he said. Cámara closed his eyes. 'At 0835 hours this morning Sofía Bodí, the well-known abortionist, was kidnapped from outside her home near the Colón market. Two witnesses saw her getting into an unmarked dark saloon car with two men.' He paused. 'Both of them were wearing *Guardia Civil* uniforms. The *Guardia Civil*, however, from the highest levels, have denied any involvement whatsoever in this morning's events.'

Cámara's eyes reopened. There was a collective intake of breath, followed by an outbreak of murmuring and swearing. *Ostias. Me cago en la puta*. People shuffled in their seats, turning their heads towards their neighbours with shocked expressions. In spite of the denials, this involved the *Guardia Civil*, the other national police force – the opposition. This was big.

Maldonado held out his hands for quiet.

'Sofía Bodí, as you all know,' he said as the voices quietened down, 'has been in the news recently thanks to the *Guardia Civil* investigation into her clinic over alleged malpractices.'

The murmuring picked up again.

'You'll find details of the investigation in the handouts you've all got.'

Cámara saw that he was missing the report, and leaned over to grab the papers from Torres's lap.

'Given the nature of what we're dealing with,' Maldonado continued, 'the implication of the *Guardia Civil*, the high profile of the victim and the timing – need I remind you who's about to visit Valencia? – the case is being led by my unit.'

As he continued, Cámara quickly got up to speed on a case which his newspaper-reading colleagues were already familiar with.

Sofía Bodí was fifty-six years old, he read, a Valencian woman originally from the Benimaclet district, the only daughter of a schoolteacher and his wife. The previous December her clinic, the *Clínica Levantina de Salud Ginecológica*, in the neighbourhood of Patraix, had been the subject of a raid by the *Guardia Civil*, who had conducted a search after clinic employees were seen carrying out bags of waste and placing them in a van. According to the official *Guardia Civil* account, at that moment the officers, from the environment-protection *Seprona* unit, suspected that an ecological crime was being committed – something to do with the waste not being disposed of in the proper way – and decided to investigate. When they raided the clinic and took away the refuse sacks, they claimed to have found the remains of foetuses up to twenty-five weeks old – three weeks over the permitted twenty-two-week limit. The officers involved, led by Comandante Lázaro, applied to the duty investigating judge to open a case, but she rejected it out of hand, saying their claims were unfounded. So they waited a couple of days, pulled some strings, until a judge they knew to be more conservative was available, and officially opened the case with him. This time the evidence was admitted.

Since then, the investigation had been continuing under intense media attention, until, two days earlier, the *Guardia Civil* raided the clinic once again, this time taking away the computers and files for inspection. According to comments overheard at the time, Comandante Lázaro, who was present, warned Sofía Bodí that the next time they would be back for her.

Despite his self-imposed media blackout – why read the papers or watch the news when you always heard in the end if something really important was happening? – Cámara was aware that the country's abortion laws had been under scrutiny over the past few months or more. The government in Madrid, he felt sure, was going to liberalise them, and make abortion legal, as opposed to simply decriminalised. Had they gone ahead and done it already? He seemed to remember images seen somewhere of large demonstrations in the capital against the move, with various grumpy old archbishops wagging their bejewelled fingers over the issue. The Pope's visit now was great timing for them.

Ahead, he noticed that Maldonado was still talking.

'. . . which is how the case was being carried out. There is plenty of evidence,' Maldonado said, taking a deep breath, 'to suggest that the Sofía Bodí investigation is politically motivated. We've already spelled out the backdrop to all this, particularly with the new abortion law and His Holiness's imminent visit.'

A couple of people sniggered. But no one was sure if Maldonado was being sarcastic this time.

'Bodí herself,' he continued, 'is a leading pro-abortion campaigner, and has been at the forefront of the movement since the mid-seventies. She's a founder member of the pressure group *Mi Cuerpo, Mi Elección* – My Body, My Choice. Then there's Comandante Lázaro. He's a known conservative – old school. And a churchgoer. There's ever more reason to suspect an ideological element to all this.'

A hand went up. Maldonado nodded for the policewoman to speak.

'But you said the *Guardia* have denied anything to do with Sofía Bodí being taken this morning.'

'Exactly,' Maldonado said, putting on the most serious face he could. 'Officially, they have said they know nothing about this; no arrest order was issued for Sofía Bodí this morning.'

Cámara was longing for a smoke, and started fingering the packet of Ducados in his trouser pocket. Sweat was pouring down his back and he was beginning to feel light-headed. He still wasn't sure why officers from *Homicidios* had been called to this meeting.

'And I believe them,' Maldonado continued. 'Which is why . . .' He looked down at the floor for a moment, as though collecting his thoughts. The guy should be on the stage, thought Cámara. '. . . we are seriously considering the possibility of a GAL-type operation being behind this.'

This time Cámara's own jaw dropped with surprise. Several years had passed since he had heard that word. He hadn't expected to come across it again, except in some retrospective articles or books on the González government – and the dirty war it had waged against ETA, the terror group seeking independence for the Basque Country.

For years, back in the 1990s, when he was still in Albacete, struggling to get promoted to inspector, people had spoken of little else. The GAL, the so-called *Grupos Antiterroristas de Liberación* – the anti-terrorist liberation groups – had been active in the mid-1980s. They were a shadowy and violent bunch of anti-ETA activists, who murdered over twenty people during their campaign. Their targets were ostensibly ETA members, but innocent people, including several across the border in the French Basque Country, also suffered at their hands. By the late 1980s their string of kidnappings and shootings appeared to have ended, but then, in the early 1990s, a group of investigative journalists began to report that the GAL's members were in fact mostly mercenaries, policemen and *Guardias Civiles*, controlled by members of the government. After a judicial investigation, Interior Minister José Barrionuevo and his deputy Rafael Vera were jailed for their part in the conspiracy. The Prime Minister himself, Felipe González, was investigated at one stage and cleared of involvement, but there were plenty who still thought he had been the mysterious '*Señor X*', the supposed leader of the GAL. It was enough to give

Spain's young and delicate democracy a serious jolt, and to lose the Socialists the election in 1996.

The fallout within the *Policía Nacional* and the *Guardia Civil* had been less visible but no less far-reaching. Older officers tainted by the scandal were moved on or forced to retire, one of the reasons, Cámara knew, why he himself had made chief inspector before he hit forty.

He became aware that the GAL comment had shocked others around him. Some were staring into space, others shaking their heads. Most were talking, either to themselves or to anyone who would listen.

'This is not mere conjecture.' Maldonado raised his voice over the hubbub to make himself heard. Feedback whined from the microphone and he had to hold it further away from his mouth.

'We've received information that I can't disclose right now that suggests that members of the *Guardia Civil* – and Comandante Lázaro may be among them – have created an illicit group to carry out acts of terror with a socially conservative agenda. If this is correct, then the kidnapping of Sofía Bodí may be their first, high-profile step. And I don't need to remind you that the GAL's kidnapping victims often turned up dead. We probably have very little time to get a satisfactory result.'

'Where does the info come from?' came a question. 'The CNI?'

Maldonado nodded. 'The intelligence services are involved, which is why I can't say any more at this point,' he said.

Cámara groaned silently. The *Centro Nacional de Inteligencia* was not especially renowned for the accuracy of its information. Years before, when they were still called the CESID, the *Centro Superior de Información de la Defensa*, he'd heard a rumour that other national intelligence organisations tended to bet against any 'information' coming out of Madrid, with consistently high returns. Changing their name had done little to improve their reputation.

Still, Comandante Lázaro already had a reputation in police circles for his reactionary views. He was a member of a right-wing officers' group, one of whose members, a few years back, had been forced into early retirement after calling on the armed forces to step in to prevent Catalonia's gradual but steady dislocation from the rest of Spain.

A hand went up. Maldonado nodded for the officer to speak.

'Is the *Guardia Civil* intelligence unit involved in this investigation? Will we be liaising with them?'

'Yes. But the *Servicio de Información* are talking directly with the CNI,' Maldonado said. 'Anything we need to know will be passed on to me.'

He walked over to a large television set on top of a wooden book-case and switched it on.

'We have reason to suspect that Sofía Bodí may have known that an attempt of some sort was being planned against her.'

He picked up a remote control and pressed a button.

'This is a recording of a news conference she gave yesterday morning.'

There was a whirring sound and colours flashed across the screen, before the image became clear. The *Policía Nacional*, it seemed, was still using video tape to record material from the television.

Cámara saw a picture of a slim, middle-aged woman with short silver hair sitting down at a table while cameras flashed on her. She was wearing rectangular, black-framed glasses – they didn't seem to make any other kind these days – and no make-up. Her face was drawn, and from the heaviness around her eyes she looked exhausted. She started reading from a prepared statement.

'*Yesterday the offices of the* Clínica Levantina de Salud Ginecológica *were raided for a second time by agents of the* Guardia Civil Seprona *Unit . . .*'

Speaking in a low, weak voice, she gave details of the 'harassment' she said she had been receiving over the past months, reminding the public of her lifelong campaign in favour of abortion, her time working in France before the practice was decriminalised in Spain in 1985, how her clinic had been one of the first to be set up in Spain after that, and her attempts to have the law changed to make abortion fully legal.

'*Though I may not wish to advertise the fact, my clinic is a high-profile target for the anti-abortion movement. I do not think this is a coincidence when we are talking about the so-called investigation that is being carried out at present. I call on Spanish society to witness what is taking place, and to make up its own mind, and not to accept the lies being fed by the conservative media. We reject all allegations being made against us, and are confident that there is no evidence to substantiate the claims being made. However, certain powerful forces are involved.*

They must understand that there will be consequences if things continue as they are. Authoritarianism is deeply ingrained in certain sectors of our country. We cannot allow them to control our lives as they once did. This is a time for action, to stand up and reject all attempts to smother a legal and ultimately humanitarian activity in the name of tradition and faith. Nothing less than the future of our democracy is at stake.'

She stood up, apparently unwilling to answer any of the dozen questions fired at her by the attending journalists. Then she stopped, leaned in to the microphone again and said:

'Right-wingers also abort.'

Maldonado hit a button on the remote control and froze the image.

'Take note of the words she used,' he said, turning to face the group. 'She mentioned "powerful forces". We're working on the hypothesis here that she had some inkling of what was going on, that there may have been more behind the official *Guardia Civil* investigation, that rogue elements may have been about to make a move on her. She stopped sleeping at her own flat, and moved in temporarily with her business partner and lover Cesc Ballester. We've taken a preliminary statement from him already, and will be conducting more interviews with him shortly. According to Ballester, Bodí was uncomfortable staying at home, and only went to her flat this morning to collect some belongings, while he went to the clinic. We suspect that it was as she was approaching her flat that the kidnappers moved in.'

He stopped, and scanned the faces looking up at him.

'Any questions?'

A few hands went up.

'If rogue members of the *Guardia Civil* are involved, why did they bother with the official investigation to begin with?'

'You expect me to explain the workings of the *Guardia*?' Maldonado said with a smirk. A few at the front tittered. 'Look, it's possible they were trying to shut down the clinic by legal means. When they saw that was likely to fail – and we understand there was a high probability that the case was going to collapse, even with a sympathetic judge at the helm – they decided to move on to plan B, as it were. That's the hypothesis.'

Pardo had been sitting quietly during all of this, but now he stood up and moved towards Maldonado, who passed him the microphone.

'As you all know, Maldonado is in charge of the day-to-day running of this investigation, while I, as head of *Homicidios*, will be overseeing. We need our best people on this. It's an extremely sensitive case. High-ranking members of the *Guardia Civil* are under suspicion. We need to be very careful, and watch what we say. Which is why all informal contacts between everyone in this room and members of the *Guardia* are now forbidden: no drinks, no chats, no off-the-record briefings. We cannot allow any leaks. They know this police investigation is starting, so they'll be prepared.'

Cámara started shuffling uncomfortably in his seat. He'd been sitting still too long, and his thighs were going numb. And for something that didn't concern him directly, the meeting was taking up too much of his time.

'The Ministry is fully aware of the situation,' Pardo continued, 'as is the government delegate in the city. We have their full support. Memories of the GAL are still fresh. No one wants a repeat of the fuck-ups of back then. This is a high-publicity case, an opportunity for us to shine. Judge José Luis Rulfo is the investigating magistrate in charge of the legal side, and you all know as well as I do that he's not an interferer, but he expects an efficient, professionally done job. It's got to be wrapped up as quickly and cleanly as possible. The Pope's coming to town, people are marching in the streets over the new abortion law. A kidnapped abortionist whose life is in danger is top priority.'

He took a deep breath, flaring his nostrils.

'Which is why I'm ordering everyone here in this room to suspend any cases they're working on. As of now you're all on this detail.'

TEN

July was the worst month. Already the temperatures were in the high thirties, but rather than slowing down people were possessed by an urgent and frantic need to get things done before the country closed for the August holidays.

He stepped out of the mobile phone shop, a new – and overpriced – charger stuffed in his pocket. The traffic was bumper to bumper, some drivers cocooned in air-conditioned bubbles, others in older cars with the windows open, breathing in hot smoke streaming from a thousand exhaust pipes as sweat dribbled down their cheeks. The sun was high in the sky, and the tall, skinny palm trees lining the avenue gave little shade. The weather was uppermost in everyone's minds at this time of year, official announcements on television reminding citizens to keep cool and drink plenty of water. Heatwaves could be lethal. They didn't want scores of the elderly giving up the ghost just as the Pope rocked into town.

Conversations tended to be monotonously alike from now until late August: someone would mention how hot it was, as though it were the strangest thing in the world, then positions would be taken between those who liked the summer, and thrived in these temperatures, and those who loathed the sticky, clammy heat, and longed for it to pass. Each one would try to convince the other that only their own position was correct. Even when it came to something as basic as the weather, his countrymen felt the need to identify with either this or that group, like political parties.

Cámara himself could bear the heat well enough, but was damned if he was going to get ideological about it. Some could cope with it, some couldn't.

A group of teenagers walked in front of him, yellow-and-white rucksacks slung over their shoulders. Publicity for the Vatican, and its front man, due to arrive in a couple of days' time. Something in him sank when he saw young kids like this being sucked into the game, each tribe – left or right, secular or religious – trying to draw them to their side, like chips in some unending poker match. He could still remember the time, back in 1978, as the country had voted on the new democratic constitution, when the priest at his school had taken him to one side.

'And if you were old enough to vote,' Father Dionisio had asked him – Cámara had only been twelve at the time – 'would you vote in favour or against?'

And Cámara, not really knowing, but remembering comments his grandfather had made back home that, despite being an anarchist, he considered a new constitution the lesser of the two evils, had said he'd vote in favour. And Father Dionisio put on the special look he used when he wanted you to know you'd done something gravely, gravely wrong: head tilted back, eyes wide open and tight, trembling lips.

'But who,' he boomed, 'has put this *porquería*, these disgusting, filthy thoughts into your mind?'

In the end, the constitution hadn't needed Cámara's pubescent vote to get through. But any doubts he might have had about the clergy were removed from his mind at that moment. True spirituality may have meant something to a handful of priests out there somewhere, but the Church was just about politics and power, like so much else in the country.

Even police work.

Today Spaniards were not firing at each other in open field, as they had done in living memory, but state forces were still engaged in a long-running, mostly bloodless war, a continuous struggle for political supremacy; a fight over the identity of Spain. Was it to be a country of tradition, of order, commercially vibrant, but which, socially at least, remained relatively static, where due respect was given to institutions which had forged the country, such as the Church and Army? Or was it a country that looked to change, eyeing with

70

envy the 'progress' of other European nations, that accepted its own social diversity and regional differences, even at the danger of breaking up and dissolving into separate mini-states?

Now, just as always, it seemed, these two forces were going head to head, and everything and everyone was supposed to declare for either one or the other.

And so began another skirmish – this time dividing the *Policía Nacional* and the *Guardia Civil*. The *Guardias* were mostly to the right politically, and for many on the left they represented the repression of the Franco era, a hangover from the dictatorship that ought to be abolished. The *Policía Nacional*, on the other hand, had been created when the country became a democracy, to defend citizens' "rights and freedoms", and was perceived as being more to the left. But Cámara had met enough liberal *Guardias* and authoritarian *Nacionales* to know the image didn't always fit.

Meanwhile *he* had a real dead body to deal with, but poor old Roures was just a paella chef. He would have to wait; even the judge presiding over his case had been forced to agree to a temporary suspension of the investigation. Political points needed scoring, and Cámara was being forced to play a part.

Abortion. First they'd legalised gay marriage – that had got them out on to the streets – now they were legalising the killing of embryos and foetuses. Few things were guaranteed more to galvanise the conservative right into action.

And Spanish democracy had still to root itself properly – you could tell by the way politicians had worn the word out through overuse.

Now he was supposed to go and look for an abortionist, one who might have been kidnapped by reactionary *Guardias* gone off the rails with their dreams of 'order and progress' – the watchwords of the Franco regime. It wasn't that he was against abortion per se, he convinced himself. On balance he probably preferred a world where you could get it done properly rather than having to deal with a quack, or travel abroad, as in the past. It was just that he had better things to do.

Alicia. God damn her. She hadn't even asked him first.

The written orders Maldonado had given him involved heading over to Sofía Bodí's flat to have a sniff around. It was clear that as a member of *Homicidios* he was being sidelined, left with mundane tasks while Maldonado's people got the more interesting jobs.

Doubtless Maldonado felt pleased with himself at this, another point scored in his ongoing feud with Cámara, but he didn't understand that this was actually a gift. For Cámara, pottering around the sidelines while the rest of the group ran after the main quarry suited him ideally. It was what he usually did anyway; he'd noticed it tended to bring in better and often faster results. Usually the problem was having to produce enough smoke to disguise the fact that this was how he was in fact carrying out his investigation. Superiors and administrators demanded a display of thorough working and methodology, like those maths tests at school, when you couldn't just give the answer, but had to explain how you'd arrived at it. But in his own experience answers came more often than not from unexpected and inexplicable sources, ones that couldn't be part of any 'method'. How could he include in the reports his dreams, intuitions, or overheard conversations in bars or buses that had nothing to do with the case at hand, but which somehow crystallised an aspect of it in his mind? Even folk tales, jokes and of course the proverbs that seemed to run through his blood had given him insights in the past. And he'd had to find a way of explaining it all, sometimes inventing stories to formulate his 'workings' in a manner acceptable and comprehensible to the force.

Now that would be unnecessary.

Yet still he felt this was a waste of time. He was in *Homicidios*, he should be dealing with Roures, a dead man, not Sofía Bodí. Not someone who made a living out of killing. The chances were she was still alive. Although, admittedly, for how much longer was uncertain.

ELEVEN

Sofía Bodí's flat was in the Eixample area near the Colón market, an expensive part of town where fashion designers tended to have their boutiques. The buildings had mostly gone up in the early twentieth century, well-built eclectic structures with decorative motifs in stone around the doors and windows. The district had a graceful, almost Parisian air, while the Colón market itself was an architectural highlight of the city, designed by a follower of Gaudí. They'd renovated it a few years earlier, trying to turn it into Valencia's Covent Garden. But from being a thriving neighbourhood market, it had turned into a den of expensive bars and coffee shops, empty but for the occasional couple of middle-aged women showing off their jewellery as they sipped on *cafés cortados* and nibbled at *madalena* cakes.

A *Policía Nacional* was standing outside the main door, in the street. Cámara reached for his badge as he approached, but the man seemed to recognise him and nodded him through the large, open door of polished dark wood.

'Second floor, sir,' he said as Cámara walked through. 'Door three.'

It was cool and dark in the entrance hall. Pink marble panels covered the walls, while the floor was made of black-and-white checked tiles.

'The, er, partner's up there at the moment,' the policeman said in a lower voice. 'Señor Ballester.'

'OK,' Cámara said. 'What time did he get here?'

'About twenty minutes ago.'

Ignoring the ornate iron lift, Cámara took the stairs. It was lighter here, the marble was a pale grey, and daylight streamed in through tall windows of frosted glass. The building felt solid, heavy, permanent. Not the kind of place you'd expect to collapse on your head at any second. It was curious, he remarked, how he seemed to have developed a sixth sense for this kind of thing all of a sudden.

He was sweating by the time he reached the second floor, but was pleased to notice he was breathing normally. He'd always told himself he'd cut back – or stop altogether – the day he got out of breath. But he was fine. Sometimes he was even convinced smoking helped clear his lungs out.

He rang the doorbell and waited. I'll make this quick, he said to himself, thoughts of the Roures case lingering in his mind. That was the investigation he should be concentrating on. Fuck the orders.

The door opened.

'What do you want?'

Cámara identified himself.

'You guys start showing up when it's too late, don't you.'

'Señor Ballester. I'd like to come in and have a look around.'

Cesc Ballester was a slightly built man, perhaps in his mid-forties, with prematurely thinning dark blond hair, the remains of which he wore long and swept back. Thick sideburns came halfway down his cheeks, but did little to soften an angular face, with thin lips and a long sharp nose. His eyes, small and deep-set, were red. Cámara wondered if he'd been crying.

'Can I come in?' Cámara repeated when the man didn't move.

Eventually, Ballester stepped to one side and let him pass.

There was something old-fashioned about the furniture and style of the flat. Cámara hadn't exactly imagined what Sofía Bodí's home would be like, but from her profession, her appearance on television, it was possible to make fairly accurate guesses about her political and social views. These didn't fit with the conservative, musty sense he got from the place as soon as he walked in, however. A large gilt-framed mirror hung from a wall in the corridor, lace curtains veiled a window at the far end, while a large, heavy wooden desk, with spiral carvings on the legs, seemed to take up most of what looked like a study.

'I imagine you're here looking for clues yourself.' Cámara turned to Ballester, who was shutting the door behind them.

'That's . . .' He paused. 'Yeah, sort of.'

He brushed past Cámara and walked into the living room, which gave out on the street. A revolving fan suspended from the ceiling was circling above, but with the curtains drawn did little to cool the air.

'I would've opened the windows,' Ballester said under his breath. 'But, I don't know. You start wondering if someone might be watching you. It's all a bit freaked out.'

He sat down in a rocking chair, beckoning Cámara to take a seat. Cámara stayed on his feet.

'Have you found any?' he said. 'Clues?'

'Isn't that supposed to be your job?'

Ballester put his head in his hands.

'Look, I've been through all this back at the Jefatura. Gave them a statement. I really don't want to talk about it any more.'

'Did Sofía give you the key?'

'What?' Ballester lifted his head and looked at Cámara through squinted eyes in the half-light.

'To get in here.'

'Well, of course she bloody did. What kind of a question . . .?' He sighed. 'She had a key to my place, I had one for here. Although I didn't come round here much. Never liked it, really. She inherited it from her parents. Hardly changed a thing. We spent more time at my place. Especially recently.'

'Was she carrying your key with her this morning?'

Ballester shook his head at the banality of the question.

'Yeah, she was coming back from my place to pick up some clothes here. I've already said.'

'So whoever's kidnapped her will also have access to your place now,' Cámara said.

'*Ostias!*' His eyes opened wide with fear. 'I hadn't thought of that. Do you think . . . ?'

'No, I wouldn't advise you to change the locks. Not yet. But you might want to be vigilant. There's no obvious reason why anyone would want to get inside your flat. But you're an employee of the clinic, and someone very close to Sofía. You may be in some kind of danger yourself.'

Ballester's attention was fully focused on him now.

'I can arrange police protection for you if you like.'

He might have been effectively demoted on this case, running around like Maldonado's subordinate rather than the chief inspector he really was, but he could still give orders himself, if necessary.

'I assume this was brought up at the Jefatura?' he added.

'No.' Ballester frowned. 'It doesn't matter. No one's coming after me. It was Sofía they wanted.'

'Who?'

'These bastards who've been gunning for her all these months!' he cried. 'Who else is it going to be? It's like a nervous tic with them. Anyone doing something they don't approve of and they've got to lock them up or get rid of them. First they cook up some charges against her. And when they saw that wasn't going to work, they pick her up off the street. I don't care how much the *Guardia Civil* deny it. It's them. She's probably down in some cell of theirs right now, but they've just forgotten to mention it to anyone, know what I mean?'

He covered his face with his hands again, shoulders heaving as the sobs took their hold.

'God knows what they're doing to her.'

Cámara left the room and went to find the kitchen. He took a glass from the drying rack, filled it with cool water from a jug in the fridge and then walked back down the corridor. A box of tissues was sitting on a counter near the door; he picked it up and carried it with him into the living room, placing it down on the table next to Ballester with the water.

'If it's all right,' he said, 'I'm going to take a look around.'

Ballester was too lost to notice.

Pulling out some cotton gloves from his trouser pocket, Cámara headed back down the corridor and into the main bedroom at the far end. The curtains were closed here too, and the air was damp with summer humidity. He flicked on the light: the walls were painted fuchsia, while a simple double bed with a shiny carved pine headboard sat in the middle. It was made, with flowery sheets, but looked as though it hadn't been slept in for some time. In fact, were it not for the heat of the day, he could almost sense a coldness about the place: a room for dying, not for living. He began to wonder if Sofía had spent very much time here at all. There was nothing in the fridge except the water jug and an unopened bottle of white wine.

He walked over to the curtains and pulled back the corner of one of them to look through the window. The glass was grimy, and it gave on to a narrow light shaft at the centre of the building, connecting with the staircase and some of the other neighbouring flats. He turned the handle and opened it a little to let in some air, sticking his head out to let it cool down for a few seconds.

Back inside he tried to take in more of the room, and the person who – officially at least – had lived here. He felt under the long, tube-like pillow and the mattress, kneeled down to look under the bed, opened the bedside drawers, flicked through the clothes hanging in the cupboard, but found nothing but the usual bedroom items. If anything it felt bare – there were no books by the bedside lamp, nothing potentially embarrassing hidden in some corner. Which was perhaps explained by Sofía taking most of her things to Ballester's place. But no one had said anything about her moving in with him.

He was aware of the similarity with Roures's home, the same absence of life-giving clutter. There was even, now he thought of it, an echo of his own flat – before it had become a shapeless pile on the ground. Each one had something functional and loveless about it, a sense of merely passing through.

Llena o vacía, la casa es solo mía. Either empty or full, my home is mine alone.

He poked his head into the bathroom. A single blue toothbrush stood in a glass by the sink next to a soap dispenser. Two white towels were folded on a rack on the wall next to the shower. Under the sink, the cupboards contained toilet roll, shampoo, some perfume in a dusty bottle that looked as though it hadn't been used in years, and a wicker basket of household drugs: paracetamol, cough mixture, and some indigestion tablets.

Back in the corridor he spotted a couple of framed photographs hanging on the wall. He saw the faces of a middle-aged man and a woman. From the style of their clothes, and the faded colour of the pictures, he had the impression they'd been taken perhaps thirty years before. Sofía's parents, by the looks of it, the people for whom this had really been a home at one stage.

The study was the last room he looked into. Dark green wooden shutters were lowered over a window giving out on to what he thought must be the side alley, but glimmers of sunlight shone through the joins, giving enough light at this brightest time of year for him to be able to sniff around without having to turn on the desk lamp; by now his eyes were accustomed to the gloom.

Built-in wooden bookshelves lined the two side walls of the square, cube-like room, and the desk stood in the middle, facing the door, like in a doctor's surgery. A black-and-gold pen stood in a stand, while the top of the desk was covered in dark red leather with gold trimming.

Cámara inspected the books: general medical tomes, works on gynaecology, many of them quite grand, but dated, he thought, as though they'd been bought more with a view to being left on a bookshelf than ever opened and read. Perhaps they were books she'd used when she was studying, and never had to refer to again.

Further across, nearer the window on the left-hand side, he noticed some smaller, leather-bound volumes. Leaning down, he noticed they were virtually identical, all with a year's date embossed in gold lettering on the spine.

He picked one up: 1987. Inside was a diary, written in neat, very small handwriting. Her mother's? Her father's? He flicked to the front page; there was Sofía's name clearly written out. He picked out another one at random, and again the same handwriting and the same name at the front.

From the living room he could hear the sound of Ballester blowing his nose. He must have stopped crying, and was doubtless wondering what Cámara was up to.

Cámara glanced down at the bookshelves to get a better look. There were dozens of diaries. The oldest one dated from 1971, then the collection stretched all the way almost to the present: the previous year was clearly visible, but then the final half a dozen copies were for future years, the dates already printed on the spines, but obviously with nothing written in them yet.

He double-checked, just in case there was more madness in this than at first appeared, just in case Sofía had written in them. But no, they were blank.

What he wanted though, and what he couldn't find, was this year's diary. That, if she was as meticulous as her handwriting might suggest, could give some interesting clues.

Back in the living room, Ballester was clearly stirring: Cámara could hear what sounded like springs creaking on a sofa.

He sat down at the desk, placed his fingertips together and let his eyes wander around the room. It was possible that Sofía had carried it with her and jotted things down during the day, but something about the neatness of the others told him she had written it right where he was sitting now, like some kind of ritual part of her day.

As if by instinct, his hand dropped down to the drawers in the desk. The first one contained envelopes and a stapler.

Inside the second was the diary. He flicked through it quickly: the last entry was from two nights before, the last time she had come to the flat.

Standing up, he placed it in his pocket. This would require time and a different space to be properly examined.

Peering round the doorway, he saw that Ballester had drunk the water, and was lying with his back to him, curled up on the sofa, his shoes on the floor.

The door gave a soft click as Cámara let himself out.

TWELVE

The restaurant had half a dozen tables outside on the pavement, where two couples of partially clothed northern Europeans were grilling themselves in the sun. Glancing at them with incomprehension, he ducked his head under the canopy and dived into the air-conditioned refuge inside.

He'd texted Torres earlier, and was pleased to see him already sitting there at their favourite table in the corner. It was a small place that did a decent lunch for seven euros – three courses with bread, wine and coffee. And best of all, you could smoke. Some kind of anti-smoking law had been passed a few years before, but it only applied to places with more than a hundred square metres of floor space. Anything smaller could opt out. So on paper the country could say it was conforming with the EU directive, while in practice everyone carried on as before. Or at least until they got caught and had to bring in a new law plugging the gap in the old one.

'They'll get us in the end,' Torres liked to say. 'You mark my words. We'll have to step outside between courses to spark up. As if we didn't have it bad enough at work. You won't be able to walk on the pavements for all the smokers blocking the way. Then people'll start getting run over, 'cause they're having to walk in the street where the cars are. And they call it progress.'

'Bad day?' Cámara asked.

'Ah, nothing,' he said with a sneer.

From his expression, Cámara recognised the symptoms: trouble at home. Torres's wife, Marga, was a quiet, intense woman who had a tendency to blow up every so often – usually now, shortly before the August break, when the speed, heat and noise could break many people in the city. What he'd sometimes suspected, but had never been able to confirm, however, was that on occasion Marga sought solace during these nervous interludes in someone else's bed.

Despite the food being good and being able to smoke, they didn't have Mahou beer on tap, so Cámara ordered a bottle. Torres opted for some red wine, which came chilled in a half-litre flask, condensation thick on the outside of the glass.

'Bring me some lemonade as well,' he called to the waiter. 'Might as well mix it into a *tinto de verano*. This stuff's undrinkable otherwise.'

They both ordered paella for the first course. Usually, as he grew accustomed to the intense heat of early summer, his appetite would wane for a few weeks, as though his body were slowing down to adapt. But today he felt hungry, perhaps, he reflected, because he had nowhere to go, no home to embrace him at the end of the day. So a feast-or-famine instinct had awakened in him, making him intent on gorging while food was available.

This being a working lunch, the paella came heaped on plates rather than served in the paella pan. Cámara looked down at the dark yellow mixture of rice, chicken, rabbit and green beans and was pleased to see there were plenty of specks of brown *socarraet* in there as well – the crispy, gooey bits from the bottom of the paella dish where the rice was more toasted, and the flavours more concentrated. It was one of the things about paella they only really got right in Valencia, and they knew him well enough in the restaurant now for him not to have to ask for it.

And despite the fact that they weren't eating it straight from the pan, he still used the more traditional spoon to feed himself. Paella just wasn't paella with a fork.

The first mouthful was delicious: enough oil as a vehicle for the myriad tastes, but the rice was still a little chalky and not overdone. Paella, he often thought, was best regarded as a combination of pan-frying and boiling: both were needed to create this unique dish.

'There's a kind of rating system for rice dishes,' Torres said. 'All part of the mystery of paella.'

'You're not going to get mystical on me, are you?'

'Paella's not just food for a Valencian; it's a way of life.'

Torres took a swig of his fizzy red drink and pursed his lips.

'You know all this already. Or at least you should do. Been here long enough.'

'All right.' Cámara held up his hands. 'No disrespect. So what's this rating system, then?'

'*Bò, rebò* and *mèl.*' Torres flicked out his fingers as he listed the words. 'It's like giving marks to the paella depending on how good it is.'

Cámara chuckled.

'Serious stuff.' Torres stared at him. 'A family can spend the whole mealtime arguing over what grade to give it.'

'All right, so what do they mean?'

Torres gave him a look.

'*Bò*, as you should know by now, is Valencian for "good". *Rebò* means "very good".'

'And *mèl*?'

'*Mèl* means "honey".'

'That's the top mark?'

Torres frowned.

'Kind of.'

'Well, is it or isn't it?'

'There's another one above that. But it's hardly ever used. Perhaps never. It belongs to the perfect, archetypal paella, like some kind of Platonic ideal. One that's been made over an open fire, using only wood from an orange tree.'

'And using Valencian water.'

'Of course. It's impossible to make paella with water from anywhere else. Doesn't come out the same.'

'And this top mark is?'

'*De categoría,*' Torres said, his Valencian accent thickening slightly, all open vowels like a yowling cat.

'You think Plato had paella in mind when he was coming up with his theory of Forms?'

'There's a Form for everything,' Torres hit back. 'Even the hairs in your nose. Or at least that's what my mate Joaquín told me at school. I never did understand much in philosophy classes.'

Cámara lifted up a spoonful of rice and meat.

'So what category's this one then? I reckon it's pretty *mèl.*'

'Get out of here. You don't know what you're talking about. This?' He pointed at his plate and frowned in concentration. '*Bò*. You can't give it more than that.'

Cámara put the spoonful in his mouth. It tasted all right to him. Perhaps a little heavy on the oil, now he thought about it.

'So what's below *bò*, then? What happens if it's a bad paella?'

Torres scowled.

'No such thing,' he said.

They only started talking about the Sofía Bodí case once coffee arrived. To have done so earlier would have been disrespectful to the food as well as to Roures in some strange way. Both knew, without having to say, how the other felt about having to suspend the investigation like this.

'By the way,' Torres said. 'There was an email from the Logroño police. The tests for blood on Victoria Luna Pérez came back negative.'

Cámara shrugged; Torres handed him some papers.

'Printout with more background on Sofía,' he said. 'Everyone's got it.'

He reached for his cigarettes.

'Don't know why, but I'm feeling less like an inspector and more like a bloody corporal or even a constable on this detail. There's a lot of orders being made, and we're just expected to run around at Maldonado's beck and call. Not sure how you can stand it, given the history between you two.'

'Anything I need to know?' Cámara asked.

Torres glanced down at the papers.

'Well, if you're too lazy to read it yourself . . .'

'Come on,' Cámara said. 'This way we'll both remember it better.'

'Quickly, then.'

'What's the rush?'

'Maldonado's scheduled a conference at three thirty. *Everyone's* supposed to be there.'

'Right. OK, what's the stuff on our missing abortionist?'

'Born nineteen fifty-three.'

'Birthday?'

Torres checked the papers.

'Twenty-seventh of February.'

'Pisces, then.'

'Oh, come on. Don't tell me you're into all that crap.'

'I knew there was something fishy about this case.'

'You can't take this seriously, can you?'

'Fish swim in the sea. Sometimes they get caught.'

Torres stubbed his cigarette out in the overfull ashtray, spilling ash on the white paper tablecloth.

'Back to Roures again?' he said.

Cámara was staring into space.

'I don't know.'

He pulled himself up.

'Anything else?'

'Father, mother . . . You know all this,' Torres went on, glancing through the notes. 'Studied medicine at the university here, but then went to France to learn about abortion. Back when it was still criminalised here.'

'When was that?'

'Seventy-three.'

Cámara raised his eyebrows. Franco had still been alive then. Leaving the country to study abortion was about more than medicine: it was a political act.

'Got an internship almost straight away at a clinic in Paris. The *Clinique Fontaine*. She stayed there until eighty-two, then opened her own place, the *Clinique Liberté*, specialising in catering for Spanish girls who couldn't get a legal abortion done back home.' He looked up. 'You got any French?'

'Studied it at school,' Cámara said. 'Enough to get by.'

Torres carried on.

'Came back to Valencia pretty quickly after the González government decriminalised abortion in eighty-five. Set up a clinic here, off the Gran Vía, then they moved to the present site in the Patraix district in ninety-eight. Bigger premises, apparently.'

She's dedicated her whole adult life to this, Cámara thought to himself. *Liberté*. That's what abortion was about – freedom. To make choices about your life. He sniffed. Or to kill.

Torres flicked through the pages, but it seemed that that was it. Cámara signalled to the bar.

'You're not coming, then?' Torres said.

'To Maldonado's conference?' Cámara shook his head.

Torres pulled out a note and some coins and gave them to the waiter.

'On me,' he said.

'Hey, look,' Cámara said, trying to thrust some cash into his hand. 'It's not as if I kept all my money under the mattress.'

Torres shook him off.

'I told you, if you need somewhere to stay.'

Cámara remembered his earlier hunch about Marga.

'I'm fine.'

Both their mobile phones buzzed at the same time. Torres pulled his out first.

'Don't bother looking,' he said.

The light from the screen reflected in his eyes as he read the text message.

'Maldonado's brought the conference forward. Wants us all to get there straight away.'

'News?'

'A communiqué from the kidnappers. "Suspend the abortion law, or Sofía dies."'

THIRTEEN

'I've realised what it is.'

'What *what* is?'

'Why you've been so miserable all this time.'

'Miserable?'

'Am I speaking to the same person? That is still my grandson, isn't it?'

'What are you talking about?'

'You've been out of sorts, depressed. Fucked, basically. For at least a year, I'd say. Perhaps more.'

'And?'

'Well, at least admit it. Helps, you know.'

'All right.'

'That'll have to do.'

'Well?'

'Well what?'

'You said you'd worked it out.'

'That's right. What's wrong with you. Came to me last night. I was reading Kropotkin before going to bed. Bit of a breeze blowing up, coming in from the sierra, cooling. Good for the brain. And, of course, Kropotkin is always good for the soul . . .'

'The soul?'

'Yes, that's what I said.'

'You're an anarchist. You're not supposed to believe in souls.'

'I can believe in the soul or not, precisely because I am an anarchist. No one's going to tell me what to believe or what not to believe.'

'Does this mean you've turned to religion? I always thought it would happen one day. Must be something to do with getting old. Getting closer to death, wondering if anything's on the other side. Hedging your bets by believing in some kind of god.'

'I'm no closer to death than you are. In fact, a damn sight further away, I'd say. You don't catch me wandering around all day with a gun strapped to my ribs talking to murderers. If either of us is walking a tightrope, it's you.'

'Yes, all right. But have you?

'Have I what?'

'Turned to religion. Found God.'

'I'm not even going to answer that. I'm an anarchist. I don't believe in belief.'

'Pretty strange kind of anarchist if you ask me.'

'What?'

'Most anarchists actually have a set of ideas, of how they want the country to be run, even if it does mean getting rid of government and money. But at least they actually believe in something. I always thought you did too. Or you gave that impression when you were active in the union. Seems that nowadays being an anarchist for you just means making it up as you go along. Accepting whatever nonsense happens to be floating around in your head each morning as though it actually meant something.'

'You might have nonsense floating around in your head. I think we established that some time ago.'

'Oh, come on.'

'But some of us have a clearer vision of the world around us. And even of things which aren't immediately around us.'

'So, what? You've become a saint now. Hearing voices?'

'Which is why . . .'

'San Hilario? Perhaps I should pray to you at night. What does that make me? The grandson of a saint? Any special concessions?'

'Which is why I suddenly realised that it's all to do with some woman in Madrid . . . Hello, are you still there?'

'I'm here.'

'Right. Thought you might have dropped the phone for a minute. Seems I'm right, then.'

'What?'

'It is. It's some *chica* in Madrid, isn't it?'

'I've never mentioned any woman in Madrid.'

'No, but you've been talking about it.'

'About what?'

'About Madrid. Keeps coming up in conversation.'

'I've been talking about Madrid?'

'Not every day. But enough.'

'When?'

'Last time you were up here, you said something about the Prado.'

'But that was you. You were talking about the Goya exhibition.'

'Yeah, but there was something about the look in your eye. Then it's been mentioned a few other times.'

'When?'

'It doesn't matter. I'm right, aren't I? There's something about Madrid that's bothering you. And the only thing that would bother you for so long is a woman. Stands to reason. Ergo you're upset about some woman who's living in Madrid. QED.'

'You should be on television. Make a mint. Hilario the great mind-reader.'

'No. I just know you. Flesh and blood. Bringing you up for all those years helped as well. Almost like knowing myself.'

'All right.'

'All right what?'

'Well, you're right. There is some woman in Madrid.'

'Hah! Knew it. What's her name?'

'It doesn't matter. It ended. Almost before it started.'

'Come on. What's her name? Names are important.'

'Alicia . . . Hello?'

'What?'

'Thought I'd lost *you* then. Well?'

'It's good. It's a good name. What happened? Why aren't you with her?'

'It's a long story.'

'They're always the best.'

'No, really. I'll tell you some other time.'

'You're holding on to something, I can tell. And it's not doing you any good. That anger, again. Always was your problem. Constipating you. Are you shitting properly these days?'

88

'There's something I need to tell you.'

'And another thing. I rang your home number last night. I wanted to tell you about my amazing discovery, about what was wrong with you. But all I got was this dead tone.'

'That's what I needed to tell you.'

'They cut you off? What's the matter? Can't pay the bills? Bastards. They don't have a right to cut you off. Not for six months at least. I looked into the laws on this. You're protected, as a citizen . . .'

'No, it's not that. The house fell down.'

'Your house fell down.'

'The block of flats. It collapsed the other day.'

'*Me cago en Dios.*' I shit on God.

'They've been building the new metro line outside, and . . .'

'Vibrations. Right. Could be. I take it you weren't inside at the time, then?'

'No.'

'Otherwise this would be a very strange conversation.'

'No. But others were.'

'Oh. I'm very sorry to hear that. Very sorry.'

'A young mother and her little boy.'

'They didn't . . .?'

'No.'

'Susana, was it? You mentioned her. That's . . . I'm very sorry . . . Very sorry.'

'The building was rotting. Wasn't connected to the sewerage.'

'What?'

'Some fuck-up years back.'

'Fuck-up or Town Hall dodgy practices?'

'What do you think?'

'Cunts. Those fucking murderous cunts.'

'. . . Yes . . . Look . . .'

'You got somewhere to stay? The police sorted you out with something?'

'Er, no. I'm OK. Friends putting me up, I'm all right. I'll . . . I'll find something. Eventually. Things are busy at the moment. Some missing abortionist. They think she's been kidnapped and they want us to find her.'

'Right, well, I won't keep you.'

'It's OK.'

'I'll call you. I've got your mobile number. Let me know when you're settled in some place.'

The diary smelt of old glue and leather. The paper was thick, and of a light beige colour; it felt like the work of an artisan: well crafted, expensive, sure of itself.

Cámara resisted a more systematic urge to start at the beginning of the year and work his way through each day till he reached the last entry. The diary might have been written like that, as most were, but thoughts and lives moved to different rhythms and he would get a better sense of Sofía and her life in recent months – perhaps even her entire life – by allowing his eyes to wander over the pages at random.

The first thing he noticed was the names. Lists of women's names on most of the days: *Inma Gutiérrez, Claudia Albornoz García, Ruth Jiménez*. He kept flicking through. They were on weekdays, with perhaps a few gaps. Four or five a day, sometimes six or seven. Always female names, never a man's.

The women she'd given abortions to?

He checked the beginning of the year. No names there, not until 7th January, the first day back at work after the Christmas holidays. Then again, during the week leading up to the *Fallas* fiesta – no names. Nor at Easter. Only on working days – the days the clinic had been open.

He pulled out a Ducados and lit it. If he were right, the diaries back at the flat contained the names of all the women who'd ever passed through her hands, stretching back to the mid-1970s. What was it? Some kind of tally? A personal record of all the women she'd . . . what? Helped? That was probably how she saw it. What about a record of all the lives she'd terminated just as they were beginning? Staring down at the names – *Marta Sampedro, Mari-Luz Ferrero Pavón, Carmen Molina Valdés* – he felt disturbed by it. It was almost as if . . . what? Was it . . . ? Was it so dissimilar from a serial killer keeping a list of all the people he'd murdered?

He stared into space and allowed himself to get lost in the experience of smoking for a few moments. Sofía Bodí a serial killer? Did part of him really think the similarity was there?

Nonetheless, there was something a little odd about this private record of hers. Was it some kind of insurance? This was information she could use in the future if she had to. 'Right-wingers also abort,' she'd said at the press conference.

Or was it something more human? These women meant something to her; they were real people.

He was confused; he didn't know what to think about it. Perhaps one day, if things turned out right, he'd get the chance to ask her.

He started flicking through the pages again. The *Guardia Civil* investigation into the clinic had begun in December, so any entries relating to that would be in the previous year's diary. But there were plenty of developments in the case to get a mention in this year's. The first few in January, before the clinic reopened, seemed to refer to it. The handwriting was harder, the pen pushing deeper into the paper, with a liberal use of exclamation marks. The *Guardia Civil* itself was referred to as *GC*, while Comandante Lázaro leading the investigation into the clinic was *Lázaro*, changing as the weeks went by into simply *L*.

> *Phone call from Lola. L is interrogating anyone who's passed through the doors of the clinic over the past year! She heard it from Jaime, who has a contact in the City of Justice law courts. Asking them straight if they had a termination beyond 22 weeks! CB thinks it's a good sign – if the physical evidence from the waste was enough they wouldn't be going to the trouble to get statements trying to 'prove' their lies.*

'CB' probably meant Cesc Ballester.

> *The mood is changing at the clinic. Everyone's very supportive – we're in it till the end. But people don't chat as much. Tole even forgot to switch on the background music in reception this morning! I think we're all feeling it a bit. We're still getting messages of support coming in. Some even from abroad. Trinidad Sánchez, the junior Interior Minister, called. She said she couldn't make a public statement of support – she has to appear to be impartial. L is one of her employees, after all. But she said she was doing everything she could. Whatever that means. She could call this off immediately, but doesn't want a big mess to clear up. They're still afraid of the old guard. L's clearly part of some reactionary 'bunker' group active in the GC. Another Tejero! They'll keep popping up until someone gets the courage to clean them out once and for all.*

Lieuterant Colonel Tejero was one of the main figures in the attempted military coup of February 1981, the man who had held up the Spanish parliament at gunpoint as a group of pro-Franco diehards in the army and *Guardia Civil* tried to take over the government.

For almost twenty-four hours the country had appeared to be on the brink of more bloody civil conflict, and tanks had even appeared on the streets of Valencia, where the leader of the coup, General Milans del Bosch, was based. In the end the plot collapsed and Spain's nascent democracy avoided being stillborn, but Sofía seemed to think that Comandante Lázaro was of a similar political breed to the men who'd taken part.

Cámara continued flicking through the pages of the diary. Later in the year, as the months progressed, and the *Guardia* investigation intensified, the entries grew shorter, except for one or two longer passages whenever new developments came along. And he noticed figures appearing at the start of each day's writing: *3, 3.5, 2, 4, 2.5* . . . At first he couldn't make it out, but over time the numbers seemed to get smaller – *2, 1.5* – and he realised: this was the amount of sleep she was getting each night. The worry and anxiety were eating into her unconscious. Over the previous week she hadn't managed to sleep more than three hours straight. Someone in her condition might be hallucinating, perhaps even getting lost. He thought for a minute. No. There were independent witnesses – two people at least had seen her being bundled into a car by men wearing *Guardia Civil* uniforms. She hadn't just taken the wrong street and collapsed under a bush in a park somewhere.

The pages turned backwards and forwards, always the same black ink, the same small, neat handwriting. Sometimes thicker and heavier, getting scrappier perhaps in recent weeks. That would be the lack of sleep.

Then something, a flash of red, caught his eye. He skipped back to the page where he thought he had seen it. Down low on the right-hand page. A mark in red ink had been made in the margin: an '*x*' and a date with a circle – *3 Nov 77*.

He checked the entry for the day next to the red mark: a Saturday back in May that year. Details of reports in the press about the *Guardia* investigation into the clinic. An editorial in a left-wing newspaper criticising the Valencian local government for not condemning the case, claiming it was obvious to 'anyone with eyes' that it was politically motivated. A reference to a meeting of *Mi Cuerpo, Mi Elección* scheduled for the following Wednesday evening.

Then at the end a simple sentence:

With CB to La Mar. Paella.

FOURTEEN

He hated skunk. Hilario's home-grown, which kept him going through most of the year, was altogether a happier, gigglier drug, the kind of marihuana you could smoke without having to worry about anything worse than a dry mouth the next morning. But what little was left to him of that year's crop had gone along with everything else in his flat, and so he'd had to score off some Moroccan kid prowling around the alleyways off the Plaza del Carmen. And skunk was virtually all they had these days. Harder, harsher, smellier; he avoided it as much as he could.

He waited until he reached the beach before rolling his first joint, picking up a packet of Fortuna blond tobacco cigarettes at a bar along the way.

The Paseo de Neptuno beach-front bars were packed and hundreds of sweating, laughing young people were milling about the esplanade. He could sense a growing photophobia in himself as the skunk began to take hold, and he carried on walking, past the concentration of bars and nightclubs and further down the walkway before crossing on to the sand.

The residents' meeting back in Ruzafa would have started by now. He'd known from the start he wouldn't be going. Better to come for a stroll and a smoke on his own out here than wallow in collective anger and pain.

The sea stretched out before him, still and black and dead. He felt his feet lower into the damp with each step, then lose their grip as he tried to propel himself forwards. Slipping, sliding, sinking. The red glow at the end of the joint seemed to point him the way.

He crossed paths with a couple of late-night fishermen heading home, an old man walking his dog wearing deck shoes and swimming shorts that got lost in the fold of his belly cascading down towards his groin. A couple of girls, assuming they were veiled by the darkness, were kissing and petting a few yards further in from the shore, their bodies silhouetted against the starry glow that came from just above the horizon.

He kept walking. There was virtually no breeze, but he felt cooler nonetheless simply by being next to the water.

The drug was swirling inside him now. He tried to forget the nausea that skunk always produced in him, drawing hard on the last remaining flakes of burning grass, the heat searing his fingers where he held the joint. Breathing in deeply, he closed his throat and held it down in his lungs for as long as he could, as the blood in the back of his neck began to thud.

The dying dog-end gave off a barely audible *pffutt* as it hit the water.

And then there was the door, staring him in the face, so suddenly he wasn't sure how he'd reached it. But a man was there in a suit two sizes too small for his hormone-pumped body, nodding him in as though recognising a kindred spirit and embracing him to some hard, rocky, loveless bosom.

Inside, red and orange lights showed him the way to the main room. A girl with shiny plastic thigh-boots gave him a smile and took his hand to lead him through. A stool at the bar found its way underneath him, and he felt his weight sinking on to it. Over the pounding music and throbbing lights he could hear voices, one of them his, negotiating for a glass of brandy.

As he waited, he rolled a new joint while glancing around the room. There were a couple of other men in there. One was sitting underneath a statue of a masturbating woman, smiling at the semi-naked shadows that were being paraded in front of him. The other man was further down the bar, a young, wealthy kid spending his father's money on cocaine and flesh through the weekend. He'd already chosen and was being led away through a doorway with flashing neon hearts on either side of it. Another line, another hit, another cunt.

The joint rolled smoothly under his fingers.

There was a chink as the brandy glass was placed on the counter in front of him. He lifted it up for a sip, and felt breath on his neck – cold and male.

More voices over the rhythmic noise bursting from the speakers.

No, he didn't know they had a no-drugs policy. Of course it wasn't a joint. Just a cigarette. He liked to roll his own.

And then there was another man. The one he'd seen on the door with the kind of muscles they advertised in certain magazines in three-for-two deals. A hand was gripping itself around his upper arm, then another was reaching for the scruff of his neck.

And he smiled to himself.

First the shock up his arm as the initial punch landed in the bouncer's ribs, then numbness in his forehead where it connected with the side of the man's face. Then more noise, shouting and screaming as his elbow followed round and smashed into his jaw. Later it was almost as if he had sensed one of the man's molars being loosened from his skull with the impact, but perhaps that was just his brain filling in the blanks.

And he heard the magic words: *Stop! Police!* And so he stopped, and the bouncer fell to the floor, a streak of blood soaking into his clean white shirt where it had spattered out from his mouth.

Not much point having all those muscles. And all that making yourself so big ever did was turn you into a larger, and easier, target.

In the silence he noticed his hand held up high, his police badge open for all to see, and everyone looking at it with open mouths.

So it was he who had shouted, 'Police!'

Of course the manager changed after that. Another brandy appeared as he drained the first, and the hand that had tried to grip his arm now kept a respectful distance. The bouncer disappeared and then returned after a few minutes in the bathroom, cleaned up, with a fresh shirt, and the swelling already beginning to show on the side of his chin. But he gave him a look of respect as he headed back outside. Probably the first time he'd ever had a proper fight.

The shadows were paraded in front of him, and he pretended to be only partially interested as he finally lit his joint and nodded at one of them, a girl with highlighted short dark hair.

Her name?

Lisa.

Alicia?

No. Lisa.

OK.

Some time later, he was back on the beach, sinking once again into the damp sand, seventy euros poorer, an opened but unused condom dangling lifelessly from his pocket.

That was the other problem with skunk, if it caught you on the wrong day. She'd tried, poor dear, rubbing his limp cock in every way she knew how, but to no avail. There'd been a moment when he thought something might happen, and he'd pulled the condom out himself, as though it might help things along a bit. But . . .

The sea was still there, inky and calm, as though inviting him to join in its darkness. You're almost part of me, she seemed to say, as lifeless and endless as these deadening waters. Just take a step and come in. Forget. Relax. Cease to be.

He thought of Roures. And Tomás.

And took a last breath.

FIFTEEN

Thursday 9th July

A blow to the back of the shoulders sent him hurtling off the bench, waking him in an instant. As he rolled across the pavement, trying not to get caught in the bushes at the other side, the sharp smell of chlorine filled his nostrils. The whine of an electric pump indicated where the blow had come from, and he looked up to see a couple of street cleaners in green dayglo suits – one with a stiff plastic broom, the other wielding the high-powered hosepipe – staring at him and laughing.

He stood up, drenched, eyes rolling as he tried to force them to work, while the cleaners hopped on to their little cart and drove off down the empty street before he could say anything, the sound of their cackling still audible above the whir of the engine.

His neck was sore from where his head had rested at an uncommon angle on the hard wood of the bench. He checked his pockets; street cleaners might be taking advantage of him sleeping rough but it seemed no one else had: everything – cigarettes, dope, wallet, phone, badge – was where it should be. With a sigh he realised he still had his old house keys in his trouser pocket. He jangled them in his fingers for a second, then spying a litter bin, threw them at it, expecting to hear a tinny clang as they landed inside. But he was still in the process of waking up and his aim was faulty, so they landed instead in a day-old dog turd at the side of the pavement, still soft

97

enough for the keys to impale themselves in it like miniature shiny darts.

Coffee and a cigarette in the first place he saw, he told himself, but he seemed incapable of finding a bar. Eventually, after the intense rising sun had almost dried him out, his shuffling feet took him back to the Jefatura.

He grabbed the shopping bags from his office and walked up the white cement staircase to the bathroom he knew Pardo had had installed next to his office. Others might have more need of it, but it was deemed necessary for a commissioner to have access to a shower and other facilities at his workplace. Not even Pardo would be there this early, however, and Cámara let himself in, watching the light reflect off the shiny green marble panels on the walls as he turned on the switch.

His dirty clothes fell into a tightly crumpled pile on the floor and he stepped into the shower. Despite feeling hot from the sun and his walk back into the city, he turned the knob towards red, allowing a cleaner, cleansing heat to soothe his body. While in his mind he began to compose the resignation letter he would be leaving on Pardo's desk.

He pulled the labels off the new clothes before putting them on. The trousers felt stiff, the shirt scratchy around the collar. He looked at himself in the mirror: he hadn't shaved for a few days now; it was time to take out his emergency sponge bag. The clothes were brighter than he might have chosen had he been buying them now. They would have to do. At the bottom of the shopping bag he noticed the iPod Almudena had bought him. It could stay there, he thought.

There was just one thing he wanted to do before bringing an end to all this. The reference to Roures's restaurant in Sofía's diary had produced a faint spark of intrigue. The place was popular and well known, and Sofía was the kind of person he could imagine eating there, so it might be nothing. But the red mark with the date pointing to 1977 was odd. What had happened back then?

He couldn't see any policeman at the entrance that morning, but the main door was open and he stepped into the hallway before taking the stairs again up to Sofía's flat. The door was locked, as he'd expected, but the window from the stairwell out on to the light shaft was open. He threw a leg over the edge and eased his body over. There was a ledge he could just reach with his toe if he stretched enough. Then from there he could get to the bedroom window into Sofía's flat which he had left open the previous day. It hadn't been deliberate at the time, but now it almost felt as if some more prescient part of him had done so deliberately to allow him future access.

His toe slipped from its foothold just as his fingers caught the windowsill. Hanging on, he looked down. High enough to break a leg, and perhaps a rib or two if he landed badly. But he was all right. No more slip-ups now. Not after last night.

He sensed something, and still hanging on to the window, he turned his head to see one of the neighbours – an elderly woman still wearing her blue-and-white floral dressing gown – staring down at him in disbelief from an open window on the floor above. He forced a smile, and was about to say something when a more determined look appeared on her face and she vanished from the window. Doubtless she had gone to make a call. Someone in the *Policía Local* was about to have their early-morning newspaper-reading shift interrupted.

The window creaked slightly as he pushed it open and hauled himself inside. The flat was the same as before; Ballester had probably left shortly after he had. The sofa still showed a dent in the cushions where he had been lying down, curled up in a ball.

He went straight to the study, allowing his eyes to adjust to the gloom for a moment before trying to find the diary he was looking for. For some reason his heart was pounding heavily in his chest. Perhaps the shock of almost falling, or the feeling that he didn't have much time before a couple of *Municipales* came knocking. Why hadn't there been a *Policía Nacional* on the door this morning? Had something happened in the case during the night? Admittedly he'd got into the Jefatura early, but he was surprised to find it as quiet as it was.

He started working his way back through the diary years, the gold numbers reflecting faintly in the scant sunlight filtering through the shutters. He'd look for 1977 in a moment; first he needed to check an entry from just the year before.

He picked up the volume and skimmed through the pages, looking for the month of May. The name he was searching for was there in the middle of the third week: *Alicia Beneyto*.

Closing his eyes, Cámara breathed slowly and deeply for a moment, then calmly returned the diary to its place on the shelf and carried on moving back through the years. He could react to this later; for now he needed to continue being a policeman.

His finger fell on the diary for 1977 before he'd even seen it: it was pushed in slightly more than the others. Which would make sense, he thought, if she'd taken it out recently to check something.

The table lamp gave off a yellowy glow as he sat down and switched it on to read. Entries for September, then October, and finally the beginning of November. He remembered what Torres had told him: she'd have been in Paris at that time, working as an intern at the *Clinique Fontaine*.

November 1. . . 2 . . . 3. Her handwriting had been slightly loopier back then, more open, not so tight and neat. He read through the entry for the day: arriving slightly late for work because of a break-down on the metro. A conversation with Dr Bouvier, her boss, about a lecture he was preparing for a conference later that month in Geneva. He'd asked her to go with him as his assistant. She'd said yes, but now, as she was writing her diary, she was having doubts. Did he want something else from her? Without spelling it out clearly, it seemed the young Sofía was worried that her employer was fishing for a romantic weekend, away from the eyes of his wife and the other workers at the clinic.

Then details of what she'd had for lunch: a chicken salad with a tarragon sauce and a glass of fizzy mineral water.

And at the end, the now familiar list of names – eight that day. Most of them were French, but three were clearly Spanish girls, taking advantage, no doubt, of the presence of their compatriot there, someone they could understand and who could understand them. He read the names aloud to himself as his finger skimmed along the page: *Josefa Fernández, Ana Pastor Sampedro, Lucía Bautista*. And there, just beside the last name, in the same red ink he'd seen in her more recent diary, was a tiny little '*x*', barely visible unless he brought the book closer to the lamp.

He heard a car pull up outside. Soon a couple of *Municipales* would be forcing their way in, sniffing around, asking questions. Should he stay here and waste time explaining? Or leave now? He'd found what he was looking for, and suddenly there was a lot he needed to do. Urgently.

He got up, switched the lamp off and ran to the open window in the bedroom. But already he could hear footsteps downstairs in the hallway; it was too late. He skipped back down the corridor and into the kitchen. It had a window looking out on to the back of the block of flats with a small balcony. Forcing the bolt, he stepped outside into the sunshine, tiptoeing around a couple of spare orange butane gas bottles to peer over the edge. As he'd hoped, the flat underneath, on the first floor, had a much larger balcony. He could lower himself over the edge from the rails where he was standing now: the drop wouldn't be too far for him to make a safe jump.

He felt his new shirt rip at the stitching under the arm as he reached over and held his weight, his body hanging like a swaying pendulum. He should have gone to a better shop than Zara.

Inside the flat, he could hear the door being opened from the hallway. Somehow the *Municipales* must have got hold of a spare key. It wouldn't take them long to find the open kitchen door out on to the balcony. He had to jump. Now.

His feet stung as they took the impact. He lost his balance and rolled back on to his haunches as the fall pushed him hard into the balcony floor below. Stumbling to get up, he could hear voices above in the flat he'd just left. He ran to the edge to find some way down to the ground floor, and the alleyway that ran along the side of the building. If he could just see some way of getting down there that didn't involve breaking an ankle. Already his bones were complaining about the first jump. He wasn't used to this kind of thing any more. Part of the problem of being a chief inspector, and being expected to get others to do the running around for you. But this was his kind of police work, on the move, adrenalin rushing, chasing his man down. Or in this case, scampering blindly to avoid the biggest problem a policeman ever faced – other policemen.

He could hear the *Municipales* pounding about in the flat above. Any minute now they would look over the kitchen balcony and see him standing there. At which point not only would he have to explain who he was, and why he was here, but also why he was acting more like a thief than a member of the *Policía Nacional*'s executive branch.

Then he spotted his way out – a disused length of television aerial cable, hanging limply from the wall where it had been disconnected. There was no time to wonder if it would take his weight: the door on to the balcony above was already being opened. He swung his leg over the railings, lodged his heel as best he could in a ledge of brick-work and launched himself towards the cable.

The skin on the backs of his fingers scraped against the masonry as his hands were propelled forwards, grasping at the dirty white plastic lifeline. He caught hold of it just as his weight started to pull him down to the greasy floor below. There was a tug, then a lurch, as he tightened his grip, only for the cable to start popping out of its brackets higher up the wall. It wouldn't hold him for long. Quickly, he slid down as fast as he could while simultaneously putting a brake on his downward progress.

Above him one of the *Municipales* was out on the balcony, casting an eye over the adjoining terraces. Cámara was partially hidden from view, but still had another three metres to go before hitting the ground. Some instinct, however, told him the cable was about to break, it couldn't hold him any longer: he had to jump.

He let go, staring down hard at the spot where he would land, calculating the roll he would need to break his fall. But the force of the impact took him unawares and his jaw cracked on his knee as his legs bent to absorb his collision with the earth. In a second he found himself lying in the dirt, face up, winded and struggling to breathe. But as his eyes adjusted to the light streaming down from the slit of sky above him, he could see that there was no face staring down at him, no *Policía Local* up on the balcony. He must have gone back inside.

He picked himself up and scrambled to get to his feet. He could feel blood welling up in his mouth from where he'd bitten his tongue. Spitting red as he emerged back out on to the main street, from the corner of his eye he could see a squad car parked outside the main door. Ignoring it, he walked in the other direction, only to be passed by the *Policía Nacional* who was meant to have been on guard duty all the time. The policeman passed Cámara at a trot, a strong scent of brandy and coffee clouding around him. He gave Cámara a bemused look as he sped past, then carried on.

The morning was turning out to be less peaceful than expected.

SIXTEEN

'You look, er, different somehow.'

Torres was sitting at his desk cross-referencing some material on *Sidenpol*, the police intranet, as Cámara walked in.

'Been on the piss?'

'Where did we put the files on the Roures case?' Cámara said.

'I mention it because you often get this weirdly relaxed, almost serene expression on your face afterwards. While we mere mortals suffer from hangovers, you seem to get a kind of cathartic release from alcohol poisoning.'

'Fuck it. We were only working on it a couple of days ago. Can't have gone far.'

'Although it does seem to affect your short-term memory. They're on the second shelf. And a couple of the later reports were still floating around your desk the last time I looked.'

'Spying on me again?'

'It's that Maldonado gets me to do it, chief. Seduces me with his bad skin and halitosis.'

'Tart.'

'So what's this? Leaving me to do all the work – yours and mine, I mean – on the Bodí case? Back to Roures? Sod the orders? To be honest I didn't see you staying the course that long, but this has to be something of a record, even for you, right?'

Cámara gave him a look.

'I need a minute,' he said.

Torres grunted and turned back to the computer screen as Cámara picked up the box file he was looking for and started rifling through the papers. Eventually he found the one he wanted and placed it out in front of him, ran through the details for a couple of minutes and tightened his lips.

'Do me a favour, will you?' he said, lifting his head to look across the office at Torres. 'Check up the clinic in Paris where Sofía Bodí used to work, the first one. Should be in the background section on your screen somewhere.'

'Do you want me to give you a foot massage while I'm at it, chief?'

'No. It'd just slow us down. The address and phone number of the clinic will do for now. But thanks for the offer.'

'No problem.'

Torres's fingers tapped away at the keyboard for a moment or two, then after a couple of clicks of the mouse, he said, '*Clinique Fontaine.* Rue Floréal. Number: 01 44 19 16 66.'

Cámara pulled out a piece of paper from his pocket – a leaflet from the brothel – and scribbled the information down with a ball-point pen in a gap between photos of bare-breasted women. Oblivious to the images of naked skin, he sat staring at the digits for a while and then reached over to pick up the phone.

'You're calling them now?' Torres said.

'Might be.'

'Shouldn't you put a request through to Interpol?'

'And die of old age before they get back to me?'

'This isn't entirely by the book.'

'You know that. But they don't.'

Cámara heard the high-pitched sound of a French phone ringing at the other end. He wanted to make contact with this lead, this urgent connection that had burst through from nowhere, even if it only meant ringing up early in the morning and hearing an answer machine at the other end.

There was a click as the ringing stopped.

'*Allo?*'

He paused. This was no answer machine. Over in Paris, someone had answered the phone. Cámara lunged desperately for the French that remained to him from school.

'*C'est la Clinique Fontaine?*'

'*Oui, monsieur.*'

'This is Chief Inspector Cámara of the Spanish National Police,' he said, continuing as best he could. 'Who am I speaking to, please?'

'My name is Madeleine Marché. I'm the secretary of the *Clinique*. How may I help?'

'I'm investigating the disappearance of a former employee of yours.'

He enunciated the words slowly, but, he hoped, correctly. Years had passed since he'd last practised, and he could understand much more than he spoke.

'Yes, Sofía. We heard. Have you found her?'

'No. Sadly not. But I do require some information from you.'

'*Bien sûr, bien sûr*. If there's anything I can do. Is this about the phone call we had from Sofía last week?'

Cámara cleared his throat.

'That was part of it,' he said. 'Could you tell me about the call?'

'Yes, of course. She rang last Wednesday. I answered the phone myself. I didn't work here when Sofía was an employee, but I've met her on several occasions at gynaecological symposia here in Paris, and in Switzerland. So we know each other, and of course there's the link to the *clinique*.'

'What did she ring about?'

'It was about a patient who had been at the clinic years ago, many years ago. It was a little strange, but she said she needed to check something. I assumed it had a bearing on the investigation they were carrying out into her. That's not you, I take it?'

'No. That was . . . others,' Cámara said. 'Different police. We're only interested in finding Sofía as quickly as possible.'

'Good. It's a sorry state of affairs when we have to be frightened of the police just for carrying out our work helping women, you know?'

'I understand. But please, you were saying – something about a patient? Could you tell me more? It's very important.'

'Yes,' came the answer. 'It was about a Spanish girl who came here back in the seventies. Can you hold on for a moment. I'll just check the record again.'

There was a hiss at the end of the line as the phone was put down and Madeleine walked away. From his desk Torres was staring at Cámara with his eyes raised, amazed that he had got so far, but sniggering at his French.

'Stop laughing at your superior,' Cámara said. 'That's an order.'

There was a shuffling back in Paris and Madeleine picked up the phone again.

'Here it is,' she said. 'Third of November nineteen seventy-seven. She wanted to know the names of the girls we saw that day. I've got the list here, but there was one name in particular she was interested in.'

Cámara waited with his pen ready.

'And that was?'

'Here it is,' she said. 'I remember. Lucía Bautista Sánchez.'

Cámara swallowed.

'She didn't . . .? Did Madame Bodí say anything about why she was interested in this particular girl?'

'No. I didn't ask. As I said, I assumed it had something to do with the investigation. That perhaps this girl – or woman as she will be now – might be able to help, or something. But I don't know exactly why. She didn't say.'

'All right,' Cámara said. 'You've been very helpful.'

'Not at all.'

'Just, er, one other thing.'

'Yes?'

'Was there any indication where Lucía Bautista was from in Spain? Is there any record of that? An address, perhaps?'

'No, we don't have that information. But Sofía herself said Lucía was from Valencia. From her own home town. She mentioned it when she rang. She said she remembered feeling homesick when girls from Valencia came to the clinic. Of course, the sunshine, the paella. It must have been hard for her back then.'

Cámara put the phone down, stood up and stared out of the window at the facades of tower blocks behind the Jefatura. A thousand lives stacked into slot-like boxes, defined and delineated by the cubic dimensions of each identical apartment. Except that human lives had the tendency to spill beyond these restricted spaces.

Behind him, Torres had got up from his desk and was looking down at the notes beside Cámara's phone.

'Lucía Bautista Sánchez? That's—'

'Roures's ex-wife. Yes.'

'Same name, at least.'

Cámara spun round.

106

'Let's check *Sidenpol* again, shall we?' He walked over to Torres's terminal. 'Come on, you're faster at this than I am.'

Torres grunted and sat down again at his desk.

'How many women with that name are there in Valencia province?' Cámara said.

'I'm on it.'

After a few moments accessing the database, three women, complete with photos, came up on the screen.

'Well, it's not her,' Torres said, pointing at a little ten-year-old girl. 'And even this one's too young. She's only thirty-five. Still wearing nappies in nineteen seventy-seven.'

'Which leaves Roures's ex-wife,' Cámara said.

They both looked at the photo of a woman with black curly hair and fleshy features, her skin pale and shiny from the over-powerful flash of the photo booth. It was the same photo on the file they had for the Roures case.

'She's better-looking in real life,' Torres said.

'She'd have been fifteen or sixteen in nineteen seventy-seven.'

'Makes sense. Got banged up. Too young for a kid, so off to France for an abortion.'

'At the clinic where Sofía Bodí was working at the time.'

'Coincidence?'

So why did Sofía mark her down in her diary? Why did she ring up her old clinic to check her name just days before disappearing? They had a dead man and a missing woman.

And Lucía was the unexpected link between the two.

SEVENTEEN

Lucía Bautista lived in a traditional El Cabanyal house on the Calle Barraca, not far from the port. The facade was tiled in blue-and-white check, with vegetal motifs over the entrance. The large wooden door had a smaller door inside which opened into the house itself. Cámara peeped through the glass, shading his eyes from the glare of the sun, trying to see if anyone was in, before lifting the Hand-of-Fátima door knocker and banging it a couple of times against the metal panel.

From the reflection in the glass he was aware that an elderly woman was watching him from the opposite side of the road. She was sprinkling the pavement outside her front door with water to draw cooler air into the haze of her home, glancing up at him as he waited to see if anyone answered his call.

'*Que no está,*' she shouted over after a couple of minutes had passed with no sign of life inside. She's out.

Cámara turned and crossed the road to talk to her, lifting his badge for her to see.

'*Policía!*' The woman dropped her eyes and shrugged. It was a common reaction among some elderly people – an instinct to have as little as possible to do with law enforcers, instilled over centuries of State and Church repression.

'Do you know where I can find her?'

'Don't know,' she said. 'She goes out sometimes. Walking.'

'Do you know how long ago?'

The woman was sprinkling the last of her water as quickly as possible on to the ground, looking for an excuse to head back inside.

'Maybe five minutes ago.' And she waved her hand in the direction of the port, as though to indicate the way in which Lucía had gone.

Cámara thanked her and set off in the same direction. It felt good to be back in this part of the city; the area had a village-like feel to it, a proper neighbourhood, and the traditional design of the houses gave it an elegance and sense of history that was hard to find in all parts of Valencia. More reason, he thought, for the Town Hall to want to pull swathes of it down. Like tyrannical rulers of the ancient world, the authorities had a crazed need to destroy anything that had been made before their rule, setting the clock to zero in order to remake the city in their own, shining, modern, reinforced-concrete image.

He smiled. These were political thoughts coursing through his mind. Not something he was accustomed to in himself. Hilario would be proud.

He looked up: above the line of the roofs stood a tower, perhaps another four or five metres higher. A *torre-miramar* it was called: one of the towers from which fishermen's families had used to attach lights to help guide the boats back to the beach; a place from which one could see the sea over the heads of the neighbouring houses. There were fewer and fewer of them left now: already a couple had been pulled down by order of the Town Hall.

He emerged from the shade of the street and out into the open space of a square near the port. Opposite, the colourful boatyards that had been put up for the America's Cup stood empty and dusty. This area had come alive briefly during that time, a couple of years before, when multi-million-dollar yachts were floating in and out of the harbour, but many of the bars and restaurants had closed now, a nosedive depression taking hold once the glamour set had moved on. Valencia had failed to turn itself into a new Monte Carlo, despite all the money that had been spent. Having marginalised neighbourhoods full of drug dealers next to the port area hadn't helped.

There was a tram stop in the square, partially shaded by palm trees. From here he could catch a lift back into the centre. Locating Lucía might have to wait till the morning.

The tinted plastic of the shelter just seemed to intensify the heat, however, and he sought refuge under the portico of a nearby block of flats. The display at the stop showed that he had another seven minutes before the next tram came this way.

So close to the sea, the air was even denser here with the humidity, but a breeze was already developing, bringing partial respite from the sticky heat. He closed his eyes as the dizziness fell away from his skin, dripping like water and trickling away along the pavement. What had he been thinking, going to the brothel the night before? He'd never done anything like that before in his life. His fingers caressed the plastic bag of skunk still nestling in his pocket. He'd find a dustbin somewhere later and throw it away.

His eyes opened as a couple walked past him, tiptoeing into the sunshine to get around him and then back into the shade. He watched as they headed into El Cabanyal, then turned his head to glance back over the square. Three minutes till the tram arrived.

A figure caught his eye: a woman wearing a white sleeveless top and beige shorts that stopped just above the knee. She was small and curvaceous, with a fleshy nose and curly hair that was almost all black save for a few white streaks.

Cámara took a step out from his shady sanctuary and crossed over towards her.

'Lucía Bautista?'

The woman stopped and looked at him suspiciously. The man had used her surname; it was clear she didn't know him.

'Who are you?'

There was a bar open on the other side of the square and she accepted Cámara's offer to go over there rather than talk in her house. No need to give further gossip material to the old woman across the road. Or others like her.

'They know about Pep. The whole *barrio* does. And they know one of your colleagues came to talk to me the other day. But even so . . .'

Cámara ordered a *café solo*, still needing the caffeine to sharpen himself up after the previous night. Lucía asked for a *bitter*.

'Any news?'

There was something soft and engaging about Lucía's eyes. Torres was right, she was prettier in the flesh than in her ID photo, but there was something tarnished about her as well, like a light that had been dulled in some way.

'The investigation is progressing,' Cámara said. 'You spoke to Inspector Torres, I believe.'

'Perhaps. I can't remember his name. Big black beard. Is there something wrong? In my statement, I mean.'

'No, your statement was fine. We just have to do some follow-up calls sometimes. Trying to pick up something we might have missed. It's perfectly normal. There's nothing to be worried about.'

Lucía gave a sigh, her shoulders dropping as she lifted her glass and sipped her bright, cherry-red drink.

'I told him as much as I could. He seemed to be interested in establishing where I was the night Pep . . . you know.'

'That's fine. And I'm not here to go over that again.'

Cámara pulled out his cigarettes.

'Do you mind?'

She shook her head.

'We need some more background on Señor Roures,' Cámara said, inhaling. 'His past, people he knew, that sort of thing. And as his ex-wife, well, you're an important part of that picture.'

'Yes,' Lucía said. Her gaze drifted away, staring out from their terrace table at the empty, mid-afternoon street. It was still too hot for most people to venture out. 'I suppose so.'

'Perhaps you could tell me about how you met.'

Lucía took a deep breath and closed her eyes.

'Pep and I knew each other from way back,' she said after a pause. 'We were at school together. Both kids from El Cabanyal. But we didn't get together until we were in our teens. He used to play *pelota* at the sports club and come round to a bar afterwards where I hung out with some of my friends.'

She swirled her glass round, watching the ice clink against the sides.

'Anyway, one night, well, you know, it just happened.'

'Do you mind if I ask when that was?'

'No, that's fine. I can tell you exactly. It was the night of the big demonstration in Valencia for the *Estatut*. The ninth of October, nineteen seventy-seven.'

Cámara remembered Valencians mentioning the date to him, the day almost the entire city had rallied in support of the region becoming autonomous rather than governed directly from Madrid. Locally, it was one of the important moments during the *Transición* – the years following Franco's death as the country moved towards becoming a democracy. Over 600,000 people from both the right and the left had marched through the streets.

'I think it was a Sunday,' Lucía continued, 'and we all met up in our usual bar, El Polp, afterwards for a drink. Pep was there, and . . . that's it.'

'And then you got married?'

'Yes. A few years later. A big, El Cabanyal wedding. They like those round here. Feels like a tribe, sometimes. So it's always good when two people from the neighbourhood get together.'

'How long was this before La Mar opened?'

'That was pretty soon after. Pep always knew he wanted to open a restaurant, and was looking for somewhere from before we got married. Then, I don't know, it must have been a few months later, that place became available – I think there'd been a bar there before – and we took it on. My father helped us out getting started.'

'Your father's dead, I understand.'

'Yes. Was that on my file?'

Cámara didn't reply.

'I'm sorry. I know, you're just doing your job. Three years ago I lost both my mother and father in the space of four months. It's just . . . There's only me and my brothers now.'

'Can you tell me what happened? Between you and Roures?'

'Why we divorced, you mean?'

Cámara nodded, stubbing his cigarette out in the ashtray on the table.

'It was the restaurant, really. It's a small place, but there were only ever the two of us. Others came and went, but we shouldered the whole thing. Living there, working there. It took its toll.'

'No kids?'

'No! No time. The idea was crazy. Besides, I don't think Pep . . . It wasn't acrimonious, or anything. We knew it had to happen, so we arranged things, Pep gave me a lump sum for my share of the restaurant, and that was it.'

'Still friends?'

'Yeah. I mean, we didn't hate each other or anything like that. But we weren't socialising either. After you've spent so many years living every second of the day with someone you need a bit of a rest. Anyway, without me at La Mar Pep was busier than ever. It's not as if we could have seen much of each other anyway.'

She paused, taking another sip from her drink. And for a moment Cámara glimpsed something of what had dulled the spark inside her.

'I used to bump into him in the street sometimes, or at the market. We'd stop and chat, catch up on things. But then he got involved more in the *El Cabanyal, Sí* thing and I hardly ever saw him at all. Last time must have been around Christmas.'

'You're not involved yourself?'

Lucía shrugged.

'Don't get me wrong – I think it's criminal what they want to do here. Pulling old houses down. But . . .' She frowned. 'I don't think there's much you can do. All right for me to say that, I suppose. My house isn't one of the ones under threat. For Pep it was different – he was right there in the cross-hairs.'

She placed her hands over her face, as though hiding herself.

'Sorry. That's not very appropriate language, is it?'

'I'd like you to tell me what you can about the abortion,' Cámara said.

Her hands remained where they were, shielding her face and eyes from the rest of the world. Then very slowly she dropped them until they rested on her knees, her eyes downcast.

'Wow,' she breathed at last. 'You really have . . . Is this relevant?'

'I know it was a long time ago, but if there's anything you remember.'

'You don't forget something like that. I think about it every day.'

Her gaze remained fixed on the floor as she spoke.

'It was a girl,' she said after letting out a deep sigh. 'I know because I developed a rash on my chest, just as my mother did when she was pregnant with me. Didn't happen with my brothers. It's a family thing.'

The sun had begun to dip a little by this point and a shaft of light was beginning to stream over part of Lucía's body, casting a twitching shadow where the vein in her neck pulsed rhythmically.

'We weren't very well off, so my aunt had to help out. My father called a doctor friend he knew, who gave us the name of a clinic in Paris.'

Cámara took out another cigarette and lit it.

'Pep had a little Renault 5, so we drove up. My mother as well. Set off in the middle of the night and we got to Paris late the following evening, driving straight through and eating sandwiches my mother had prepared to save money.'

'Do you remember how much it cost?'

'I think it was about fifty thousand pesetas. It was a lot of money, particularly back then.'

'How long were you in Paris for?'

'Just a couple of days. We stayed the night in some *pensión* on the outskirts of the city, went to the clinic the next morning. They carried out the procedure, and we had to go back in the afternoon for a check, to make sure everything was all right. Then it was back in the car and poor old Pep driving through the night to get back here.'

'Do you remember what the clinic was called?'

'No. No, I don't.'

'Any other Spanish girls there?'

'Yeah. One or two. I remember the girl who went in before me. Catalan, I think she was. Very nervous. They had problems with the anaesthetic and she was screaming.'

She lifted her eyes.

'I was only fifteen. I was way too young to have a child. I didn't know what I wanted to do with my life then, but I was thinking of going to university, I don't know. Just not, you know, settling down, having a baby. My parents thought about adopting it, bringing it up as their own, but they were already quite old by then. There was nothing else we could do.'

'And no solutions here in Spain.'

'No way. I mean, everyone knew where to go for a back-street job, but . . .' She rolled her eyes. 'There was no guarantee you'd get out of there alive.'

'Yes, I've heard,' Cámara said.

'I haven't talked about this for a long time,' Lucía said, taking a sharp breath. 'And now here I am telling all my secrets to a policeman. Anything else you need to know while I'm at it?'

'How've you kept yourself going since the divorce? Financially, I mean.'

'Ooh. You're serious, aren't you? You're going to tell me now you're not from *Homicidios*, but actually a tax inspector.'

'No, I'm not from *Hacienda*. But all of this does help us build up a picture, and brings us closer to finding who killed your ex-husband.'

'If you put it like that.'

She shivered and let out a sigh.

'Oh, what the hell. I've got a little sewing business. From home. Mending people's clothes, that kind of thing.'

'Cash in hand?'

'Hey, you just told me you're not interested in that.'

'You're right. And I don't think it's important here.'

'I should bloody well hope not.'

'Any other emotional attachments since the split with Roures?'

She looked at him sharply.

'I'm sorry, but I have to ask.'

'Men . . . come and go,' she said, looking away. 'Nothing serious. And nothing at all for the past couple of years.'

Cámara got up and went to pay the barman, then returned to the table. Lucía was finishing the last of her drink.

'Still,' she said as she got up to go. 'I'm glad to see you're really concentrating on this.'

'It must be hard for you.'

'He was my husband. It's been a long time now since we split up, but when someone you've been close to dies . . . And suddenly and violently like that . . .'

'I'm very sorry.'

'Yes. So am I.'

She reached out to shake his hand.

'Will I be seeing you again?'

'I don't know,' Cámara said. 'There may be some loose ends to tie up later on. One of my colleagues may be in touch.'

'If there's anything I can do.'

'You've been a great help.'

She let go of his hand and made to leave.

'One other thing,' Cámara said.

She turned and looked him in the face.

'Has someone called Sofía Bodí been in touch with you at all recently?'

She squinted.

'Sofía Bodí? What, like the woman in the news?'

Cámara nodded, catching sight again of the pulse in her neck.

'No,' she said with a frown. 'Not at all.'

EIGHTEEN

'I wasn't sure if you'd show up.'

In her text message she'd said the Bodeguilla del Gato restaurant. Ten o'clock. Cámara knew it well, tucked away down an alley behind the Plaza del Negrito in the heart of the Carmen area. In a moment's rush to the head, he'd booked a room for the night at a small boutique hotel around the corner. Something far more expensive than he would otherwise choose. Just in case. Yes, a double. He'd need somewhere to sleep anyway.

The restaurant did the best *patatas bravas* and *rabo de toro* he'd tried anywhere, but his stomach felt tight-squeezed like a sponge as he stepped into the cramped, rosy-lit space. Couples perched on stools at the bar, bodies engaged, gaze distracted as they sipped on cool red vermouth, condensation pouring down the glass and dripping on their laps in spite of the dry cold draught blowing from the air conditioning unit. A blur of faces soaked into his eyes until he found one that appeared clear, delineated, silent. Alone.

Alicia hesitated before looking up. Cámara sat down at the table as she busied herself with a cigarette, fishing it out of the packet with dark-painted nails and taking three strikes with the lighter to catch a flame. Then finally, as smoke drained from her nostrils, her eyes met his.

'I wasn't sure either.'

Cámara took in the details of her face: the upturned nose; the slight, endearing gap between her front teeth; crow's feet around her eyes, perhaps a tad deeper than when last he'd seen her. She was keeping her hair longer, he noticed, not the short, wiry crop of when he'd first met her, at the start of the Blanco case. Her skin was darkened by the sun, shiny and inviting, and her breastbone was decorated with a black-and-silver necklace with a deep red stone at the centre. Moroccan, by the looks of it. He felt he'd seen the design before, perhaps in a market in Fès, or Tangier. He couldn't say.

And then there was a certain glow about her, something he'd perceived the moment he'd first seen her. Other men, he could sense, were drawn to it as well, an energy, an eroticism, a way of looking at the world with a cheeky, playful grin. That, more than anything else, had intoxicated him back then, an attraction that went not to the heart, but which seemed to get under his nails and seep into his blood. As he absorbed and observed her now, an inner sense momentarily more active than his outer ones, he could see it was there, just as before, but less brilliant, perhaps, of a slightly duller, less intense hue.

'I'm glad you came.'

The waiter walked over and Cámara ordered a bottle of Mahou; Alicia a gin and tonic.

'I need something cold,' she said.

'And strong.'

She grinned.

'You're right,' he said. 'I could do with one myself.'

He called the waiter back and changed his order. A moment later, two tall tubular glasses of fizzy, slightly fluorescent liquid stood on the table between them.

'*Chin-chin?*' she asked, raising hers.

Cámara hesitated, then lifted his and tapped it lightly against her glass.

'Going to be like that, is it?' she said. She took a long drink, emptying almost half of it in one. Vapour was rising from the ice cubes, while her lip was wet from where the gin had splashed against the side.

'OK, it's not just a social call,' she said. 'Although it is . . .'

'I realised that. Let me guess, the paper in Madrid has sent you over here to write something on The Case of the Missing Abortionist.'

'Yeah, I suppose we could use that as a headline, but it's a bit clichéd. Sounds like Sherlock Holmes meets Stieg Larsson.'

'Well, it's a good job I'm not a journalist, then.'

She pulled on her cigarette and looked him in the eye.

'I didn't know what to expect, really. Thought you might be, well, a bit hostile, a bit sharp. But it's been over a year. Are you so angry at me?'

Cámara waved her comment away.

'It's just our usual banter,' he said with a grin.

'Yes. I suppose it is.'

They decided to order some food. Thick peppered gammon served on a wooden platter, leeks soaked in vinegar, and, of course, a serving of *bravas*. If they were still hungry afterwards they might order the oxtail as well. They opted for a bottle of Somontano wine to accompany it.

'Go on,' Cámara said as they started eating. 'I know you're itching to. Ask me about the case.'

Replying to her questions, he confirmed the Maldonado theory, that a GAL-type organisation was behind the kidnapping, and that, nominally at least, he was part of the investigation team, that all other cases had been suspended to bring manpower to this. He told her what he knew about Sofía, about her background, her history as a pro-abortion activist. Much of this Alicia already knew, but she was fascinated by his description of Sofía's old-fashioned flat, and the curious, foetus-like behaviour of Ballester, her lover. About the diaries, however, he remained silent.

'You know the Pope's arriving tomorrow morning, right?'

Cámara's eyes opened wide.

'Christ, I'd almost forgotten. Tomorrow already.'

'Pretty strange timing, don't you think?'

'It'll have been planned for months, years.'

'Not the visit. I mean kidnapping Sofía.'

'That's part of the thinking,' Cámara explained. 'We find Sofía as quickly as possible so that as the Pope's here preaching anti-abortion the *Policía* arrive on a white horse saving the abortionist who's now in the headlines.'

'I get that,' Alicia said. 'Although it is a bit far-fetched for the police to cast themselves as heroes of democracy all of a sudden; they've hardly got a clean record themselves. What I mean, though, is why, if you're a bunch of hard-line conservatives, would you kidnap Sofía just as the Pope's arriving? Doesn't it just embarrass him?'

Cámara shrugged.

'Oh, come on. You're not going to tell me the thought hadn't crossed your mind.'

Cámara stabbed a fork into the gammon.

'This *lacón* is delicious.'

'Or is it just because Maldonado's in charge that you're not taking the idea seriously.'

'Here. Try some.'

'You're not going to answer me, are you?'

'Listen,' he said, dropping his fork on to the plate. 'Right now it's a united police force working tirelessly together to solve this as fast as we can. That's the public image they want, that's what it's got to be for now. All right?'

Alicia held up her hands in a defensive gesture.

'OK. I get it.'

She lifted one of the leeks on to her plate and started cutting into it.

'Although it's hardly that tireless if you've got time to have dinner with a journalist the night before you-know-who shows up.'

'I've switched off my phone,' Cámara said with a grin. 'Besides . . .'

'What?'

'Nothing.'

Cámara drained the last of his gin and tonic and poured them both some wine.

'You going to be doing any other stories while you're over?' he asked.

'Like what?'

'Like, I don't know, this whole El Cabanyal thing?'

She pursed her lips.

'That's turning into a big story, a national story,' she said. 'It's like we can't believe that kind of old-fashioned, bulldoze-it-all develop-ment is still going on. Most people have realised we spoilt whole swathes of coastline by building as fast as we could, and that this needs to stop, but in Valencia there's this old-style mentality insisting on razing anything old and characterful and replacing it with concrete blocks of flats.'

'Creatures of habit.'

'Bloody dinosaurs, you mean.'

'Jobs for the boys?'

'Oh, yeah. That's part of it as well. You know Javier's on the Valconsa board of directors?'

'Gallego? Your ex?'

'That's right.'

'On the board of the construction company?'

'Yes, the people working on the El Cabanyal project.'

'He's still editor of *El Diario de Valencia*, I take it?'

'Very much so.'

'Which is why you never read any criticism of the bulldozing in the paper.'

It was Alicia's turn to shrug.

'Or on regional TV.'

'Well, that's totally controlled by Emilia's party,' Alicia said. 'Has been for years.'

Cámara frowned.

'We have elections every four years,' Alicia said with a starry-eyed smile. 'We're a member of the European Union, we even criticise other countries for their lack of transparency or human rights records. Yet back home we have politicians and judges from Franco's day still in their jobs and a corrupt, politically manipulated media.'

'I can see you're feeling at home at your new paper, then.'

Alicia sighed.

'Yes, it's a little more to the left, but newspapers are newspapers. You're going to get the same tensions and squabbles wherever you go. And no one's feeling safe these days. I got in just before a whole load of the workforce got the chop. But at least I don't have to censor my own stories any more.'

'As a bullfighting correspondent?'

'That was only part of what I did. Although you'd be surprised.'

For a moment, Cámara's thoughts turned to the hotel room he'd booked for the night. He wanted to kiss her.

'How do you like living in Madrid?'

'It's fun. Bloody freezing in winter, but there's a lot going on. The people are great.'

'So you've . . . made some new friends?'

'One or two. Work keeps me busy, so I can't get out as much as I'd want.' Alicia smiled at him. 'It's good to be back here, though.'

'Are you over for a while?'

'I've got to get back tomorrow.'

'Staying at the flat?'

'Yes. It's empty.'

There was a pause as the conversation lost momentum and they ate in silence, Cámara watching as the light reflected from the silver dolphin ring on her finger.

'So how did Gallego end up on the board of Valconsa?' he asked.

'He's friends with José Manuel Cuevas, the CEO,' Alicia said. 'Who in turn is the brother-in-law of Rafael Mezquita.'

'The new urban development councillor?'

'That's the one. Clean churchgoing type. Emilia put him in to replace García Ramos, remember?'

'Someone mentioned it. Something about a scandal involving a goalkeeper's wife.'

'It was a big blow for Flores – Ramos was one of his disciples.'

'So now the head of development in the city is related to the head of the company that's going to pull down El Cabanyal?'

'Cuevas is married to Mezquita's sister. They were in the FES together at university.'

The *Frente de Estudiantes Sindicalistas* had been a Fascist youth movement back in the seventies and eighties before it was absorbed into the Falangist party. Former Prime Minister José-María Aznar had been a member before joining the *Partido Popular*.

'So you do think there's a right-wing conspiracy afoot?'

Alicia smiled.

'The forces of evil are out to get us,' she said theatrically. 'They're everywhere.'

Cámara took a sip of his wine, masking his face.

'Seriously,' he said. 'There's a personal angle to the abortionist story for you, isn't there?'

Alicia's smile dropped. Without finishing her food first, she placed her fork down and started looking in her handbag for her cigarettes.

'I mean, this is the clinic where—'

'Max!' She held up a hand. 'Stop there.'

'We never had a chance to talk about it.'

'Look, I . . .'

She lit her cigarette and stared out into space.

'So what do you want to say?' she asked.

The moment of anger seemed to have passed, and Cámara fell silent.

'You want to know what I think's happened to Sofía?' he blurted out as the idea took hold in his mind of a sudden. 'I think some disgruntled would-be father who never got a chance to say what he thought about his child being aborted has decided to exact some revenge. You're right, we don't need any conspiracy theory to understand this. There's motive enough, thousands of them. One for every life she snuffed out. I've seen Sofía's diaries. She wrote down the name of every woman she carried out abortions on, like some death register.'

The cigarette was twitching in Alicia's hand.

'Or life.'

'Life?'

'I met Sofía. She was the kindest person you could imagine, only interested in helping people in difficult, painful circumstances. Those women were given control over their lives by what she was doing.'

'Only by killing—'

'What? By killing what, exactly? Children? Babies? What do you think they are? Do you think they're actual people? Biologically they're less complex than the pig whose flesh you're chewing on right now.'

They were both raising their voices and looks were being cast in their direction from neighbouring tables. Cámara closed his eyes.

'So what are we talking about?' Alicia continued. 'The soul? Do you think embryos and foetuses have souls? You've got religious all of a sudden?'

Cámara had picked up his glass and was swirling the wine around inside it.

'Come on,' Alicia said, lowering her voice as she realised that they were becoming the focus of attention. 'Do you even know yourself what you think?'

She took a deep breath and sighed.

'Don't imagine I didn't go through all this myself. Or do you think I skipped happily into the clinic with a bloodthirsty glint in my eye at the thought that I was about to abort something that had grown from an act of love, of intense, joyful love?'

Cámara wanted to look her in the face, but his eyes remained fixed on the circling wine.

'I could probably have done things better. But that's the case with almost everything we do. What should I have done, though? Tell you I was pregnant?'

Cámara nodded.

'And would that really have been fair on you? You were still confused about that other woman, admit it, Max. I was very close to falling in love with you. There. I've said it. But we'd only slept together once. I was busy working out how to get away from Javier and the suffocation of *El Diario*. I didn't know what you wanted, what you felt. You're a policeman, you're hardly classic father material.'

Cámara put the glass down on the table, but found that he still couldn't look up.

'What was I supposed to say? Hey, look, we've only just met, and we had sex once and, oh, by the way, can you help me raise this child? And then what? Stay in Valencia? Have the child and move in together? Get married and live *felices como perdices*?' Happily ever after.

Ash was beginning to fall on to the table from her cigarette.

'Yes, that might have been how things turned out, but I just couldn't see it. What I saw was me being stuck in Valencia, at a crap local newspaper, with a father to my child whose most outstanding characteristic was that he was never around.'

'You could at least have told me.'

'I did.'

'Before the abortion.'

Cámara could feel a tightness in his shoulders, a fuzziness in his brain that he usually took as a warning sign that any thoughts at that moment were best left alone, unvoiced and ignored. But anger and indignation were getting the better of him.

He looked up. Alicia was staring at him incredulously.

'What? So you could hold my hand? You're not listening to me. There was no way I could have told you before. Who would I have been telling? I barely knew you. I barely know you now.'

'I was the fucking father.' Cámara's voice lowered as he spat the words out. 'Doesn't that count for something?'

'This isn't about the child, or the foetus, or whatever you want to call it,' Alicia said. 'It's not some moral thing. It's about you not being able to control the situation.'

Cámara's eyes widened.

'There was no solution here. No opportunity for Chief Inspector

Cámara to come along and solve the problem. That's what pisses you off. Yes, it was yours as well, but it was growing inside me. I was the one who would give birth to it and raise it. Disappearing, giving up, only taking care of it at weekends – these weren't options for me like they were for you.'

'I . . .'

Cámara tried, but couldn't speak.

'What? You would have been a great dad? Maybe. But that's easy to say now. More difficult when there's an actual child that needs taking care of.'

She paused.

'Look,' she said, 'whatever pain it caused you, whatever angst you went through, believe me, it was worse for me.'

The fuzziness seemed to be intensifying inside him. Just say nothing, he told himself. Don't speak.

'This isn't about whatever happened to you in the past, that big dark secret you never want to talk about. This isn't about Cámara the policeman, the murder detective desperately trying to undo the deaths that have scarred him so deeply. It was about you and me and a little group of cells that was about to cause a huge mess.'

He walked her to her old flat. There was no point mentioning the hotel room.

He stepped away as she unlocked the main door, making it clear he wasn't expecting to be invited up, but she moved towards him and kissed him softly on either cheek.

'I've thought a lot about us this past year,' she said, gripping his arm affectionately.

'So have I,' he said.

'But it's within you. Whatever it is that holds us apart is in you.'

She moved back towards the door and stepped inside.

'Come and find me,' she said, glancing back for a moment. 'If ever you're ready to tell me about it, come and find me.'

NINETEEN

Friday 10th July

He stepped into the first bar he found, dizzy and foggy-headed. He'd woken early, hunger lifting him out of his leaden, skunk-induced sleep, paid for the hotel room in cash, and crashed out into the bright sunlight outside, looking for somewhere to have breakfast. The bar was just around the corner in the next street.

Flores's puffy face wasn't the first thing he wanted to see on any day, but less so that morning. Nonetheless, there he was on the TV, in a beige summer suit with a lemon shirt and a pink, black and white striped tie, frowning at the journalist who had dared corner him to ask a question. Cámara ordered a *café con leche* and some toast with olive oil and salt and then glanced up at the screen screwed to the wall opposite, wondering if the world had turned upside down while he'd been asleep. But no, this wasn't Valencian Canal 9 – they would never have the temerity to buttonhole one of their paymasters in this way; it was a national channel, one less pervious to the censoring tendencies of the local ruling party.

He sipped on his coffee, trying to ignore the man who had organised violent attacks against him during the Blanco case. Flores had been trying to slow Cámara's investigation down, using him as a tool in the campaign to get Mayoress Emilia Delgado re-elected. But since then, apart from a few fines for supposedly not paying his car tax, Flores had left Cámara alone. If Vicent was right, he wasn't as powerful as he once had been, not as close to Emilia. Perhaps someone else had replaced him in her bed.

He drained the coffee, ordered another one, took a bite of the toast, and glanced back up at the screen. Flores looked angry.

Journalist: '*You've ordered the removal of an exhibit at an art show that the Town Hall itself organised.*'

Flores: '*The piece in question was grossly indecent and insulting.*'

Journalist: '*And you've also banned an anti-Pope rally organised for this afternoon. Aren't you stifling a constitutional right to freedom of expression?*'

Flores: '*Freedom comes with responsibility. We have to maintain standards of common decency.*'

Journalist: '*But the demonstration?*'

Flores: '*It's illegal. The application for permission came in after the deadline.*'

Journalist: '*A deadline you only made public after the application had been made.*'

Flores: '*That's a lie!*'

Journalist: '*What do you say to allegations that public money spent on the Pope's visit has been siphoned off . . .*'

But Flores wanted no more. He pushed past the girl with the microphone and stepped into a waiting car to be whisked away. The image cut to a photograph, the anchorman explaining that this was the exhibit that the Town Hall had ordered be removed from the exhibition at the modern art gallery. Cámara stared up at a montage showing a naked, crucified Emilia, blood tricking down her torso, a group of praying Town Hall councillors circling beneath her. On one side a figure representing Flores himself was placing a fig leaf over Emilia's mouth, while below a man with Mezquita's face superimposed over his head was busy anointing her feet.

A TV commentator was speculating whether the image hadn't reached a wider audience by cack-handed attempts to censor it. Then they cut to a different Town Hall spokesman, one Cámara hadn't seen before, writing off the accusations against them as a smear campaign by the opposition parties. They would only be happy, the spokesman insisted, when Emilia was woken up in the middle of the night, put against a wall, shot and buried in an unmarked pit.

The parallel to the killings of the Civil War period was obvious, and the shock at hearing such brutal language quickly stifled Cámara's laughter. The wounds were still too open, too fresh, for talk like that.

As the images cut to show the recent demolition of more houses in El Cabanyal, he turned away from the screen, his belief in the corrosive effect of news media further strengthened. Inflaming, depressing or exciting, all it ever did was pull at lower emotions, making people twitch like puppets while rarely passing on truly useful information.

The phone in his pocket vibrated twice in succession as he finished his toast and drained the last of his coffee. The first text was from Maldonado, threatening to have him formally disciplined if he failed to report to him by ten o'clock that morning.

The second was more interesting: Captain Herrero, the *Guardia Civil* he'd met on the beach when they'd fished out Roures's body from the sea, was asking to meet him later that morning at a bar near the railway station.

Outside, it was as if two rival football teams were about to go head to head, with yellow-and-white flags for the Pope's fans, and red-and-white banners hanging from the windows of the more anti-clerical persuasion. From the flatter, darker, more Asiatic faces that had suddenly appeared in the city, it felt as though half the population of Latin America had been parachuted in to fill out the Vatican's numbers.

Cámara pushed his way through the crowds of excited teenagers and elderly ladies lining the sides of what was later to be the papal route through the city and crossed the old river bed in the direction of the Jefatura.

'Don't tell me,' he said to Torres as he walked into their shared office. 'Pardo wants my head on a plate.'

'On a plate with a nice *salsa verde* and a side helping of *allioli*. Just to give it some flavour.'

'He knows how to eat well, you've got to give him that.'

'I'm sure he'll be flattered to hear it, chief,' Torres said. 'Did you manage to find Roures's ex?'

But Cámara wasn't listening. Sitting down at Torres's desk, he started clicking his way through the web pages of *Sidenpol*, checking up information on Valconsa.

'I thought you said you didn't know how to use that thing,' Torres said, glancing over his shoulder.

'I lied.'

Torres started playing with his packet of Habanos cigarettes. It was time, he was trying to signal, for a smoke downstairs outside the emergency exit. But still Cámara wasn't paying him any attention, his concentration fixed on the screen.

'I'll, ei, go down on my own, then,' Torres said.

But he didn't get a chance to make it across the office floor. As though drawn by a scent, Pardo walked in at that moment and slammed the door shut behind him.

'*Buenos días, jefe,*' Torres said. Pardo wasn't in the mood for pleasantries. Glancing about the office like an arsonist about to set fire to the place, he stepped over the piles of reports and box files and wandered over to Cámara's desk, where he slumped down in the chair and started spinning around.

'Do you want to go through the whole your-job's-on-the-line routine,' Cámara asked, standing up, 'or shall we go straight to the explanations?'

Pardo kept spinning, not saying anything.

'You look like you need to let off some steam.'

Torres threw Cámara a look. Pardo placed his feet on the ground and stopped, keeping his back to both of them, staring out through the window at the monotone brick facades of the block of flats in front.

'They really didn't give you the best view, here, did they?' he said at last. 'I wonder why that was?'

He spun round in the chair to face them.

'Take a seat,' he said.

Torres sat at his own desk; Cámara perched on the edge of a table.

'Right, here's the deal,' he said calmly. 'You're both – that's right, both – facing disciplinary hearings. I don't need to explain why in your case,' he said to Cámara. 'But you,' he nodded in Torres's direction, 'for covering for him.'

Torres froze, his face turning a pale, waxy colour.

'That's right, Cámara. It's not just about putting your own neck on the line any more. You want to run around making your own rules, it's the people around you that's going to feel the consequences as well this time.'

Pardo started rolling his tongue around in his mouth as he chose his words.

'Half the Interior Ministry's poring over every piece of paper we produce on this case. Meanwhile Madrid's itching to send over a special investigations unit 'cause they reckon we're out of our depth on this one. Want to turn it into a nationwide thing. Can't believe there are rotten apples only in the *Guardia Civil* here. Must be everywhere, they reckon.'

Cámara shuffled on his perch; Torres sat motionless.

'So while you two are playing Cowboys and Indians, not only are you making the investigation look a fucking mess, you're giving them the excuse they need to come down here and take over the entire fucking show.'

Cámara made to speak, but Pardo held up his hand.

'Wait your turn,' he barked. The anger was rising in his chest, despite his efforts to dampen it down, and he was beginning to breathe heavily.

'Now I know,' he said through tightened lips, 'that you're a good policeman.' He turned to Torres. 'You're both good. So this is what we're going to do: you're going to tell me in very simple language what the fuck it is you've been doing for the past couple of days while the rest of us have been running around like headless chickens trying to find Sofía Bodí before the fucking Pope flies into town.'

He nodded at Cámara to speak. Cámara gave a cough.

'I'd really prefer it,' Pardo butted in before he could start, 'if you sat down on a proper fucking chair.'

Cámara grabbed a spare seat from the other side of the office, hauled it over in front of Pardo and sat down.

'There, that's better,' Pardo said. 'See?'

'There's a link,' Cámara said, pressing his fingertips together.

'A link,' Pardo echoed.

'Between Bodí and Roures.'

For the next few minutes Cámara outlined what he'd learned: about Sofía's diaries; about the entries for each day with the names of the women she'd carried out abortions on; about the mark next to a recent entry when she'd gone for lunch at La Mar, and how that mark had referred to an abortion carried out back in 1977 on Roures's ex-wife, Lucía Bautista. Pardo sat in silence, listening, his eyes cast down towards the floor.

'There were no other marks in the diary like it,' Cámara said. 'We're looking at something exceptional, something tying her in with our murdered paella chef just weeks before she herself goes missing.'

'Anything in the diary to suggest she knew who might be about to kidnap her?' Pardo asked.

'Nothing from what I read. The entries were getting shorter over time. She wasn't sleeping. She was probably close to breaking down, physically and mentally.'

Pardo signalled for him to stop, thinking the information through in silence for a moment.

'You've talked to this Bautista woman?'

'Inspector Torres carried out an initial interview,' Cámara said. 'I spoke to her again yesterday.'

'And?'

'Claims she's had no contact with Sofía Bodí. Said she'd only heard of her from the news stories. But she confirmed the abortion back in seventy-seven.'

Pardo rested his cheek against his knuckles, his eyes unfocused.

'All right,' he said, getting up from his chair. 'It's good enough for me. Too much coincidence – don't like it. You've got my permission to keep at this. But you've got to work quickly. Keep a proper record of everything – I mean everything. I'm going to keep a lid on this for the next few hours, but once you find something we're going to have to go official, which means no spelling mistakes and no missing commas. Right?'

He looked over at Torres.

'No more wasting time covering for this arsehole, got it? I need you both working flat out. And I need a result by this afternoon. There's enough to start with, but we're going to need more to convince the top floor.'

Cámara was familiar with this particular version of Pardo – no longer a *comisario* but one of the boys, pretending to get his hands dirty while making common cause against the 'bosses' upstairs.

'What about Maldonado?' Torres asked. 'Do we need to—'

'Fuck Maldonado,' Pardo snapped. 'He can look after himself.'

He moved towards the door. Cámara took a step after him.

'One thing, chief,' he said in a low voice.

Pardo opened the door and turned to him.

'This is only ever between you and me. Don't ever do that to Torres again.'

Pardo's eyes widened in disbelief.

'What the fuck?' he spluttered. 'You threatening me?'

'*Pecado de mucho bulto no puede estar siempre oculto,*' Cámara said in a low voice. You can't hide a big sin for ever.

Pardo's expression of disbelief shifted from one born of rage to one sustained by fear. He held Cámara's gaze for a moment and then stepped out into the corridor, slamming the door behind him.

Cámara moved back to his desk and sat down in the chair Pardo had just vacated.

'Chief,' Torres said. Cámara kept his head down.

'Have you got some dirt on Pardo?'

Cámara shrugged as he flicked through some forms lying on his desk.

'Looks like I do now.'

TWENTY

Captain Herrero was not in uniform, but Cámara recognised him immediately from his tall, angular body and sharp features. He walked purposefully into the bar, ordered a *café solo* from the barman, then crossed over to where Cámara was sitting in the corner as though he'd known he was there from the start.

'I shouldn't be here,' he said as he sat down.

'Neither should I,' Cámara said. 'Specific orders.'

Herrero's mouth twitched into a grin: they understood each other.

'Any fallout from the other day?' Cámara asked.

'The body on the beach? No, not really. Who was he, anyway?'

'Pep Roures. Used to run a paella restaurant in El Cabanyal.'

'La Mar?'

'That's the one.'

'Yeah, I heard about that case.'

'But you haven't come here to talk about that, have you?' Cámara said.

Herrero paused as the barman brought over his coffee and placed it down on the table in front of him. Cámara was already halfway through a *café cortado*; the skunk felt to be pretty much out of his brain by now, but he eschewed a usual mid-morning beer in favour of more caffeine to keep him sharp. On the television set above the bar, images were being broadcast of the Pope's arrival at Valencia airport, the King and Queen welcoming him along with a host of local politicians. Emilia was there, smiling as broadly as she could, a yellow patent leather handbag swinging from her arm.

Herrero didn't speak until the barman had gone back behind the bar and was well out of earshot.

'They transferred me out of *Servicios Marítimos* the next day,' he said. 'Some reorganisation of personnel. Or at least that's what they said.' He gave a cynical laugh. 'I was virtually the only one not on sick duty for depression and they pulled me out. I mean, what's the point?'

'We get the same kind of bullshit,' Cámara said.

'Anyway,' Herrero continued.

'We didn't come here to moan about the demotivational skills of our respective superiors,' Cámara finished for him.

'Yeah,' Herrero said. 'Listen, they shunted me into an office in the *Comandancia*. It's comms and protocol stuff mostly, like a kind of hub.'

'Got it,' Cámara said.

'Well, look, something interesting passed by me yesterday, records of a phone tap.'

Cámara raised an eyebrow. Already Herrero was sticking his neck out more than any other *Guardia Civil* he'd encountered. Even if the information turned out to be useless, this was already important in itself.

'Are you sure you want to . . .' Cámara said. 'We can stop right now and forget everything about this. It's not too late.'

'You need to know what I'm about to tell you,' Herrero said. 'If we've got some nutters on our side running around kidnapping civilians I want them flushed out as much as you do.'

Cámara nodded. It seemed that Maldonado's 'GAL theory' was common currency.

'OK. Go on.'

Herrero put a spoon into his coffee, stirred it for a couple of seconds, then took a gulp.

'Right, as I said, this office I'm in, it's just light stuff mostly. And as the new boy they weren't going to show me anything sensitive. But yesterday I was there on my own. I reckon the others thought I'd picked up enough to know the score and they could bugger off to the beach for the day. So this pink envelope comes through – that means class 2 security – and I had to process it.'

'You use pink envelopes for top secret?'

'No that's red. Pink's one down. But, yeah, pink. I know what you mean. Not the kind of colour you associate with the *Guardia Civil*, right?'

He looked down into his coffee, as though weighing what he was about to say.

'OK, look, I've just got to tell you this, all right?' he said, launching himself into it. 'Sofía Bodí's phone was being tapped.'

'Right,' Cámara said. 'Probably to be expected given Lázaro's investigation into the clinic.'

'Yeah, yeah,' Herrero raised his hands as though to slow Cámara down. 'That's what I thought. Comandante Lázaro was behind the tap, but what I was looking at was a list of all the people who were receiving the transcripts.'

'Go on.'

'We use codes to denote who they are. I know them by now; they were people you might imagine: Lázaro's superiors, a couple of people in Madrid, one or two others.

'But,' he went on, 'one code was different. An emergency code, not one for someone inside the *Guardia*.'

He reached over for a paper tissue from the metal dispenser at the side of the table, fished out a pen from his shirt pocket, and started writing in small, heavy lettering. When he'd finished he turned the paper round and showed it to Cámara, keeping his finger on the paper.

Cámara looked down and saw: *X46125201*5.

'Yeah,' Herrero said. 'It wouldn't have meant much to me a week ago. But I'm a fast learner. Look, we can break it down.'

With his pen, he drew a line down after the '*X*', separating it from the numbers.

'That's *X* for external. We know this is going to someone outside. But where?'

He drew another line, this time after the numbers '*4*' and '*6*'.

'Forty-six. That's the first two digits of the Valencia city postcode.'

Cámara pursed his lips.

'That was easy,' Herrero continued. 'The next bit was more complicated. But I had a breakthrough last night.'

He turned the paper round and started writing again.

'Let's assume each letter of the alphabet has been assigned a number.

134

A equals one, B two, and so on. Now the only letters that would make sense out of the remaining digits here would be these.'

He drew his pen down, dividing the numbers into four groups: '*1, 25, 20, 15*.'

'One is A,' Cámara said.

'Twenty-five is Y,' Herrero continued. 'Twenty is T. And fifteen is O.'

He wrote each letter out as he explained: '*A*', '*Y*', '*T*', '*O*'.

Cámara's eyes stayed fixed on the paper.

'And we all know what that means,' Herrero said.

Ayto. It was the common acronym for *Ayuntamiento,* the Town Hall.

Cámara took a breath.

'Listen,' Herrero said. 'I can't do anything with this. I'm not even sure these days who I could mention it to. Know what I mean? Everyone's on edge at the moment. The last thing anyone wants is a *Policía Nacional* investigation into the *Guardia Civil.* It's got people paranoid.'

Cámara had pulled out a Ducados and was lighting it, his gaze fixed on the piece of tissue paper on the table in front of him, with Herrero's proprietorial finger still pressed down on it.

'I owe you one,' Herrero said. 'From the other day. I know you're on this case.'

'I suppose that's how you got my mobile number as well,' Cámara butted in.

'I'd be a pretty hopeless *Guardia* if I didn't.'

Cámara smiled.

'The point is,' Herrero said, 'this needs to be known about. You need to know this. Whatever you do with the information from now on is your affair, though. This cup of coffee, this bar, this meeting, none of it exists.'

Cámara nodded. 'Don't worry about it.'

He was busy trying to memorise the numbers on the piece of paper, wondering if Herrero was ever going to lift his finger off it and let him keep it.

'I just wish I could get my hands on those transcripts,' he said under his breath. 'Find out what Sofía was saying, who she was talking to.'

Herrero put a hand into his back pocket and lifted out a wad of folded papers, placing them in front of Cámara.

'Yeah,' he said. 'I thought you might say that.'

TWENTY-ONE

In the end there was no reason not to. Seeing him walking down the street with Herrero's papers in his hand, the bus driver thought Cámara was flagging him down as he skipped on to the melting tarmac around the edge of the bus stop in order to get past the two old women blocking the narrow pavement. And so when the vehicle came to a stop, and the doors opened with a long hiss, Cámara wondered for just a fraction of a second before hopping on and letting himself be carried by the wave that had unexpectedly come his way. He needed somewhere he could read the transcripts in peace anyway. And there was always the chance that Herrero was being watched by his own team. Which meant a tail might be following him now.

Quien peces quiere mojarse tiene. He who wants to catch fish has to get wet.

He sat in the higher seat at the back, checking that no one else was getting on board with him, studied the street for watching eyes and then, as the bus jerked back into motion, opened up the folded papers, barely conscious of the cool blow of conditioned air blowing down the back of his neck from the vent above his head.

Sofía had made dozens of calls over the course of the week before she'd disappeared. At the top of each conversation was typed the time and date, her name and her mobile phone number, along with the number and identity of the person at the other end, and *outgoing* or *incoming* to denote whether she had initiated the call or not. Cámara flicked through the pages, searching for names that jumped out. There were several to Ballester, Sofía's partner – quick calls to arrange the shopping for dinner, an apology for arriving late for a meeting at the clinic, discussions of their defence against the Lázaro investigation. And, less frequent but more important, comments of mutual support and affection. Stripped of their true context and subtleties such as tone of voice or the length of a pause, phone-tap transcripts often seemed pathetic and sad, Cámara thought, like a badly written – if realistic – play, built around the unthinking set phrases that made up so much of everyday speech.

Cámara continued skipping through the pages, avoiding lingering too long on any one detail as he tried to grasp a sense of the whole, the generic picture of Sofía's days leading up to the kidnapping, before going back to read in more detail. Calls to and from other members of the clinic, names he recognised from the notes he'd read back at the Jefatura; a misdialled number which had caused her much anxiety judging by the subsequent conversation she'd had about it with Ballester. Was she being stalked? Ballester had done his best to calm her down, but Cámara could sense the paranoia that was taking hold of both of them.

Sofía: '*Do you think . . .*'

Ballester: '*. . . What?*'

Sofía: '*This phone could be tapped.*'

Ballester: '*It's possible. Quite likely, I should say.*'

Sofía: '*What should we do?*'

Ballester: '*Keep talking. You've done nothing wrong. Let them listen, if the sons of bitches want to.*'

And then there it was, the name that jumped out and grabbed him by the throat. The name that somehow, without knowing, he'd known he would see.

Sofía: '*¿Hola? Is that Lucía Bautista?*'

Cámara stared at the name to make doubly sure, before reading on.

Lucía: '*Yes. Who's this?*'

Sofía: '*My name's Sofía Bodí. You may not remember me. But we met, years ago. I used to work at a gynaecological clinic in Paris in the nineteen seventies.*'

Lucía: '*How do you . . .? How did you . . .?*'

Sofía: '*I'm very sorry to be calling you like this. I wouldn't do so if it weren't extremely important. For you as well as for me.*'

Lucía: '*I don't know what you're talking about. I'm putting the phone down.*'

Sofía: '*No, please . . . I saw Pep Roures just a few weeks before he died.*'

Lucía: '*You met Pep? What's going on?*'

Sofía: '*Look, can we meet? It's vitally important. There are things I don't want to mention on the phone . . .*'

And so Lucía had been persuaded; they'd arranged to meet that very afternoon at the Montblanc café in El Cabanyal, not far from Lucía's home.

What had they talked about? Had Lázaro sent someone along to spy on them? If so, had his agent overheard the conversation?

The bus was racing down the long stretch of the Avenida del Puerto, the driver jumping three or four lights as they were turning red. Cámara looked up at the small television screen suspended from the ceiling showing a graphic of the route: he was on the number 2, heading away from the city centre towards the harbour. In a couple of minutes the bus would be swinging to the left and entering the narrow grid of streets of the fishermen's quarter that stretched out along the beach front to the north. All roads, it seemed, led to El Cabanyal.

The screen changed to a slide-show newsreel, showing the Pope's smiling face, while text alongside quoted a statement he'd made about Sofía Bodí's kidnapping. The Holy Father was said to be 'appalled' at the news. However, the newsreel text continued, the Vatican had no plans to curtail his planned anti-abortion comments during his visit, a decision that had been welcomed by the Town Hall.

Cámara stared absent-mindedly through the window.

Hot damp sea air swamped him as he got off the bus. He darted across the road into the shade of a palm tree, using the cool of the air conditioning still clinging to him for a precious few seconds to get his thoughts together. The heat had intensified over the course of the morning, passing the crucial 37-degree mark when the air became hotter than blood.

Why had Lucía lied about Sofía? Her house was a two-minute walk from where he stood; he could go there now and ask her directly. But coming here unexpectedly had moved some other piece inside his mind, and he decided to explore a different route first, to check on something he'd missed the first time.

*

'So you've come back. I haven't heard anything new, I'm afraid.'

Mikel Roig was sitting behind his desk, talking on the phone, but he interrupted his conversation to beckon Cámara in. Fold-up metal chairs were arranged in rows, filling up the remainder of the large ground-floor room. At the far end a banner was scrawled with the slogan *El Cabanyal, Sí – Especulación, No.*

Cámara remained on his feet. He could hear Roig trying to bring his phone conversation to a close, but the person at the other end kept talking. Roig rolled his eyes in a look of mock desperation at Cámara, before finally he was able to hit the hang-up button.

'Admin stuff,' he said with an apologetic sigh. 'Takes up so much time.'

'You're having a meeting?' Cámara asked.

'Later this evening. We don't usually hold them on a Friday, but we've heard there's going to be another wave of bulldozing. Imminent.'

'How many houses are they planning on knocking down?'

'This time? I don't know. There's at least one building for certain, but they might come in and take half a dozen. You can never be sure.'

'And in total? What's the actual plan here?'

'Over fifteen hundred houses have been marked for demolition,' Roig said. 'They pulled the first one down a couple of years ago. Just to show they could, you know. Some sort of power thing. It was a beautiful place. Had this magnificent wooden mirador looking out on to a hundred-year-old palm tree. Someone even used it as the location for a film years back, it was that special.'

Roig pointed to a nearby chair.

'Here, do you want a seat?'

Cámara shook his head.

'Have they knocked any more down since?' he asked.

'They took a couple of houses the week before last,' Roig said. 'The *Municipales* make a cordon round them, the demolition team comes in and they're gone in a couple of hours.'

'What about the residents?'

'So far Valconsa are only pulling down what they've already bought on behalf of the Town Hall,' Roig said.

His phone rang again. He picked it up, looked who the caller was, then hit the reject button.

'So how does it work?' Cámara asked.

'They could take the whole lot using the land expropriation laws,' Roig said, putting the phone back on the desk. 'They give them power enough.'

Cámara had come across Valencia's controversial land-grab laws, which gave the local government almost total powers to take whatever they wanted and even, in some cases, to force the owners they were depriving of their property to pay for part of the subsequent development costs. No one had been able to do much about it until a Scandinavian MEP with a holiday home on the Costa Blanca found himself having to fork out for the new dual carriageway running through what had once been his front garden. He took the case to Brussels, where officials forced the Valencian government to change the law. So the Valencian representatives went away, tweaked their legislation, gave it a new name, and carried on virtually as before.

'The problem is, though,' Roig continued, 'that would mean having to give a set rate of compensation to the owners. And we're talking about a lot of houses here; it would cost too much.'

'So?'

'So they run the area down. They buy the houses they can, then let them out to Gypsies and immigrants. These people have no connection with El Cabanyal – they don't care if this neighbourhood lives or dies. And they bring with them their own culture.'

'Meaning?'

'Meaning that in ten years El Cabanyal has gone from being a relatively quiet neighbourhood to becoming the city's drug supermarket. I can tell you exactly where to go at exactly what time and who to talk to to get whatever drug you want. Soft, hard, anything.'

There was nothing in Roig to suggest that he was some xenophobe or racist. This was not, Cámara could tell from the man's demeanour and way of speaking, anything to do with a problem with skin colour. He was simply describing a reality, and the reality was that large sections of the Gypsy community were involved in the drug business. He'd known enough about it himself from when he'd been in narcotics, five years before. There had been indications the dealers were moving out of their usual haunts in Natzaret and La Coma back then. El Cabanyal had been one of the areas named as a new drug centre.

'So the area gets run down,' he said.

'That's it,' Roig said. 'Things start going downhill; dealers and junkies everywhere, people lighting bonfires in the middle of the street, a few skirmishes between rival gangs. No serious violence yet, but it's enough to make people living here uncomfortable. Enough so that when Valconsa comes along offering to buy their property for next to nothing, they're happy to sell.'

'At a lower price than if they'd got compensation.'

'You got it,' Roig said with a resigned grin.

'Aren't these houses protected?' Cámara asked. 'This is like an open-air museum, with all this old tilework on the facades.'

'Yes, they're protected. But only until the Town Hall decides otherwise. Which, not surprisingly, they do on a regular basis.'

Cámara got up and Roig went to join him at the door, stepping out into the street. The sun was intense and felt as though it were burning the skin off their backs.

Cámara frowned at the death-threat graffiti that was still staining the front walls of the building.

'It's really nothing,' Roig said. 'We've had worse. The other day they smashed the windows and broke in. They didn't take anything because there's nothing to take.' He laughed. 'Of course we reported it, but the *Municipales* . . .'

Cámara noticed a wooden board covering a hole in the window.

'Who do you think it was?'

'The Valconsa lot,' Roig said.

Cámara raised his eyebrows.

'Trying to intimidate us, I suspect. Cuevas, the boss, used to be *Guardia Civil*. The company's hand in glove with the Town Hall. They've even got the contract to build that big stage down in the river bed where the Pope's saying Mass later on.'

'Have you got anything that might show it was someone linked to Valconsa?' Cámara asked.

Roig shrugged.

'No,' he said. 'But who else would it be?'

TWENTY-TWO

Cámara braced himself against the heat and set off, heading deeper into El Cabanyal. He glanced at the clock on his mobile phone: there was just enough time for him to check out something else.

The public sports club was a ten-minute walk away, but in the glare of the sun it felt as though the pavement was sticking to his feet, clawing at him to stay and melt into the earth. Ignoring it as best he could, he zigzagged his way through the side streets, on to the main road.

Eventually he found the large, deep-red brick building and crossed over to the gated entrance, passing a couple of open-air basketball courts before he found the shelter of the porch. The door was open and he stepped inside.

A girl at the front desk pointed him in the direction of the *trinquete* – the *pelota* court – past the changing rooms and towards the back, taking up one whole side of the building.

Cámara poked his head through the open door and looked out on to a white rectangular chamber about ten metres wide and fifty metres long. A net, drooping in the middle, was slung at around head height, like some kind of afterthought. The steps along one side of the court indicated where the spectators sat, forming part of the actual playing area; if the ball fell among them they simply allowed it to bounce down through their feet back to where the players were standing and the game carried on.

Cámara had seen *pelota* on local television often enough, the players dressed in white trousers, smacking the ball with ungloved hands from one end to the other. Usually there were two players on either side, but it could be played as a singles game as well; you often saw them with bandages wrapped around their hardened, swollen fingers. And it was mostly played in courts like this, although occasionally games took place in the street, the traditional location for *pelota*.

He remembered chancing on a match one Sunday afternoon in a side street just around the corner from the flat. It was around midday, a couple of hours or so before lunch, and he was taking a stroll. Where had he been going? He couldn't recall. It was as if all memories of his life there were seeping from his mind and getting lost.

He stared out at the long empty court, an awareness of his home-lessness striking him like a blow to the backs of the knees. He shut his eyes. It wasn't that he forgot about it: the experience was burnt into him like the branding on an animal's rump. But he distracted himself from it – with the investigation, a visit to the brothel, a chance dinner with Alicia. He'd thrown himself into that, he realised now, not just because of the emotion of seeing her again, but because it gave him another opportunity to block out the pressing issue of where he should live. Another night sorted, a hotel bed, perhaps with Alicia by his side.

Except that it hadn't turned out that way. Was she still in the city, or had she gone back to Madrid already? He imagined her somewhere in the centre of town, arranging to interview people, sitting in her flat with a laptop computer, writing out her notes. She might still be here, close by, close to him. Perhaps he could call her. A call he knew he would never make, but which briefly took form in his mind. Her voice on the other end of the line. Yes, I'd been thinking about you as well. I really enjoyed . . .

He sat down on the steps at the side of the court. His fingers were already searching in his pocket for the plastic-wrapped ball of dope nestling in the heat of his groin. Absent-mindedly, he found a cigar-ette, pulled it to his mouth, licked it along the edge and then started to pull it apart, making sure the tobacco fell into the well in the palm of his hand. Then he unwrapped the skunk and placed a large pinch of it into the tobacco and started mixing them together with his fingertips, forming the dried leaves into a sausage shape. He placed a cigarette paper on top, flipped it over like a pancake, then rolled it into a joint, slipping in a piece of rolled cardboard torn from the cigarette packet to act as a makeshift filter.

Pulling out a lighter, he flared the joint into life and inhaled deeply, glancing up with a frown to check for any smoke detectors. There were none, and with a nod of approval he noticed that large windows at the top of the court were open; no one would be able to tell someone had been smoking in here, he told himself.

The skunk worked its way from his lungs into his blood. First a welcome chill as his blood pressure dropped, a slight sense of nausea which he did his best to ignore, and then the dizzying rush as he closed his eyes and the weight seemed to fall away from his body.

It was enough.

He stubbed the joint out on the back of the step while it was still only half-smoked. The damage was done, but there was still time to limit it.

He got up and stepped back into the corridor. It was black in comparison to the brightness of the court, and he stumbled and swayed for a couple of seconds.

Faces smiled and grimaced out at him from the walls. He stopped and looked. Photographs from previous *pelota* teams that had played here over the years. 1997. No, not that one. He shook his head, calling up wakefulness from somewhere as the reason for his coming here began to rise up and take hold, only to slip from his grasp.

No. Further back. Other years.

1983.

He focused on a group of boys in their late teens, wearing the long-sleeved outfit of the *pelota* player, hair flowing down almost to their shoulders. The Socialists of Felipe González had already been in power for a year by then.

But no. Further back.

1979. The faces glared at him. No.

1978. No.

1977.

There.

A flash of red hair caught his drifting eye. He looked down at the name. Yes. Pep Roures was younger back then, but the future creator of so many well-appreciated paellas was recognisable, his features slimmer, his body longer, it seemed. Lucía had been telling the truth about that: he had played *pelota* here.

He tried to look into the boy's face. Was there some part of Roures back then that knew how he would die, as though his destiny had been programmed at birth? Would he, Cámara, be able to see it in his eyes through the lens of this thirty-year-old photograph?

He saw nothing. Just the serious, self-conscious expression of a red-haired teenager, with thoughts of little more than girls and *pelota*.

He turned away, but as he did so he knew at once he had to look again at the photo; there was something else there he needed to see.

Roures was in a group of three other boys: two at the front and Roures with another boy at the back. He checked their faces but didn't recognise any of them.

He shook his head again. The dope was swelling inside him like the body of a rotting fish and he was struggling to register what his eyes were seeing.

He glanced down at the names of the four boys typed on a white card underneath the photo. There was Roures's name again, jumping out at him and blocking out the others. But he forced himself to read, first one, then another, then . . .

Clarity hovered around him like a fly. He read the fourth name once, twice, then a third time before looking up at the face to whom it belonged.

It had changed over the years, but yes, yes, he could see it now.

It was the last person he expected to find.

TWENTY-THREE

The traffic had been cut off along Avenida Reino de Valencia and crowds were pressed tight in around the top of his street. Cámara nudged his way through as best he could. A fleet of police vans was parked up on the far side of the pavement, while members of the *Policía Nacional* had taken up positions at the front of the throng, holding people back from what might otherwise turn into a stampede. Over five thousand officers had been drafted in for the papal visit, many bussed over from other cities to make up the numbers. High over their heads two police helicopters flew in wide, slow circles, cameras trained on the heaving mass below.

Yellow-and-white flags fluttered everywhere, clutched in little girls' hands, used as a pin for one woman's hair bun, waved high in the air by a group of smartly dressed teenagers, climbing a lamp post in their enthusiasm as they tried to catch a better glimpse.

Across the street a *Policía Local* was angrily pulling porn magazines down from the display of a newsagent who'd defied the temporary ban on public images of naked people during the Pope's stay in the city. The newsagent shouted back at the policeman, waving his own red, yellow and purple Republican flag in his face. A small act of defiance which would only serve to increase his chances of getting a fine.

Cámara pushed his way through till he got to the corner of Vicent's bar. Showing his badge, he was let through the cordon and into the inner group of dignitaries, security men and residents of the street who were allowed to be this much closer.

The block of flats had fallen down so soon before his arrival that the Pope, or someone in his team, had decided it would be a good idea for him to make time in his schedule to come and visit the scene of the city's recent tragedy. Not to have done so, Cámara pondered, would have looked bad, uncaring. So the Pope was about to show up, to say a few prayers and throw some drops of magic water on a pile of rubble that had once been his home. And home to Susana and Tomás.

This was the latent anarchist in him, he thought, years of being brought up by an active member of the once-banned CNT union. Hilario would be proud of him standing there, stoned and silently swearing at the Pope, so close to where the Bishop of Rome was about to appear. This was nothing more than public relations. So far nothing had been done in the wake of the building's collapse four days earlier, no responsibility admitted, no charges brought for criminal negligence. Emilia posed for the photos but you didn't see her actually talking to any of people affected by this, not even to Susana and Tomás's relatives. The Pope's hosts – the smiling officials forgetting for the moment while the television cameras were switched off that this was supposed to be a solemn occasion, and that frowns and tears were more appropriate – were happy to use the pageantry of his visit to cover up for the fact that no one was going down for what had happened.

At the far end a sudden buzz of excitement was gripping the crowds; they were looking to the side, along the length of an adjacent street, cheering and stretching their necks to see. The Pope was pulling up in his Popemobile, complete with sixteen-vehicle entourage, and would soon be stepping out and walking towards them.

A smaller group of people was standing next to the pile of rubble. Emilia Delgado was there, wearing a dark blue summer suit with large shoulder pads and gold nugget-like earrings. In her hand swung her patent leather handbag, brushing backwards and forwards over her knee as she stood waiting for the Pope to arrive and to welcome him to the site of the accident. She wasn't happy doing this, he could tell. Far better to use the Pope's visit to showcase all the recent advances in the city: the new museums, the America's Cup port. Training the world's cameras on this scene of destruction and ineptitude had not been part of the grand scheme. But there was no avoiding it.

She looked at her watch a couple of times, double-checking on some detail of security with a man with sunglasses and a wire in his ear who was standing close by. Cámara didn't recognise him; doubtless the Town Hall was mixing its own men in with those of the *Policía Nacional*. They'd be lucky if the two security bodies didn't start shooting at each other.

Behind Emilia and her entourage he caught sight of Esperanza, his neighbour. She may have been made homeless, but the old *beata* wasn't going to give up a chance like this to meet Christ's representative on Earth in the flesh.

Doubtless Esperanza would be promised a beautiful home in the next life in exchange for the cramped, rotting one she'd had to put up with in this. That would make her happy, probably speed her up a bit in her sad shuffle towards death.

The hullabaloo at the other end was reaching a crescendo. Cámara found a corner from which he had a relatively clear view of the street and the ceremony that was about to take place in front of his old home. So much had happened in the past few days that he struggled to remember his former life in the space up there that had once been his. Not that he could ever have imagined that one day some old man with a stiff walk, wearing a white frock and bright red shoes, would come strolling down here and pray in front of it while millions watched from around the globe.

He took a deep breath and looked up into the cloudless sky. The humming inside his skull hadn't abated, although the coffee he'd swallowed hot and whole on his way over was helping to bring back a certain sharpness. He still felt dislocated from himself in some way.

A flash from the other side of the street caught his eye and he looked up. Someone was opening a window from Vicent's bar, and it had reflected the sun on him for a second. But a breeze blew the window wider open than intended and it swung out until it rested almost flat against the outside wall of the building. The reflection of a group of people came into focus: a middle-aged woman with a cloth hat and sunglasses staring down the street with open mouth in anticipation of the Pope's imminent arrival; a tall thin young man wearing a white-and-yellow T-shirt over sunburnt skin speaking into a phone, watching the television cameras closely to see if he could appear in one; a man in his forties, the only one not concentrating on events further down the street, with a knotted, angry look in his eye. The glass in the window wasn't entirely flat, so the image was distorted slightly, but it seemed as if the man were staring back at him with a cynical sneer, his shoulders rounded with self-imposed stress, a shadow around his chin where he hadn't shaved that morning, grey-brown bags under his eyes. He looked as though he were there under duress; not a believer, but someone who had come simply to leer arrogantly, as though searching for confirmation of his superiority by watching others forget themselves in the emotion of some meaningless ritual.

The Pope arrived, and all attention was directed on to him. Emilia, at the head of the welcoming committee, took a step towards him and curtseyed, kissing the holy hand, then backed away, beckoning the Pope to come forward and see for himself the scene of the collapsed block of flats. They exchanged a few words, a few other councillors bowed and kissed before him, and then the man in white was introduced to Esperanza. Even from where he was standing, thirty or forty metres away, Cámara could see the tears forming in her eyes. This made it worth it, this made losing her home and neighbours worth every moment. She would have eaten her own tit just to be here.

Neither the Pope nor the Town Hall people were keen for this to go on for too long. A few words were said in the direction of the rubble, the Pope held up his hands as though in supplication, a couple of priests on either side of him waved some incense burners, and that was pretty much it. With a smile the Pope turned around to face the thousands of people crammed into the street to see him. The ritual cleansing was over: no more tears; they could get back to the job of adoring his person now.

Cheers went up and Cámara was jostled as a middle-aged woman on one side and a young boy with a T-shirt in the Vatican colours on the other jumped up and down for joy, crashing into him as they lost their balance. They were so happy.

From the corner of his eye, Cámara could see that the cynic reflected in the window opposite was also being buffeted by the crowds around him.

Gradually, however, as the initial excitement abated, and the bodies stopped jostling so much, he began to see. And the sense of dislocation within him simultaneously both intensified and faded.

How could he not have recognised his own reflection?

He stood stock still, staring in disbelief at the form he had been so dismissive of only moments before. Everything he had seen was true. That was who he had become: a snarling, judgemental, unforgiving shape, so wrapped up in his own distress that it had cut him off both from people around him and from himself – his truer self. For this wasn't him, this wasn't the person he knew he could be. It was a monster that had taken control.

He looked down at the ground, gathering himself, breathing slowly and calmly, feeling the air inside him as though for the first time, and then looked up again at the window. Someone had moved it, and now, instead of seeing himself, he saw a man further down the street. A tall man wearing a light grey suit, gazing out with a devoted stare at the Pope as the pontiff moved away from the empty space where Cámara's home had once been, and started to walk over to greet members of the crowd.

The man in the suit smiled.

Cámara smiled.

It was time he spoke to Rafael Mezquita.

TWENTY-FOUR

But for his crooked nose, Rafael Mezquita, head of urban development at the Town Hall, would have made a handsome man. He was striking enough, with his tall frame, and shining, almost tearful eyes, but the near pin-up looks were spoilt by the slight disfigurement, a bend at the centre of his face where nature demanded rectitude. There were those who touted him as someone to watch, a future mayor himself, perhaps, or president of the Valencian regional government. But closer political observers tended to rule out such heights. Voters, they argued, would never vote en masse for a man with such a facial flaw, even if it was only minor. Things like that went deep, were instinctive.

Cámara pushed his way through the people watching the Pope, slowly taking his steps towards the crowd. Mezquita was standing still, not having to strain as much as the others to see over their heads. What he hadn't noticed, however, was that a white plastic cup dropped by someone in the crowd had blown over and got stuck on the end of his foot; the orange liquid that it had once contained now oozed out over his black leather shoes. It had a slightly comic effect, like some cartoon toecap, or a scene from an old slapstick comedy.

Mezquita cocked his head slightly to the side and gazed down as Cámara introduced himself.

'Chief Inspector,' he said. 'A pleasure. What can I do for you?'

His eyes glanced back towards the Pope as he spoke, anxious that his attention should not be distracted for too long.

'I used to live there myself,' Cámara said, nodding at the rubble pile.

Mezquita's eyes widened in sympathy.

'Oh, I'm so very sorry to hear that,' he said, looking at him more closely. 'This must be a very emotional time for you.'

Cámara shrugged

'It's been a shock,' he said. 'For everyone. Especially losing neighbours like that.'

'Susana and Tomás,' Mezquita said. 'Yes, I'm very sorry for your loss. It's been a tragic time. For the city as a whole. I think we're all in mourning in one way or another. But particularly for you, their neighbours. Their family.'

'Did you go to the funeral?' Cámara asked.

'I did,' Mezquita said. 'I represented the Town Hall. Very sad.'

'I couldn't make it.'

'No, of course. Listen, you must let me know if there are any hold-ups in getting you rehoused, or the compensation process. I know these things can take longer than we'd all like. But you can call my office any time.'

His eyes resumed their flicker between Cámara and the Pope as he spoke, not wanting to lose sight of his important visitor.

'I appreciate that,' Cámara said. 'But I wanted to talk to you about something else.'

Mezquita gave him a quizzical look.

'I'm investigating the murder of Pep Roures,' Cámara said.

'I used to know him,' Mezquita said. 'Years back. You're talking about Pep Roures who ran La Mar restaurant, right?'

'That's correct.'

'Another tragic story. We used to play *pelota* together, when we were teenagers.'

'I've just come from the El Cabanyal sports centre,' Cámara said. 'I saw the photo of the two of you.'

'Oh, is that still there?' Mezquita said with a smile. 'Yes, that was some time back.'

He placed his hand to his crooked nose.

'That was just before this happened.'

'Your . . .' Cámara hesitated.

'My nose was as straight as an arrow back then,' Mezquita said. 'As I'm sure you'll have noticed. But it got broken shortly after. It was Pep himself, actually. Shouldn't speak ill of the dead, but it was a mis-hit from him one day. It went straight into the side of my nose and broke it pretty badly. The doctors were never able to get it right again.'

He chuckled to himself.

'I was devastated at the time. You get over these things, but I thought I'd had it. No girl would ever look at me after that.'

He grinned.

'By the way,' he said, suddenly changing his tone. 'Is this a formal interview? If so, perhaps it could wait for another time.'

And he nodded his head in the direction of the Pope, who was now walking towards them, reaching out to brush the hundreds of hands and fingers trying to touch him.

'I'm just getting some background,' Cámara said. 'I saw you here and thought we could have a quick chat.'

'Yes, of course.'

'I suppose Roures would have felt quite bad for what he did.'

'Pep?' Mezquita said. 'Did you know him?'

'I went to his restaurant a few times, but can't say I knew him. I'm building up a picture of the kind of man he was.'

'Yes, that's right. He was a noble sort, was Pep. And he was very cut up about what happened. I was young at the time, and probably didn't spare him his blushes, if you see what I mean. I could have handled things differently, done more to make him feel less bad about it. But I think he felt he owed me something after that, as though he were indebted to me in some way.'

'Did you ever call the favour in?'

Mezquita frowned.

'No. No, of course not. I forgave him. It was an accident. But perhaps not until he'd bought me a couple of drinks.'

He grinned again, then turned his attention to the Pope as he walked within a few feet from where they stood.

'It's funny,' he said as the cheering soared around them. 'I hadn't thought about Pep for years until the story came out about him being killed. And now here you are asking me about him as well. He was a tremendous cook, made some of the best paellas. This city has lost one of its greats.'

Cámara raised his voice to make himself heard.

'Of course, La Mar was due to be demolished for the El Cabanyal building project.'

'The price of progress. Pep would have been compensated well, but he chose to hold out. It's a shame. That neighbourhood has been run down, and these people trying to hold on to the past are simply dragging it down even further. They need to understand that they are the problem here, that they're stopping the rejuvenation of the area.'

Cámara remained silent as the screaming and cheering got louder around them. It was becoming more difficult to hold a conversation.

Mezquita seemed to register that their chat was coming to a natural end, and he grabbed his chance.

'Do call my office if there's anything else I can help you with, Chief Inspector,' he shouted into Cámara's ear. 'Delighted to meet you.'

And he slapped him on the shoulder.

Mezquita headed back to the nucleus of Town Hall officials concentrated around Emilia's person, while Cámara found himself being drawn along by the crowd of security men following in the wake of the Pope as he continued his impromptu walkabout. Rather than breaking out, he went along with them, displaying his badge to a quizzical man wearing dark glasses and with a weapon-sized bulge in his ill-cut suit. The team looked nervous: the Pope, he imagined, was expected to head straight back to the Popemobile, not mingle like this. But in the few years of his pontificate, the old man had become increasingly known for his erratic behaviour.

Cámara shuffled along, curious that he should find himself close to someone who meant so much to millions. Hilario would appreciate hearing about this, he thought to himself. But would probably complain that Cámara hadn't at least thought about assassinating the Pope while he had a chance. He looked around; it wouldn't be that easy even if he were so inclined: the security men were packing sub-machine guns. He'd be dead before he even got his finger around the trigger.

They progressed along the street slowly as the Pope tried to make contact with as many outstretched hands as possible, stopping to talk occasionally for a few moments with the faithful. Cámara spotted a gap in the railings further on where a uniformed policeman was holding back the crowds. Once they reached the spot he'd slip away.

He turned back to watch the Pope, who was standing just a few feet from him now. He looked hot in his robes, and the skin on the back of his neck was shining with sweat, made more brilliant by the lights of the television cameras. But the smile, which Cámara could only partially see as he stood behind him, appeared to be fixed as he glanced at the ecstatic people, holding out hundreds of mobile phones to record images of the event. When this kind of thing happened to young rock stars, he thought, they usually ended up in rehab. What did Popes do to counter the corrosive effect of so much adulation?

He glanced back at the spot just in front of the slowly moving group where the policeman stood. Something had registered in the corner of his eye, but he couldn't see now what it might have been. He looked closely at the faces: three heavily made-up teenage girls were straining to get closer, but the officer was holding them back, placing his hands on their naked shoulders as politely as he could to keep them from jumping on the Pope. As they swayed back and forth, he saw someone else there, squeezed in between them, the only person in the crowd not smiling.

He took a step forward. The security men around him sensed that something was wrong and began to twitch. One of them tried to barge his shoulder between the Pope and the crowds, but the outstretched hands got in his way. As the group reached the policeman, his hands full with the three teenage girls, a streak of colour seemed to break out. A man in a deep red T-shirt pushed his way forwards and darted towards the Pope, too quick for the policeman to stop him. Cámara was caught at the side of the group, but pushed his way around the security men to reach out. One of them was already grappling with the attacker while two others were doing their best to drag the elderly Pope away before he'd even realised what was happening.

There were screams. From smiling and cheering with joy, the teenage girls were holding their hands to their mouths, unable to utter a sound. Around them, quicker members of the crowd were already calling out in fright as others pushed in even tighter to see what was happening.

Two security men had dragged the attacker down and were pinning him on the ground as he struggled to get free. The first one was grappling to hold him still, while the second reached into his jacket for a can of pepper spray to blow into the man's face.

Cámara clambered over and held him back.

'Stop!' he cried, pulling out his badge.

The security man shot him a look of anger, his wrist held tight in Cámara's solid grasp, his finger twitching to press on the spray can.

'I know this man,' Cámara said.

And he lunged forward, pushing the first security man off the attacker and leaning in to pin him down himself.

'*¿Qué cojones?*' What the fuck?

The uniformed policeman was standing close by, doing his best to hold back the crowds. Cámara leaned over and pulled him down with him.

'You help me with this,' he said to him. 'Keep him immobilised. Otherwise these idiots will rip him apart.'

He turned to look down into the face of the attacker.

'Señor Ballester,' he said. 'We're taking you to the Jefatura.'

He hauled Ballester up on to his feet and with the help of the policeman started dragging him away. In the chaos of screams and people he overheard a voice. Mezquita was looking in to see who had attacked the Pope.

'*Es el xic de l'anti-mare eixa,*' he explained to someone next to him. The boyfriend of that anti-mother woman.

TWENTY-FIVE

There was a queue of people outside wanting to catch a glimpse of the man who had tried to swing a punch at the Pope. Not only that: he was the partner of the missing abortionist they were now all supposed to be looking for, the reason why they had all been taken off their other duties.

Inside the interrogation room, Cesc Ballester sat with hunched shoulders, holding a bag of ice against his bruised face where the security guard had managed to hit him.

'Fuckers,' he swore under his breath.

Cámara stood behind him, while Maldonado stepped back and forwards in front, sleeves rolled up, his hands in his pockets, snorting through his nostrils like a beast. Near the door stood Pardo, a rare sight in interrogation sessions. But no one wanted to miss out on this.

'You should be dead,' Maldonado muttered to himself as he marched up and down. 'By rights you should have been pulled to shreds by the Pope's gorillas. God knows it would have saved us all a headache, if it hadn't been for El Cid here stepping in to rescue you.'

He glanced up at Cámara. Pardo pinched the bridge of his nose, keeping his eyes concentrated on the floor.

'I mean, what the fuck!'

Maldonado leaned in on the table separating him from Ballester and bawled into his face.

'What the fuck almighty were you thinking?'

Ballester averted his eyes.

'What did you think? That by strolling up to the Pope and landing him one you'd somehow bring your girlfriend back?'

'They banned the anti-Pope rally,' Ballester said softly.

'What?'

'Emilia. She banned the rally against the Pope. We were supposed to march—'

'What the fuck's that got to do with anything?' Maldonado screamed. 'You couldn't stage a demonstration, so you went and took your anger out on the fucking Pope himself? What was he supposed to do? Talk to Emilia on your behalf? Get her to change her mind?'

Ballester closed his eyes.

'Or did you think you'd just stage your own one-man rally instead? Make a stand for democracy by taking a swipe at the Holy Father in front of millions of people watching on TV.'

'That wasn't my idea,' Ballester mumbled.

'What? That wasn't your idea. Well, thanks very fucking much. But please do enlighten us, I mean, what the fuck was your idea? Hey! Did you even have one?'

Maldonado pulled himself away from the table and placed his hand over his eyes in a gesture of frustration.

'*Me cago en la madre que le parió,*' he grunted. I shit on the mother who gave birth to him.

'Do you realise the amount of crap you've just thrown at us? You've fucked everything up. Trying to save Sofía? Well, you've done that cause a lot of fucking good. How do you think her kidnappers are going to react to seeing her boyfriend assaulting the Pope? Do you think it's going to help? Huh? Do you? Really? Did you even stop to think about the consequences of what you were doing?'

Ballester hung his head in his hands.

'We're here sweating blood trying to get her back to you alive.'

Maldonado looked up at Cámara.

'Well, most of us are,' he muttered to himself. 'And then you come along,' he continued more loudly, 'and screw everything up.'

'It's all his fault!' Ballester shouted, looking up from his seat.

'What?' Maldonado screwed his face into a sneer. 'Whose fault?'

'The Pope's,' Ballester choked. 'The Pope and all those sycophantic bastards that surround him, inflaming people against us, against Sofía and people like us, and gays, and whatever. It's all just hate spewing from their mouths. Have you heard them?'

Maldonado gave a cry of mocking disbelief.

'It's the Pope's fault, you say? The Pope what done it?'

'Not the Pope himself,' Ballester said. 'I didn't say that. But the people who believe in him. They all listen to him, and his talk of the family and having to save it, and that it's under threat. He spurs them on, makes them do things.'

'Incites them,' Cámara said from behind the chair.

'Yeah,' Ballester said, looking round. 'Incites them.'

'So, what? He's your fucking lawyer as well as your saviour now?' Maldonado said. 'Telling you what to say?'

From his corner, Pardo scraped his foot on the floor as he lifted it to scratch his ankle. A wordless message to Maldonado – keep it on track.

Maldonado sat down in the chair in front of Ballester and put his fingers to his lips. The blotches on his face, old acne scars which were scarcely visible normally, were beginning to redden. Cámara had only ever seen him like this once before, when years back they'd ended up in a fight. At least, Cámara had punched him in the chest and Maldonado had ended up on the floor. Some squabble over a pay review. Or that's what he told people. It hadn't really warranted the word 'fight'.

'So what happens now?' Ballester asked after a pause.

'What happens now? Maldonado asked.

'Are you going to repeat everything I say?' Ballester said, a rush of confidence seeming to come over him.

Maldonado leaned over and pressed his finger hard into Ballester's throat.

'Don't start getting *chulo* with me. None of that cockiness. You're in serious fucking trouble.'

Pardo took a step towards the table. Maldonado withdrew his hand.

'You'll be charged with assault,' Pardo said. 'That's basic enough. How bad it's going to be for you depends on how far you cooperate with us now in trying to find Sofía.'

Ballester shook his head.

'Finding Sofía? I don't understand. All I've ever wanted to do was to find Sofía.'

'Right,' Maldonado said. 'And a fat lot of good it's done us so far. The kidnappers have sent a message to the newspaper in the past half-hour.'

Cámara shifted in his spot. He hadn't heard anything of the kind. This was a bluff, he felt sure.

'They're not happy about what you did. Pretty fucking pissed off. They've given a deadline. If the government doesn't repeal the abortion law by tomorrow Sofía's dead.'

Ballester covered his face with his hands and started to shake.

'What do I have to do?' he asked eventually.

'Firstly, you're staying here. You're not going anywhere. On bail or in any other form,' Maldonado said.

'Secondly, you agree to do everything we tell you. If we need to feed you to this lot to get Sofía back, we'll do it. And you'll go along with it.'

Ballester placed his hands down on his knees and nodded, as though agreeing to his own death sentence.

'We'll also need you to agree to a statement we're preparing,' Pardo said. 'The grief of losing Sofía has pushed you off balance. You aren't quite all there at the moment.'

'Are you saying I'm *loco*?'

'Some would say trying to lash out at the Pope is proof enough. And we've got a police psychologist who'll agree.'

'It's about limiting the damage you've already caused,' Maldonado said. 'If you ever want to see Sofía again, this is how it's going to be.'

But it was unnecessary to press the point further: Ballester was already broken. He wouldn't be arguing any more.

He nodded his agreement and Maldonado got up to leave. Outside, the corridor was quickly emptying, the onlookers realising that the show had ended. As Pardo opened the door, Cámara caught a glimpse of Torres's black beard by the noticeboard.

Ballester looked up at him.

'One quick question,' Cámara said as he glanced at the doorway, and the exiting form of Maldonado. Pardo looked round, saw that Cámara was talking to Ballester, and quickly ushered Maldonado out, closing the door behind them.

'Before the kidnapping, about six weeks ago, you and Sofía went to La Mar restaurant in El Cabanyal, right?'

Ballester shook his head.

'What? What are you talking about?'

'Think, man. This is important. It was a Saturday, in May. Sofía and you went for paella at a place not far from the beach.'

Ballester paused, then started to nod, gripping his forehead with his hand as he did so.

'Yeah. Hang on. Yeah, I remember now. The paella place.'

He looked up.

'What about it?'

'Did either you or Sofía speak to the owner at all while you were there? A red-haired guy called Pep Roures.'

Through the small reinforced window in the door, Cámara saw that Maldonado was trying to see what was going on back inside the interrogation room, while Pardo did his best to distract his attention.

'Come on!' Cámara grunted.

'I remember a red-haired guy. Yeah, the one who served us. Is it his restaurant then?'

'Yes, look, did you speak to him?'

Ballester was still dazed from everything that had happened and was struggling to think straight.

'No, I didn't speak to him. Except to give the order, I suppose.'

'What about Sofía?' Cámara said urgently. He could hear the doorknob rattling as Maldonado tried to get back inside.

'I don't know,' Ballester said. 'Wait. Yes, I remember now. She went up to pay at the counter. I remember because I was in a hurry to go home and watch the practice for the Grand Prix, and she was taking her time. She was talking to the bloke with the red hair. Yeah, that's right. How did you know?'

'What did they say?' Cámara asked. 'What did they say?'

The door was already opening in on them.

'I don't know,' Ballester said. 'She didn't tell me.'

The door opened and Maldonado walked in, the blotches on his cheeks now bright crimson.

'Barely said a word for the rest of the afternoon,' Ballester said to himself, 'now I think about it.'

Cámara stepped into his office, seeking solitude and a moment to think. There was somewhere else he needed to go, someone he needed to talk to, but for a minute or two at least he could stand here, undisturbed.

He had almost lost control earlier on, he could see that now; almost strangled Ballester as he'd pulled him away. That was why the security men had allowed him to take over: not because he was a policeman or had more authority than they did, but because there was a more intense aggression in him that they responded to instinctively, and respected.

It had only been for a second, but it had been enough, and Ballester was still ruffled by it.

Getting stoned on duty: he couldn't remember doing anything so idiotic.

The skunk was buried deep in his pocket. He lifted it out, crushed it in his hand and dropped it in a grey plastic bin at the side of his desk.

That was it. No more.

He'd seen enough of himself, enough of what he was in danger of becoming.

TWENTY-SIX

The Pope was deemed to be shaken, but unharmed, and it was agreed that his schedule should continue unchanged. After celebrating Mass and visiting the scene of the collapsed block of flats, he had a late lunch and a lie-down at the archbishop's palace next to the cathedral before being driven through the city streets once again in the Popemobile to the old river bed, where a vast stage had been erected for him to preach to a crowd numbering hundreds of thousands, all sizzling in the intense afternoon sun.

The bridges and avenues leading up to the venue were closed to traffic and lined with police vans back to back, while the helicopters were in the air again. All taxi and bus services in the city centre had been stopped, as had the metro line where it coincided with the papal route, in case of underground bombs. As he strolled in the shade of the pine trees, Cámara could sense, rather than see, the marksmen crouching on the rooftops. His old friend Beltrán, the best shooter in the force and the man who had saved his life only a year before, had mentioned being roped in for security duty. Back in the Jefatura, staff levels were below the supposed minimum, while the other police stations around the city were standing practically empty. After the incident with Ballester, no chances were being taken, and only Maldonado and his immediate team were spared from 'Pope duty'.

Already the voices of dissent were making themselves heard: 15 million euros had been spent on security and they still hadn't prevented that morning's attack. Far better to use the money on hospitals or schools than on some old man who couldn't be trusted to look after himself. Around the city, people protesting at the Pope's visit were leaning out of their windows and banging pots and pans as loudly as they could.

Others more commercially minded, meanwhile, were happily using his trip to make some extra money: flats with balconies near where the Pope was going to speak were being rented out for the day, and wealthier members of the faithful were paying up to 18,000 euros to watch, a safe distance from their sweaty, less affluent fellow believers below.

Coming out from the shade of the trees, Cámara walked past a kilometre-long line of grey plastic portable toilets before crossing a bridge and descending into the old river bed itself, once the home of the unpredictable waters of the Turia and now an arch of parkland around the city centre. Wending his way through the multitude, almost all wearing yellow-and-white caps and sipping bottles of water handed out for free by Town Hall and Church volunteers, he used his police badge to cross the various checkpoints designed not only to protect the Pope, but to separate the audience into categories of 'ordinary', 'special' and 'very special'. Cámara was looking for the 'very special' section.

He was pointed in the direction of an area cordoned off close to the main platform, which had been constructed on top of a bridge crossing the old river bed. Next to it, a temporary white cross, thirty-five metres high, towered above them. The Pope himself had yet to arrive, but all seats were taken and proceedings were about to begin. Cámara climbed up an incline to arrive at a gateway manned by two *Policías Nacionales*. Cámara didn't have an invitation, and the timing was strange. But he outranked them.

José Manuel Cuevas was sitting at the end of the third row, wearing a dark suit with a white shirt and a black-and-ochre striped tie. A silver pin in his jacket lapel seemed to denote membership of some fraternity – religious, probably – but Cámara couldn't make out the detail. His short greying hair was slightly out of place owing to a moderate breeze that was mercifully blowing in from the sea. Unlike most of the others present, with their fixed smiles of anticipation, he had a more pinched expression, his lips tight, his eyes reflecting something more like anxiety than joy.

Sitting next to him, in a grey suit, his skin tanned to a deep bronze and his hair dyed black, was Javier Gallego, the editor of *El Diario de Valencia*.

Cuevas looked suspiciously at Cámara's badge as he introduced himself.

'You want to talk to me *now?*' he said.

On his other side, Gallego took a while to notice that something was going on, but then turned his attention on Cámara, looking at him as though trying to remember who he was.

'This is important,' Cámara said. 'I'm conducting a murder investigation.'

Cuevas sat immobile; Gallego indicated the still-empty papal platform in front.

'*Pero, hombre,*' he said. 'This can wait. We're here to see the Pope.'

'I'm investigating the murder of Pep Roures,' Cámara insisted. 'He used to own the La Mar restaurant.'

Cuevas looked ahead, ignoring him.

'In El Cabanyal.'

'If this is something to do with the El Cabanyal project,' he said with a sigh, 'then you'd better talk to my aides. We do these things through the usual channels, not by charging up to someone on a day like this. I'm afraid I can't help you.'

But Cámara didn't budge.

'Valconsa is responsible for the bulldozing of the El Cabanyal area,' he said.

'Very good, er, Chief Inspector. Didn't you hear me the first time?'

Gallego was still staring at Cámara as he dipped a hand into his jacket pocket and pulled out a mobile phone.

'I'm calling your superiors,' he said. 'What did you say your name was?'

'Cámara. Chief Inspector Maximiliano Cámara, of the *Grupo de Homicidios.*'

Cuevas turned around, as though looking for someone he might call over to eject the intruder. But the policemen were smart enough to have their backs to what was going on. Disturbed glances from the others sitting in the VIP area were equally unsympathetic.

'Valconsa,' Cámara continued, 'was also responsible for building the block of flats that collapsed the other day in the Ruzafa area.'

'What?' Cuevas spluttered. 'You're talking to me about some place that was built, what? Fifty years ago?'

'Fifty-seven years ago,' Cámara said. 'By your company.'

'What's going on?' Cuevas said. 'Would you mind getting to the point. Look, the Pope's meant to be arriving any minute.'

Beyond him, Gallego was holding his phone but had yet to dial a number.

Cámara pulled out a clipping from the newspaper showing photos of a young woman and a little baby boy.

'These people were killed when your building fell on top of them,' he said.

'Yes,' Cuevas said. 'It . . . yes, sad business. Very sad.'

'They were my neighbours.'

Cuevas's eyebrows twitched, and he looked back towards the empty stage. Next to him, Gallego gave an awkward cough.

'Look, what is this?' he said. 'You said this was a police matter.'

'It *is* a police matter,' Cámara said. 'We're looking to see if there's scope for an investigation into criminal negligence. Señor Cuevas may be responsible for the deaths of these two people.'

'Me?' Cuevas said. He stood up and tried to push Cámara away. 'Me responsible? You'd better have a bloody good reason for coming down here right now and throwing allegations like that around, or I warn you—'

'Valconsa was also the company contracted to carry out sewerage work on this building shortly after it was built,' Cámara said. 'Work that it got paid for by the Town Hall, but never carried out.'

'What the hell are you talking about?'

'The fact that our building wasn't connected to the drains wasn't discovered until a few weeks ago, thanks to the work on the new metro line,' Cámara continued. 'For all these years our drain water has been seeping into the ground underneath the building.'

'So it's a problem with your drains now?' Cuevas said. 'Call a fucking plumber.'

Around them, no one was saying a word. All eyes were fixed on the two men arguing while priests scrambled around the edge of the stage in preparation for the Pope's arrival. On the other side of Cuevas, Gallego was also standing up to join in. To the side, the two policemen were watching from the corners of their eyes but maintaining a distance.

'Over fifty years of waste water sitting under the building,' Cámara went on. 'Do you know what that does to the foundations, Señor Cuevas? I imagine you do, because you're in construction. It's not very good, believe me,' he said. 'The building starts to rot. Damp in the walls. Cracks start appearing. And then, one day, all of a sudden, it falls down, collapses like a sandcastle being kicked by a dog.'

Cuevas's lips were turning white, but he said nothing.

'And the biggest problem is that anyone inside at the time tends to end up like the building itself – crushed, finished, just another pile of rubble that needs to be got rid of, buried in a hole and forgotten. It's a miracle only Susana and Tomás were in there at the time. Otherwise there would be a lot more blood on you.'

Some of the people sitting nearby were starting to stand up and move away, uncomfortable both at the scene that was taking place, and of being associated too closely with Cuevas.

'The Town Hall's happy to shut down the city so people can hear a sermon about the evils of abortion, but they don't make so much of a fuss when a mother and child die because of criminal malpractice by one of their associates.'

'I know who you are.' Gallego stood up and leaned across Cuevas towards Cámara.

'You're that policeman fantasy fuck that Alicia had a while back. Hah!'

He dug Cuevas in the ribs.

'What's the matter, didn't work out in the end?' Gallego continued. 'Yeah, she told me about you. Always was one of her things. Still, I suppose she got it out of her system. Took her a while, though. She had a few other fantasies to play out first. There were a few happy faces in the fire brigade for a while, I remember. The stupid little tart. Believe me, you're better off without her. I certainly am.'

And he gave another forced laugh.

'Don't worry about this one,' he said in Cuevas's ear, loudly enough so that Cámara could hear. 'I've come across him before. We've got enough on him.'

'Look, what is this?' Cuevas said. 'I'm responsible for every death in the city now, is that it?'

'You had a motive.'

'A motive for what?'

'Señor Roures's restaurant was getting in the way of the El Cabanyal building project, which Valconsa is also involved in.'

Cuevas was trying to stifle a smile.

'Look, Chief Inspector whatever-your-name-is.'

'Cámara.'

'Right. I'm not sure what you think you're doing coming down here like this. But if you think I'd murder someone just so I could finish off some development project, then I think the heat must have gone to your head.'

The background volume from the crowd increased as word spread that the Pope was just about to come out to give his sermon: a few people gave a cheer; others clapped.

'Five years ago Valconsa made a statement saying it would begin the El Cabanyal development project by this year,' Cámara said, 'and took out restructuring loans based on that assumption. There are less than six months to go before this year ends. I imagine both your creditors and your shareholders will be getting nervous. The construction industry isn't going through its most lucrative phase at the moment. I'd say there's a lot riding on the El Cabanyal scheme.'

From the corner of his eye, Cámara caught a glimpse of white cloth as the Pope finally emerged on to the platform and moved towards the centre, his arms raised to receive the cheers of the crowd.

'I hear you built all this as well.' Cámara raised his voice, indicating the temporary structure put up for the papal visit. 'Another Town Hall project. It must help having your brother-in-law as the head of urban development.'

'Arrest me!' Cuevas shouted, his voice masked by the cheering. 'Arrest me or get out of here! You haven't got anything, so just fuck off. Another policeman playing politics. I've got whole offices of lawyers to deal with crap like this.'

From an unhealthy shade of white, the flesh around his cheeks had turned a deep burgundy.

'I suggest you start running now.'

Cámara looked around. Many of the other seats had been vacated as the faithful had stood up to watch the Pope, finding gaps between the chairs or along the adjacent passageways. Anywhere but next to Cuevas and Gallego.

Gallego was now starting to look uncomfortable; he'd put away his phone unused and was pointedly averting his gaze. Cuevas was still facing the insolent detective who had dared approach him in the VIP box. From the loudspeakers came the sound of the Pope's voice as he began to preach. Cámara turned to leave.

'Thank you for your time, Señor Cuevas,' he said. 'You've been very helpful.'

TWENTY-SEVEN

Going to Enrique's place had been a fall-back plan since the beginning. When finally he called it was as if they had been waiting all this time for him to show up.

'Where've you been sleeping? Under a bridge somewhere?'

Cámara gave a laugh as Enrique embraced him in the doorway.

'OK,' Enrique said. 'I understand; no more questions.'

As well as having green and white tiles on the outside facade, organised in an elegant zigzag design, the building's inside walls were tiled with hundred-year-old *Modernista* vegetal patterns in blues and yellows. The bright, shiny surfaces were well suited to the hot weather, giving an impression of coolness. Most of the windows were open, while the main door on to the street was left ajar, and a slight breeze was blowing through from a small patio at the back of the house that faced in the direction of the sea.

Maite, Enrique's wife, was sitting outside on the pavement in a fold-up chair talking to her neighbours, her small baby, Carlos, nursing at her breast, while her two other boys, despite it being almost midnight, were kicking a ball in and out of the parked cars a few feet away.

'Another boy!' The woman sitting at the next-door house grinned at Cámara as he passed.

'*¿Qué le vamos a hacer?*' he replied. That's the way it goes. 'I'm sure they're delighted, though, boy or girl.'

'Of course we are,' Maite said. 'A girl would have been nice. But if it's meant to be a boy, I wouldn't have it any other way.'

'I'm glad you're here at last,' Enrique said as he and Cámara stepped inside, away from the street gossipers. They passed through to the kitchen, where Enrique pulled out a couple of bottles of Mahou beer from the fridge.

'Everything arranged for tomorrow?' Cámara asked.

'Yeah, virtually,' Enrique said with a belch. 'Ceremony at the church around half twelve, then we've booked a table at La Pascuala.'

'Excellent.'

Cámara leaned back against the ledge.

'You gonna be around? In the morning, I mean.'

'Don't know. Might have to head off, then come back later on.'

'Sure. But don't be late. You're the godfather, remember.'

'OK.'

'And besides.'

'What?'

'Maite's sat you next to Marina.'

'Marina?'

'Yeah, come on. Marina. You met her last time you were over. Nice woman. Lives near here. Divorced.'

Cámara's mind was blank, but he feigned recognition.

'Oh, that Marina,' he said.

'Yeah. She likes you, you know.'

'Come on, Enrique.'

'Look, just sit down next to her and try to be nice, that's all. You might find you like her as well. Can't have you moping for ever over Almudena.'

'What? Oh . . . yes.'

'What did I say?'

'Nothing.'

They went and sat down in the patio. Candles had been placed in among the plants; it was a calm, soothing place.

'I thought the boys would be down playing near the beach,' Cámara said.

'They usually do. They used to like to hang out in all those old boatyards near, you know, La Mar.'

'What, they don't like it any more?'

'Dunno. Seem a bit scared by the whole thing. Spooked them out a bit, as though Pep's ghost was hanging around there, or something.

I don't push it. They prefer to stick around here. That's fine by me. Easier to keep an eye on them.'

Cámara's phone rang; he saw the time as he pulled it to his ear: 11:30.

'What's the matter, Torres?' he said. 'Having a late night?'

'My wife prefers it this way.'

'All right,' Cámara said. 'I shouldn't have asked. If you need somewhere to sleep . . .'

'What? You going to offer your place? Thanks, but I think I'll give it a miss.'

'You know about Pardo's bathroom suite, right?'

'I know about it. We all do. You reckon you're the only one who nips in there early in the morning to freshen up?'

'OK. I'll shut up. What's up?'

'Two things. Firstly, I found Ramón the fisherman, the one Mikel Roig mentioned had been arguing with Roures.'

'What did he say?'

'Well, according to Ramón, it was someone from Valconsa who pressurised him to start threatening Roures about his fishing lines.'

'What?'

'Yeah, he wasn't hard to crack open. Just started telling me straight away. He said that after he'd sold his house Valconsa came back to him saying that they'd given him a good deal for his property and that he owed it to them to start squeezing Roures.'

'Who from Valconsa? Who was it?'

'He didn't know. Some guy in a suit. But he'd seen him before, during the sale of the house, so he knew he was from Valconsa.'

'A fisherman on their side would have been more of a threat to Roures, I suppose. Could have shut his night-fishing operation down.'

'But we're only talking about an annoyance. Not something big enough to make him give up and sell.'

'How did he seem, this guy?'

'Frightened. I think he was expecting us. Everyone knew about him and Roures. Then Roures ends up murdered. Doesn't look great for him.'

'You think he's telling it straight?'

'He's had time to come up with the Valconsa story if he wanted to. But my gut feeling says he wasn't lying.'

'OK. What's the other information you've got?'
'I got hold of Roures's medical records.'
Cámara leaned forward in his seat.
'Go on.'
'Turns out he got a bad case of the mumps when he was sixteen.'
'Mumps.'
'Yeah.'
'And your point is?'
'If the infection spreads down to your *cojones* that's it, you're infertile for life.'
'Yes, I've heard that. But did it?'
'What?'
'Did the disease spread to his balls?'
'Says here that it did. The mumps developed into orchitis. Caused permanent damage.'
'Sounds painful.'
'It is. And I reckon that's why he and Lucía didn't have kids.'
'Hold on,' Cámara said. 'How old was he when this happened?'
'I told you. He was sixteen.'
'So he can't have been infertile then.'
'Why?'
'Because he got Lucía up the duff when he was eighteen and they had to race off to Paris for an abortion. Look, just because someone says they're infertile, or there's a chance they might be, doesn't always mean they are. Believe me, I know about these things.'
'I didn't realise you were an expert on male fertility problems, chief.'
'Look, cut the crap. Trust me, all right.'
'So why didn't they have kids then?' Torres said.
'Because of the restaurant. They were too busy keeping a restaurant going. I don't know, perhaps they decided they didn't want any after all.'
'Did she tell you that?'
'What?'
'About the restaurant, about them not having kids because of that?'
'Yes, as a matter of fact, she did.'
'Well, I suppose you've got to believe her, then,' Torres said.
He rang off. Cámara leaned back in his chair and allowed his eyes

to be captured by the flame of the candle on the ledge opposite, a trail of smoke rising as it shuddered in the breeze for a moment.

She'd lied about Sofía.

Saturday 11th July

Torres grabbed him and dragged him back out into the corridor as he stepped into the office.

'Hey, about what you were saying last night—' Cámara said.

'No time,' Torres interrupted him. 'Urgent meeting. Now. Run!'

Cámara fell into step next to him. The incident room was packed; Maldonado was standing at the front, waiting to start the briefing. He glanced up at Cámara and took a breath, as though about to utter some sarcastic comment, but saved it: there were more important things to do. And with something approaching a grin on his face, he began.

'As I speak, a rapid-response GEO team is being assembled to move in on an address in El Cabanyal.'

He looked down pointedly at his watch.

'They'll be leaving in three and a half minutes. All of us here now will be going in behind them. *Zeta* squad cars are ready outside and I've given orders for their engines to be left running.'

He lifted his head and looked one or two of them in the eye, flaring his nostrils for dramatic effect.

'This is it. We've got the tip-off we were hoping for. Sofía Bodí is being held in a house on the Calle San Pedro, number ninety-five, and we're going to get her.'

He clapped his hands.

'Come on! Let's go!'

As people rose to their feet, he called over above the hubbub and pointed at Cámara and Torres.

'You two are coming with me,' he said. Then in a lower, but still audible tone, he added to a colleague nearby, 'It's the only way I can guarantee they'll show up.'

The squad car shot off from the Jefatura in the direction of El Cabanyal, Maldonado in the front next to an officer driving, Cámara and Torres in the back. The air conditioning was switched on, but although it cooled the front passengers well enough, it failed to reach the whole of the inside of the car. Cámara pushed a sweaty finger down on the button on the door, but his window stubbornly refused to open.

'You'll be asking yourselves what this is all about,' Maldonado said, keeping his eyes on the road ahead. Cámara and Torres gave each other blank looks

'A certain Corporal Navarro of the *Guardia Civil* has confessed to being involved in the kidnapping of Sofía Bodí,' he continued.

'We're holding him?' Torres asked.

'No. He's only talking to his own people. For the time being.'

'So how . . .?' Torres started. 'Oh.'

Maldonado grinned.

'Yes, I've got someone passing on information.'

He glanced down at his mobile phone, as though expecting another text message from his *Guardia Civil* insider, and slipped it back into the holster on his belt. Then he leaned across and turned up the volume of the police radio in the centre of the dashboard; messages were coming from the central command room, and other squad cars were giving their position as they moved in towards the Calle San Pedro, but there was still no word yet from the GEO team.

'Should have arrived by now,' Maldonado mumbled to himself.

'So what's this Navarro saying?' Torres asked.

'The interrogation's ongoing,' Maldonado said. 'The most important thing is he's admitted to being involved in the kidnapping, that he drugged her, and he's given the address where he took her.'

He rubbed his hands together.

'I've tipped off the TV. If we get this right the first images will be being broadcast just as the Pope's jumping on his plane to leave. He's off in a couple of hours.'

'Has he said who else was involved?' Cámara asked from behind Maldonado's seat.

'We're getting there, Cámara,' Maldonado said. 'Don't worry. There won't be any loose ends that need tying up after this case.'

'Whose orders was he following?' Cámara insisted, ignoring the sarcasm.

'There's no obvious link to Lázaro at the moment,' Maldonado said.

'You don't know, do you? This is supposed to be some organised conspiracy by right-wingers, and all we've got is a *Guardia Civil* corporal acting on his own?'

'He was not on his own!' Maldonado shouted. 'That much is clear. This is unravelling as we speak, Cámara. Information is still coming through. In the meantime we've got a chance to find Sofía and prove that we're up to this. Or would you rather we let her sit there and rot until we put all the pieces together? For fuck's sake.'

The radio spluttered more street names and squad car numbers, but still the GEO were silent. They were on the outskirts of El Cabanyal now, moving away from the tall brick tower blocks of the more modern city development and into the narrow lanes of colourful two-storey houses. Graffiti were sprayed on many of the walls, most of them telling Emilia where she could stick her bulldozers.

'What do we know about Navarro, then?' Torres asked.

'Doesn't seem to be the brightest sort,' Maldonado said, sitting back in his seat and watching the road ahead. 'Still a corporal aged thirty-five. Joined the *Guardia Civil* straight out of school. Clean record, nothing unusual, but known right-wing sympathies – carries a keyring with Franco's face on it. But as I said, no obvious links with Lázaro or anything – hasn't served directly under him as far as we can tell.'

'So Lázaro's not involved?'

'He's not in the clear yet. We'll see what everyone has to say for themselves once we get hold of Sofía.'

The car swung into the top of the Calle San Pedro, one of the more run-down parts of El Cabanyal. Many of the houses had already been pulled down and empty spaces stood where lives had once been lived. Flashing lights were visible up ahead, and the driver accelerated.

'One interesting thing about Navarro, though,' Maldonado said as he undid his seat belt in preparation for jumping out of the car. 'He did serve under a Lieutenant José Manuel Cuevas years back. Bloke's the head of Valconsa now – the company that's trying to pull all this down.'

He placed his hand on the dashboard to support himself as the car braked hard at the edge of a group of other police vehicles. The dark GEO vans were pulled up on the other side. Maldonado got out of the car, quickly followed by the others. More police cars were coming down from behind them, and from the other end of the street. Someone handed Maldonado a loudhailer.

An officer in black GEO kit, with a helmet and body armour and a sub-machine gun strapped to his thigh, walked up to Maldonado. It was Cámara's friend, Enric Beltrán.

'Chief Inspector?' Beltrán said.

Maldonado nodded. 'Right, brief me,' he said. 'I was expecting to hear from you earlier over the radio.'

'You need to see something,' Beltrán said. He led Maldonado through the maze of police vehicles, with Cámara and Torres behind. They came out into an empty space in the street, where the rest of the GEO team were standing around with their arms crossed.

'Are you sure you got the right address?' Beltrán said bluntly.

'What are you talking about?' Maldonado said. 'I gave it to you very clearly. Calle San Pedro ninety-five.'

Beltrán grabbed him by the arm and pushed him forwards.

'Well, that's number ninety-five,' he said, pointing ahead.

Maldonado fell silent: in front of him was an open space reaching through to the next street along.

'What the hell . . .?' Maldonado muttered.

'Got pulled down two days ago,' Beltrán said. 'At least, that's what a kid riding past on his bicycle told us. And before you ask,' he carried on, 'yes, of course we've checked the other houses. Empty, most of them. There's an old lady living three doors down, very friendly, and she did invite us in for coffee, but there was no sign of your missing woman anywhere. Unless she chopped her up and fed her to her cats, of course.'

Maldonado's face had dropped, gripped by a white fear of looking ridiculous. From further up the street a television van with satellite dishes on its roof was pulling in to get some shots.

'Looks like you got dodgy info,' Beltrán said, brushing past as he walked back to his men. 'Either that or you've been seriously stitched up.'

TWENTY-EIGHT

He walked away from the police cars and television vans, passing through a gap that had once been a house, and slipped into the streets of El Cabanyal. The church was a ten-minute walk from here. He might even arrive a bit early.

Maldonado had done his best, but the truth was that the operation had been a disaster. Searches were ordered of the other houses, until almost the entire street had been covered, but nothing, no sign of Sofía, emerged. Meanwhile, teams of officers were sent around the neighbourhood to talk to residents to see if anyone had seen anything on the day Sofía had been kidnapped, leading up to the day of the house's demolition.

'Perhaps Navarro did bring her here,' the comment went among the policemen at the scene, 'but she was then moved somewhere else before the house was demolished.'

If so, who had taken her, and where? Was she even still alive?

The *Guardia Civil* had meanwhile got wind of the *Policía Nacional*'s fruitless swoop on El Cabanyal, and whoever it was who had been feeding Maldonado information from inside had fallen silent.

'They're closing ranks.'

'We'd do the same.'

'Yeah, but we're the ones looking like idiots right now. *Nos han jugado.*' They've played us along.

And so, when he got a chance, Cámara pulled away and melted into the streets; he was needed more elsewhere than here.

Para aprender, perder, ran the proverb in his mind. In order to learn you have to lose. The police had lost face. Was there anything they could gain in all this?

The Iglesia de los Angeles was set in a small square in the northern part of El Cabanyal, an unexceptional, baroque church with a brown-and-white painted facade of columns and statues. Enrique and Maite were standing outside with Carlos, their two other boys looking more subdued than the night before in their ironed shirts and black trousers.

'I haven't had a chance to change,' Cámara said as he strolled up to the family group. Enrique smiled, clearly glad that the godfather had not only arrived, but had done so before the ceremony had actually begun.

'It's all right,' he said. 'It's only a baptism after all. Not a wedding. It's a good job you and I have the same shirt size,' he joked, 'otherwise you'd still be wearing yesterday's smelly rags.'

'Yes,' Cámara said, 'I need to get myself sorted out.'

'Don't worry about it. Our sofa's got your name on it for as long as you need. And you can have as many clothes as you want. *Donde comen tres, comen cuatro*,' he added. Four can survive on the food for three people.

'Or in your case, *Donde comen cinco, comen seis*,' Cámara laughed. Six instead of five. 'You'd better start thinking about family planning soon if you don't want to fill the house up.'

'Shh,' Enrique hissed with a smile. 'The priest might hear you. He's feeling more anti-contraception than ever, what with the Pope's visit. Got to kiss the holy one's ring, apparently. And yes, I'm talking about the one on his hand.'

'It's you who's having Carlos baptised.'

'Maite wanted it,' he said with a shrug. 'What the hell, gives us an excuse for a party.'

With the other guests – members of the family, along with a few friends and neighbours – about two dozen people were gathered outside the church door, many having a last-minute smoke before heading inside.

'Who's the godmother?' Cámara said as he stubbed his Ducados out on the edge of a column.

Enrique gave him a look.

'You mean we didn't tell you?'

'Maybe you did and I forgot.'

'She's over there.'

Enrique pointed to a woman with dyed blonde hair and red-rimmed glasses, wearing a low-cut denim dress and black high heels, standing on the other side of the doorway, smiling at them.

'Max,' Enrique said, walking over to her, 'you remember Marina.'

It was a relief to get out. Rather than going through the motions, the priest had insisted on giving them the longer version of the baptism rite, with a full-blown Mass and sermon about the respon-sibilities of the parents and godparents to the baby now embraced into the bosom of the mother Church. The monotony of the man's self-importance was relieved only by Enrique singing a beautiful *nana* – a flamenco lullaby – for his new baby boy towards the end.

> *Who can tell my child about the water,*
> *With its long tail and its salt of green?*
> *Sleep, O carnation, the horse does not want to drink.*
> *Sleep, O rose, the horse is beginning to cry.*

The words were by Lorca; the great Camarón had sung it in the past.

Cámara sought the shade of a nearby tree as photos of the baby were taken in front of the church door.

'Oh, Ducados,' a voice near him said. 'Can I have one?'

He and Marina had exchanged a couple of ironic glances through the course of the ceremony, both aware that neither of them was well suited to the role of spiritual guardian that the priest was busy trying to spell out for them in Carlos's life.

'Did he specifically say we couldn't smoke?' Cámara asked.

'I'm sure it would be frowned on,' Marina said. 'Especially in the child's presence.'

'Perhaps we should turn our backs.'

'God will still see you all the same, remember. And punish you!' She widened her eyes dramatically.

'*Joder!*' Cámara laughed. 'Carry on like that and you'll end up converting me.'

'That's the plan,' she said. 'Here, give me a light, will you?'

She grabbed his hand and brought the lighter to the end of her cigarette.

'There,' she said as a trail of smoke drifted up into the tree above their heads. 'That's better.'

They were encouraged to sit together when they arrived at La Pascuala restaurant. Cámara was happy to be with her; she was fun and friendly, but in the back of his mind was a concern that there might be an imbalance in what each was hoping to get from the encounter. His head was filled with too much else to be able to consider anything more than just a few drinks and a chat. A question kept playing through his mind: what had Sofía talked about with Lucía? What had been so important that she'd sought her out and called her like that? Was it something Roures had told her when she'd visited La Mar? There was no choice: he would have to confront Lucía directly about it. Now that Maldonado's operation had run into the sand he might be able to grab a moment to go over and talk to her. But he'd like to find out from other sources, or at least find a clue from elsewhere, first. He preferred not to go in hard and cold.

Except with Cuevas. But that was for Susana and Tomás's sake.

Yes, Cuevas. His *Guardia Civil* connection with Navarro was interesting. He thought for a moment about texting Torres to get him to look into it more, before stopping himself. This was time off – a baptism party where he was the godfather. He owed it to Carlos and Enrique to forget about things at least for the next couple of hours. He needed the rest himself, anyway.

Besides, the chances were that Torres was on to it already.

He shivered, despite the heat: Torres, he realised, was the nearest thing he had to a stable relationship.

La Pascuala was more a *bodega* than a restaurant, a bar and wine cellar where they served freshly cooked food in workers'-sized portions at prices the locals could afford. Only open until lunchtime, it was packed virtually from the moment things got started at seven in the morning to around four in the afternoon, when the last of the lunchers finally made it out through the door.

'It's an El Cabanyal institution,' Marina said. 'Look at the names of the sandwiches on the board up there.'

He glanced up. The paint was faded and dirty, but he made out names like *The Republican* and *The Bribe-Giver* and chuckled to himself. More irreverent Valencian humour.

'Emilia wants to pull the place down,' Marina added. 'It's in the firing line for her development plan.'

They ate paella; the chef brought it out in an enormous flat pan and presented it to them for their approval before hauling it over to a side table where he and a helper dished it out on to individual plates.

'La Mar must be close to here then,' Cámara said. A waiter was placing a jug of *sangría* down on the table between them and he had to lean out of the way to let him through.

'Just a couple of blocks further down,' Marina said, refilling their glasses. Above their heads ancient bottles of brandy covered in thick layers of dust and grease stood in long rows along the edge of the wall. A black-and-white photograph of a local group of *pelota* players was cocked to one side where the hook from which it was suspended had come loose in the plaster.

'Enrique said you were working on the Roures case,' Marina said, moving closer to speak in his ear.

Cámara sniffed.

'It's all right if you don't want to talk about it,' she said. 'It's work. I understand.'

They ate their paella to the background clatter of a dozen other conversations around them, Cámara picking up pieces of rabbit with his fingers and teasing out bone splinters from the meat.

'He was a lovely guy, Pep,' Marina said after a while. 'I'll miss him.'

'Everyone in El Cabanyal seems to have known him, or at least known of him,' Cámara said.

'That's the great thing about this area – it's like a village. Everyone knows everyone else. Its got its bad side as well – it's hard to have secrets. But . . .' She shrugged. 'I wouldn't have it any other way.'

'Did you use to eat at Roures's . . . at Pep's place?'

'Often enough,' Marina said with a smile. 'I've known him for ever. We were at school together.'

She leaned over and looked him in the eye.

'And you know what? He gave me my first kiss!'

She giggled for a moment and then stopped, her face taking on a more serious expression.

'It's strange that,' she said. 'It makes me feel old just saying it. The man who gave me my first kiss is now dead. It's as if he's taken a tiny little piece of me with him.'

Cámara filled her glass with more *sangría*. It was getting hotter and noisier inside the *bodega*, and they were drinking it like water.

Marina was still facing him, but her eyes were unfocused as she remembered.

'It was outside the El Polp bar,' she said. 'I was sixteen. I remember because it was the day of the big march for the *Estatut*. It felt like a party. Everyone had been out on the street. We loved it – it gave us a chance to go out and get properly drunk for the first time. And we were still too young to understand, but I think it was the first time that we really felt that Franco was dead. I mean, we knew he'd died a few years before, physically, but that was when we got the sense he'd actually gone for good. Do you remember?'

She focused on him again as she was brought back to the present.

'Oh, I forgot. You're from Albacete, aren't you? And just a little bit younger than me.' She squinted her eyes at him playfully. 'But I suppose you must have been through something similar, right?'

Something must have happened, he thought to himself. He'd barely noticed. A murdered sister and a crumbling family had smothered everything, almost all of his certainties.

'Albacete isn't Valencia,' he said.

'No. No, it isn't.' She grinned.

'Was Lucía there?' he asked. 'At the bar when you got your first . . . kiss?'

'Lucía?' Marina looked surprised. 'Of course. You mean Pep's wife? Well, she wasn't Pep's wife at the time, obviously . . .'

'Yes. That Lucía.'

'Oh, yes,' she said. 'We were all there, all our crowd.'

'So she and Pep . . .'

'No, no. She didn't like redheads. She told me. Pep came over to our table. He was still wearing his *pelota* kit. I think he'd come over from practice, or a game, or something. And he was chatting to me, and then he went away to get his mates, and Lucía said, she told me, she said, "He's cute, but he's got red hair!" I think she was drunk. Didn't stop her later, though, did it?'

Cámara felt a buzzing in his pocket as his phone began to ring.

'So she and Pep . . .?' he said. 'That night?'

'No. I told you. That came later. Pep was after me that night.'

Cámara lifted his phone out, but kept looking at Marina.

'And he was very much the gentleman,' she went on. 'Only kissing.

Nothing more. I was a bit disappointed, to tell you the truth. The drink, the party, I could have done anything that night.'

The phone was insistent in Cámara's hand. He could sense the call was important and that he'd have to take it, but still he refused to look down at the screen to see who it was.

'What about Lucía?' he asked. 'What happened to her?'

'Oh!' Marina thought for a moment, as though trying to remember. 'No,' she said at last. 'She wasn't left on her own. There was a boy in Pep's group. I didn't know him. She went off with him, I think. I'm not sure now. It's a long, long time ago.'

She raised her eyebrows and smiled.

'Do you remember anything about him?' Cámara asked. She seemed to catch the tone of urgency in his voice.

'Not really,' she said. 'I don't know. Perhaps there was something about his . . .'

Her eyes went vacant as she tried to recall, and she lifted her hand to her face.

The phone was about to divert the call to voicemail. Cámara glanced down at the screen.

It was Flores.

TWENTY-NINE

Torres came running up to him as he entered the Jefatura.

'Chief, I've got something.'

'So have I.'

'OK, you first.'

They found the lift and started heading up to their office.

'Flores wants to come in and make a statement,' Cámara said once the doors closed and they were out of earshot.

'Flores?' Torres did not have the most demonstrative of faces, not least because most of it was covered in thick black hair, either from his beard or his eyebrows, but the surprise in his expression was evident nonetheless.

'In person,' Cámara said. 'I've had him on the phone just now asking for a formal interview.'

'What did you say?'

It wasn't a facetious question: they both knew from experience that Flores was not the kind of person who did anything without various other motives – ulterior or otherwise – being in play.

'I told him to come down right away, but that I would only do it here and with Pardo present as well.'

The doors pinged as they reached their floor.

'I'd like you to join us.'

'My pleasure,' Torres said. They stepped out on to the corridor, but remained standing for a moment before walking towards the incident room, where other officers were milling around.

'What do you think it's about?' Torres said in a low voice.

'Well, I don't think he's coming to discuss the arrears on my driving tax.'

'Yeah, I got that.'

'So what's your news?'

Torres glanced down the corridor, then back at Cámara.

'This Navarro guy,' he said, 'and his connection with Cuevas, the head of Valconsa. You remember Maldonado mentioned it in the squad car?'

'Yes,' Cámara said. 'What did you find out?'

'I was digging around. Maldonado was right – Navarro served under Cuevas in the *Guardia Civil*'s intelligence unit, the *Servicio de Información*, ten years back. It was the last position Cuevas had before he quit the *Guardia Civil*.'

'And walked into the job at Valconsa.'

'Right. They made him director of communications at first, but he took over as CEO five years ago. Well, look.'

Torres pulled out a paper he was holding and showed it to Cámara.

'These are the names of the other people who were in the unit with him at the time.'

There were half a dozen of them. Torres placed his finger under one of them.

'There's Navarro,' he said. He moved his finger down the list.

'And then there's this one.'

Cámara read out a name: 'Juan Antonio Guisado López.'

He looked at Torres.

'He left the *Guardia Civil* as well a few years later,' Torres said. 'Got a job in security as a driver and bodyguard.'

'Who does he work for now?'

'Cuevas's brother-in-law.'

'Cámara!' A voice called out from the other end of the corridor. They both looked round: it was Pardo.

'One other thing,' Torres said quickly. 'Maldonado didn't pick this up: Cuevas had a second-in-command. He stayed in the force. Guess who it was.'

'Who?'

'Comandante Lázaro.'

Pardo was insistent.

'Get over here,' he shouted. 'He's arrived.'

Flores's skin looked almost pale under the harsh strip lights. But the fluorescent glow only heightened the eye-watering contrast of his olive-green suit with a bright orange shirt and a chequered rose-and-lemon tie. An officer had already ushered him into an interview room, where he was sitting on his own, his hands on his lap, looking relaxed, if determined. Pardo had ensured they were put in a room where the recording equipment actually worked and would be switched on.

'Whatever this is about,' he muttered in Cámara's ear as they were about to step inside, 'forget the history between you two and let the man speak.'

Flores glanced up as they opened the door and entered.

'Three of you,' he said with a grin. 'I'm honoured.'

Cámara took a seat in front of him, Pardo sat beside him and Torres remained standing.

'You've brought the hairy one along as well, I see,' Flores nodded. 'Frightened that I might try to break out? Oh, I forgot, you're the one with the violence issues.'

'You called us, Flores,' Cámara said. 'We're here because you want this.'

'There was a bit of a bust-up at a brothel near the beach the other night, I hear,' Flores continued. 'Funny, because the description that was passed on to me of the one causing all the fuss reminded me so much of you. He even identified himself as a policeman, apparently. But you wouldn't do something so stupid, now would you? Not unless . . . No, I refuse to believe all those years in narcotics turned you into a drug user.'

'Have you come here to make accusations against one of my police officers?' Pardo butted in. 'If so, we're too busy to hear it now.'

'Oh, no,' Flores smiled. 'No, I'm not here about that. Although I do worry about your chief inspector sometimes, Commissioner. He does have a habit of getting himself into trouble. I hear there was quite a fuss yesterday at the Pope's event.'

'Ballester,' Pardo said with an impatient sigh. 'Yes, we got him. The Pope was unharmed.'

'Thank fuck for that.'

'It was Chief Inspector Cámara who pulled Ballester down,' Torres said. 'And brought him in.'

'So it speaks, does it?' Flores jerked a thumb in Torres's direction. 'Amazing.'

'*Basta de gilipolleces,*' Cámara said, clapping his hands together. That's enough bullshit. 'What are you here for?'

'Yeah, right,' Flores said. He leaned forward and laid his hands out on the table as though about to say something, but remained silent. Cámara exchanged a glance with Torres.

'You're still working it out, aren't you?' Cámara said. 'Whatever it is, you're still calculating all the possibilities and eventualities of what you're about to say. Funny to see you so unprepared.'

'Shut the fuck up,' Flores snapped. 'As you said, I'm the one who asked for this, and I'm going to take my time if I have to.'

'Señor Flores, perhaps I didn't make myself clear,' Pardo barked. 'We don't have a lot of time. Now get on with it or get out.'

Flores leaned back in his chair.

'Perhaps he's upset he's no longer the one shagging Emilia,' Torres said. 'And he needs someone to talk to.'

'Could be that,' Cámara agreed.

'No one to tuck him in at night.'

'Oh, for fuck's sake,' Flores laughed.

'That's enough!' Pardo shouted. He leaned over and grabbed Flores by the lapel.

'Start telling me something fucking interesting or I'll have you arrested!'

'All right, all right,' Flores said. 'Calm the fuck down.'

He unwrapped Pardo's fingers from their grip on his jacket and placed his hands together.

'I know,' he said, looking Cámara straight in the eye, 'that you know that someone connected with the Town Hall was receiving transcripts of the *Guardia Civil* tap on Sofía Bodí's phone.'

There was a pause.

'And?' Pardo said.

'I want to do a deal with you,' Flores said.

'There is an ongoing and urgent police operation into the whereabouts of Sofía Bodí,' Cámara said. 'If you have information that can facilitate that operation it is your civic duty to pass it on. We're not here to do deals. A woman's life is at stake.'

'Hear me out first,' Flores said.

'We've got a ticking clock,' Torres said. 'The kidnappers have said they'll kill Sofía by today if the government doesn't change the anti-abortion law.'

Cámara frowned; perhaps Maldonado hadn't been bluffing with Ballester after all.

'You want to hear what I've got to say, all right,' Flores said. 'Just run with me on this one.'

'How did you find out?' Cámara asked.

'What? About you knowing about the phone tap?'

Flores gave a self-satisfied grin.

'I'm afraid I can't tell you.'

'Right,' Pardo said, standing up. 'I've had enough. Inspector Torres, go and fetch a charge sheet. This man is wasting police time. And I've got a murder squad to run.'

He moved towards the door.

'No, no, no!' Flores said. 'Sit down, you've got it all wrong.'

Pardo didn't stop; Cámara got up to follow after him.

'It wasn't me, you see?'

Cámara paused and turned to look back at him. Pardo was already at the door, but his hand rested on the handle.

'What wasn't you?'

'Sit down, will you?' Flores said.

Cámara sniffed, then sat.

'What wasn't you, Flores?'

'It wasn't me receiving the transcripts.'

Cámara remained silent; Pardo turned back to face the room.

'I know you think it was me.'

'How do you know I found out about the transcripts?!' Cámara shouted.

'I have a contact inside the *Guardia*. Come on, Cámara, you can work that one out yourself.'

'Herrero?'

'No. Not Captain Herrero. He'll be facing the usual disciplinary measures for his indiscretion, but you don't have to worry about him. Look, it doesn't matter, the point is I knew you wouldn't believe me if I simply denied being the one receiving the transcripts.'

Pardo moved away from the door and towards the table, but remained on his feet. Still in his earlier position, Torres crossed his arms.

'You're pretty full of yourself, aren't you?' Pardo said. 'Why would we assume it was you getting the transcripts?'

'Because it's my job to know stuff. That's my role in the Town

Hall. And I know you know that. Which is why you thought I was the one reading about Sofía's phone calls. Am I right?'

Cámara shrugged.

'You are an obvious candidate,' he said.

'See?' Flores said. 'But I also knew that if I denied that you wouldn't believe me.'

Cámara didn't react.

'Hold on,' Torres said. 'I know what's coming here. You want us to do some dirty work for you, don't you.'

'I was coming to the bit about a deal.'

'That's what you were spouting on about last time you were here, getting other people to do your dirty work for you.'

Torres took a step forwards.

'We're policemen,' he said. 'We're not here to fuck around with cunts like you. I'm going to get that charge sheet.'

'Wait!' Pardo said.

'Just one thing,' Cámara said. 'Why did you come to me? Why not get in touch with Maldonado? He's your inside man with us, isn't he?'

'Maldo's useful at times, it's true,' Flores said. 'But I don't want him getting above himself.'

There was a slam of the door as Torres left the room.

'He won't be long,' Pardo said. 'Now hurry the fuck up.'

'What do you want?' Cámara asked.

Flores tapped his fingertips together.

'Silence. About this conversation.'

He took a deep breath and sighed.

'Lázaro's caused a lot of problems for all of us with his stupid investigation into the clinic,' he said. 'And things have got out of control. There's going to be a lot of fallout when this story breaks.'

'And it's going to break soon?'

'Oh, yes.' Flores leaned in.

'Why?'

'Because I'm about to tell you who was reading the transcripts of Sofía's phone calls,' he said. 'And I just want to be sure the shit lands on the right head.'

THIRTY

The problem was where to look; not only for the murderer of Pep Roures, but for the man behind the disappearance of Sofía Bodí. If he was the same person, he had killed once: had he done so again? And if not, could they get to him in time?

As it was, though, Rafael Mezquita was nowhere to be found.

'He's been tipped off,' Torres said when searches of the Town Hall and his home proved fruitless.

'Who by?'

'His brother-in-law's ex-*Guardia Civil*, isn't he?'

'*Navarro ha cantado*,' said Cámara. Navarro's told everything. 'He knew we'd be on to him soon enough. At least we got Guisado, his driver.'

And after a full half a minute of pressure, during which it was explained to him that not only would he go to jail, but that he'd lose his salary, unemployment benefit and pension too if he didn't cooperate, Juan Antonio Guisado had also sung for them. And unlike Navarro, who had only been interrogated by his own people so far, Guisado had fallen into the hands of the *Policía Nacional*, who were all too happy to be able to get their teeth into a member of the *Guardia Civil*. Although not literally, at least not quite.

Guisado had told them everything as quickly as he could: how Mezquita had told him to kidnap Sofía and take her to an address in El Cabanyal. A new campaign, Mezquita had told him, was about to begin against the left-wing liberalism that was corroding the conservative, Catholic values the country was built on. If the government in Madrid wanted fully to legalise abortion, they would have to face the consequences. Guisado was given a chance to be there at the start of a new beginning for Spain, to have a crucial early role in what would snowball into a mass movement, turning the clock back and restoring the decency that had once prevailed. Kidnapping Sofía Bodí was just the first step in a concerted strategy that would quickly take root across the rest of the country. Guisado was to play a vital, initial part for this large, nationwide, but very secret body.

So it seemed it had been Mezquita's idea to make the kidnapping look like an arrest by the *Guardia Civil*, knowing that thanks to Lázaro's investigation into Sofía's clinic, and the high profile the case had, this was likely to arouse fewer suspicions. At least initially. Guisado had fallen for it, getting in touch with his old *Guardia Civil* colleague Navarro. Your chance to play a part in making history, mate. Navarro had provided the car and a uniform for Guisado.

Sofía had looked nervous, and ruffled, Guisado said, but hadn't struggled in any way, assuming that her kidnapping was in fact the arrest she had long feared coming. A blow to the back of the head had blacked her out, then once they'd got her into the abandoned house on Calle San Pedro, chaining her to a pillar in the attic, they'd injected her with a barbiturate to keep her unconscious. A bottle of water, and some bread and sausage, were left nearby for when she regained consciousness. And a bowl for pissing and shitting. They didn't have to worry, Mezquita had told Guisado. Their job would finish there. Someone else would come later and take over once they'd left.

Hadn't anyone seen them going into the house?

That part of the street was virtually deserted, especially in the heat of the daytime. Only a few junkies looking for shady corners to jack up.

But less than two days later the house had been demolished, as Mezquita, the head of urban development, would have known. There was no one in the house when the bulldozers moved in: a preliminary check was routine, even when dealing with places that were almost falling down on their own, and the technicians at Valconsa had confirmed this. So Sofía had been moved elsewhere, presumably by Mezquita himself.

Where either of them was now, however, remained a mystery.

While everyone was put on alert, running up and down the corridors, jumping in and out of squad cars as they followed up reported sightings or possible leads, Cámara sat in his office, staring out the window, his hands held together, twisting gently from side to side.

It was time to stop. Do nothing. Not even think. Just let what he already knew rise to the surface.

'Chief!'

It was Torres at the door.

'Emilia's holding a news conference on TV. Mezquita's been sacked with immediate effect and she's saying she'll cooperate fully with the police investigation.'

'OK. Thanks.'

'We're moving in now on Mezquita's parents' house. You coming? Get a chance to meet his old fascist father.'

'You go ahead.'

Torres didn't argue; he'd seen that meditative, pregnant expression on Cámara's face before.

He closed the door behind him, muffling the sound of urgent feet outside.

Maldonado had been right – almost. There *was* a GAL-type organisation behind Sofía's kidnapping, but only in Guisado and Navarro's minds. There the conspiracy ended; it was no more than Mezquita's invention to make them take the first step on his behalf in what was a purely personal, grubby affair.

First Roures, then Sofía. Mezquita was the link between the two.

How would Roures have worded it? His phone records had shown that he'd called Mezquita's office. Was it a straightforward blackmail attempt?

You're head of urban development now, Mezquita. You can stop all this, you can stop them bulldozing my home and my restaurant, what I've spent my life building up. You can stop the barbaric demolition of a great swathe of this historic barrio.

Because if you don't, I'm going to tell everyone your little secret. Now, just as the Pope's arriving.

But Mezquita was supposed to be the man who would finally implement the El Cabanyal development plan after years of being bogged down in the courts and the sex scandal that had crippled his predecessor. He was Emilia's new star, perhaps even her new lover after Flores had fallen out of favour. He wasn't about to turn Town Hall policy on its head. This was Emilia's pet project, her chance to leave a stamp on the city she had begun to regard as her own personal fiefdom. There was no way out.

Ultimately, he suspected the problem hadn't been about El Cabanyal in Mezquita's mind. Cuevas was right: you didn't murder someone over a demolition project, no matter how damaging that might be. What troubled him was the prospect of losing face, and being made to look a fool.

The Pope was about to arrive in order to head the World Families Conference, with its strictly anti-homosexual, anti-abortion message. And if, on the morning his plane touched down at Manises airport, news broke that a leading member of his welcoming committee had arranged an abortion himself years back for a child he had conceived out of wedlock?

Stop the demolition, Roures would have said, or your secret's out: it was your child Lucía aborted in Paris back then, not mine.

Good old Roures. Mezquita had said how Roures had felt indebted to him after breaking his nose. Did Roures feel that he'd redeemed himself by sorting out Mezquita's complicated problem for him? Whisking Lucía off and pretending that *he* was responsible? Certainly Mezquita's right-wing, conservative family, with strong links to the dying Francoist regime, would have been unsympathetic. Mezquita was young and ambitious back then, already a member of the far-right Falangist FES movement. He wasn't going to marry some girl from El Cabanyal that he'd slept with. An abortion was the only option available. And in the circumstances, he probably had no one else to turn to.

So Roures had stepped in, driving Lucía up to Paris in his Renault 5. Perhaps it was the kindness he showed her then that had changed Lucía's mind about redheads. Accompanying a girl to carry out an abortion wasn't an obvious way to start a relationship, but he could imagine Lucía craving another person's sympathy at that time, someone she was familiar with, someone from El Cabanyal. They shared a secret themselves after that. In a tightly knit community, it could be enough to draw two people together.

But in the end Roures had decided to break his debt of honour with Mezquita and played his strongest hand – his only hand. Had he not expected some kind of backlash? Perhaps faith in the rightness of his cause had blinded him to the danger he was putting himself into.

For a moment, Cámara felt the blood throbbing in his neck as he imagined the murder taking place. There was something botched about it, Quintero had said. What had Mezquita done? Looked up a web page on how to stab someone from behind? They could check his computer later.

Roures had been removed, and the threat had been eliminated.

Except that it hadn't. Not entirely. Sofía Bodí had carried out the abortion all those years before. Trained in Paris, at the very clinic Roures had driven Lucía to. There was no reason for her to have known then who the real father was. Or subsequently, even. Besides, Mezquita was still just a teenager in the late seventies, not the rising Catholic politician he was today. But what if she found out? That was Mezquita's problem – the rot could easily spread. What if Roures had told her before Mezquita murdered him?

And he almost certainly had. Ballester had mentioned Roures talking to Sofía when they'd gone to eat at his restaurant. What would he have said?

You and I have a common enemy. There's something you need to know.

Mezquita hadn't known about that, but the fear that the two of them might have spoken at some point would have haunted him. He couldn't walk up to Sofía and ask her, though; if he was to regard her as a threat he needed some way of finding out what she knew.

The phone tap.

It had been clear once Flores started talking that he didn't know everything, despite his air of omniscience, but he was aware that Mezquita was involved in the Sofía case in some way, and that his receiving the phone tap transcripts was damning in itself. As head of the committee in charge of the papal visit, Mezquita had insisted he be given a copy for security reasons: the pro-abortion lobby, he argued, might be planning to stage something while the Pope was in the city. The phone tap was already in place. It would be irresponsible of him not to take advantage of an important source of information like that.

The excuse had been taken at face value at the time. Only Flores had had his doubts.

The Pope had been and gone. Then Navarro was arrested. Flores saw which way things were about to fall. And helped push them along, against the interests of his Town Hall rival.

Cámara wondered for a moment if Flores had been back at Emilia's side during the news conference.

He stopped circling in his chair and stood up. A small patch of sky was visible from his window and he stared at the irregular shape of cloudless space formed by the edges of the nearby buildings. From one end, high above, the vapour trail from an aeroplane was slowly streaking a double white line in its wake, cutting across his little azure parcel and splitting it in two.

His eyes jerked to the side: another plane had appeared and was moving in at the same time, almost at right angles to the first. With a frown he realised that the two were on a collision course, that in a matter of seconds they would crash into each other.

He held his breath and watched: the two planes crossed paths almost directly above his head, merged into one . . . and then continued along their respective routes, unharmed, the vapour trails hovering motionless behind them now in an 'X' shape.

He smiled. From where he stood down there near the ground he'd been right: to all intents and purposes they were about to crash. Only his perspective had been wrong: what he couldn't see was that one of the two planes had been flying at thousands of feet higher than the other. There was never any collision course to begin with.

But he'd been blind to that.

There was no one to bother him as he walked down the corridor to take the lift: almost everyone was out trying to locate Mezquita – and Sofía. The fire exit at the back on the ground floor was left permanently half-open these days to allow smokers quicker access in and out. And the air conditioning in the building was so poor it barely made a difference if hot humid summer air was allowed to waft inside.

He pulled out a cigarette and lit it, leaning against a white cement pillar as his eyes lazed on the scattered remains of a thousand other smokes that had taken place out here.

What had Mezquita seen in the phone tap transcripts? He'd seen the one thing he'd hoped never to see: proof of contact between Sofía and Lucía Bautista. Two women who had only met briefly once thirty years before, now convening at Sofía's insistence after she called the clinic back in Paris to double-check what Roures had told her, and what her diaries said – that Sofía had given Lucía an abortion. There was only one thing they had to talk about, one thing they had in common. Did Lucía confirm to Sofía that Mezquita, not Roures, got her pregnant?

He had to assume that she had, for Mezquita had then seen Sofía on television, making a statement in the wake of the Lázaro investigation, commenting on her past, her time in Paris, and 'consequences' if the harassment continued. 'Right-wingers also abort,' she said. Maldonado had been right – it was a threat. But not to the people he imagined.

And so Mezquita had put in his plan to have Sofía kidnapped, another attempt to stop the spread of the rotting infection. Guisado and Navarro had played their parts well. Until Navarro had cracked.

What was the idea? To keep her locked away for the duration of the Pope's visit, to prevent her making embarrassing public comments about Mezquita? But the Pope had left a couple of hours before. If Mezquita hadn't killed her already, they had very little time to get to her first.

Now at least they knew who they had to find. They just didn't know where to look.

The cigarette was burning low and beginning to singe the skin on his fingers. He cast his mind back to his conversation with Mezquita when the Pope had visited his street.

Don't think about it, part of him was saying. Just let the thoughts come.

But there was nothing, no clue. Just a fairly straightforward chat. Mezquita had seemed helpful and genuinely concerned.

He stubbed the cigarette out and went to step back inside. Close by were the stairs leading down to the cells in the basement. Ballester would still be down there, he imagined, all but forgotten in the chase to find Sofía, another victim of the country's illiberal laws on detainees' rights. He wondered for a moment about heading down to tell him about the morning's developments, but stopped himself: better not give the man false hope; they didn't know yet whether Sofía was alive or dead.

Ballester. Part of him understood what had led him to lash out at the Pope like that. Not that he had anything against the Pope. Not really. But the sense of rage, of helpless, nihilistic rage. He knew, because he had it in him himself. It was what separated him from Alicia.

He had seen the disgust in Mezquita's face as they hauled Ballester away. Ballester at least gave wild, uncontrolled release to his anger. Mezquita had been nursing his, building it up, even. Had he ever forgiven Sofía for killing his child – even though he himself would have demanded the abortion?

He stopped still. There was something of himself in that image. How had he felt towards Alicia? Anger, frustration. But as she'd said – not so much at the loss of the child, but at not being able to resolve an irresolvable situation. And over time the anger had begun to fester, until he'd become infected by it.

He breathed deeply as he saw how close he'd been to becoming a reflection of the man he'd been searching for.

What had Mezquita uttered as they dragged Ballester away from the security men?

He was the lover of Sofía, the lover of – it was a curious phrase – *'l'anti-mare'*, 'the anti-mother'.

The phone slipped from the sweat on his fingers as he tried to dial a number.

'Torres. Get over here right away. I know where she is.'

THIRTY-ONE

A greasy black cloud was ballooning up from the restaurant as they braked hard and Cámara leaped out. The police cordon still wrapped around the door was beginning to melt and flames were visible licking at the upstairs windows.

Torres had already spoken on his phone to raise the alarm.

'I've got to go in,' Cámara called.

'No!'

'Sofía's in there!'

He pulled off his jacket to wrap around his hands so he could touch the door, but before he reached it Torres had wrestled him to the ground.

'You'll be burnt alive.'

'Let me go, you bastard. She's in there.'

But Torres only tightened his grip harder, wrapping his arms and legs around Cámara's torso till he could barely breathe.

Immobilised, and with his face pressed hard into the pavement, Cámara stiffened as the acid smell from the fire filled his nostrils. Tears were falling down his nose and he coughed, a hacking, sickened cry rising up from his guts. A few days ago he could barely have cared for the fate of Sofía; now he would throw himself into the blaze just to see if she was in there.

He was strong, and although Torres was no wimp, Cámara could probably throw him off if he drew up enough force, but a weakening resignation seemed to be descending on him. And as long as Torres sensed Cámara might throw himself in there, he wasn't going to loosen his hold.

Cámara could hear the first sirens racing in towards them now, growing steadily louder until they drowned out the humming, cracking sound of the fire. The hardness in his body began to lessen. By the time he realised he could move again, Torres had already stood up and was briefing the wave of policemen surging in in the firemen's wake.

He leaned against one of the squad cars, his back to La Mar as he heard the sound of the front door swinging open and firemen running in. There was a cruel, evil irony to Mezquita coming here. La Mare, people had called it – the mother, as though it were some kind of birthplace. Where else would he want to take the woman who threatened him now – the woman who had aborted his unborn child?

Someone was pushing a bottle of water into his hand. He lifted it to take a gulp, then poured the rest over his head, as though trying to rid himself of the putrefaction of the scene.

A few yards away Torres was talking to the fire chief, nodding. He spied Cámara and walked over to him.

'They've found one body,' he said. 'It's a female.'

Flecks of ash were beginning to fall from the sky. Cámara wiped them from his face where they were sticking to his wettened skin.

'Sofía,' he said flatly.

'Almost certainly.'

Had she been killed first? Dear God, let her not have burnt to death.

'Just one body?' he said.

'Yes.'

He gave a start.

'Get in the car!' he shouted.

He broke into a sprint as he rushed across the street, Torres following close behind.

'We might just make it.'

There was only one other place in his mind that Mezquita might go, one other mouth, in his desperation, that he needed to silence.

It took them less than five minutes to get there, racing across to the other end of El Cabanyal. The door to Lucía's house was open and the old neighbour from across the street was peering in suspiciously.

Cámara pulled her as gently as he could away from the doorway.
'We're from the police,' he said.
'I know you,' she said, startled.
'Is Lucía in? Please, it's very important.'
'I can smell smoke,' she said.
'Yes, there's a fire. It's under control. But right now I need to know if Lucía's in there.'
'I don't know,' she said, pulling away from his grip on her arm.
'But you were looking in through the door,' he said.
'She's my neighbour. There's nothing wrong with—'
'*Señora,*' he interrupted her. 'This may be a matter of life or death. Why were you looking through her door? Did you see something? Something unusual?'
'I just wanted to see who that man was,' she said, looking away. 'Never seen him before. Thought he might be one of your lot. Just walked in. We've got to be careful. There's been robberies round here.'
'Is he still in there?'
'What?'
The old woman was beginning to look disturbed, her hands shaking.
'Did you see him leave?'
'No. I thought, I don't know. I just wanted to see . . .'
Torres had already pulled out his service weapon, and was poised at the door and waiting for Cámara's nod. Cámara edged up to the other side of the doorway, signalling for the neighbour to back off to the other side of the street, but in the confusion, she didn't understand. At that moment a younger woman carrying shopping bags came around the corner. Cámara waved to her; she saw Torres's gun, the two men poised outside Lucía's door, and in an instant took in the situation. Dropping her bags where she stood, she ran over and escorted the old woman away.
Cámara took a breath; they could either do what they were expected to do: stand here and call for backup, another GEO team, perhaps even get Beltrán with a bit of luck. And arrive too late once again.
Or they could do what they should do: go in now.
He pulled out his own pistol, looked across at Torres, then in a low voice counted: *uno, dos, tres.*

The front room was empty. Torres came in behind him and searched the bathroom to the side as Cámara kept his gun trained on the entrance to the patio at the back of the house. Nothing, either in the tiny bedroom, or the kitchen next to it, although a drawer full of chopping knives had been left open. Cámara signalled a flight of stairs leading up to the next floor. Torres took over watching the back exit as Cámara crept up the steps, keeping his head as low as possible.

The first bedroom was empty, as was the bathroom next to it.

He sensed the blood before he saw it, an earthy, metallic smell.

Lucía was sitting on the floor of the second room, propped up against the side of the bed, eyes closed, face pale grey, a deep gash just above her breastbone. She'd lost litres of blood already and it was coursing in rivulets across the tiled floor.

'Torres!'

But putting pressure on the outside of the wound itself wasn't enough. Torres ran in and pushed Cámara aside.

'It's deeper inside,' he said. 'I've got to find her artery.'

Without pausing for breath, he slid two fingers of his right hand deep into the wound.

Lucía opened uncomprehending eyes for a moment, then they closed again.

Cámara had already pulled out his phone and was calling for an ambulance.

'I've found it,' Torres said. 'I think I've found it.'

Cámara hesitated. Torres was holding Lucía against him, taking her weight and keeping her upright.

'You can't do anything else here,' he said. 'Go!'

Cámara paused, then raced down the stairs, his feet slipping from where he'd stepped in Lucía's blood. Pausing at the bottom, he quickly wiped his hands and gun handle dry on the tail of his shirt, then resumed his search.

Outside in the patio, a roof tile had fallen and smashed to the floor.

He ducked to the side of the glass door leading out, fell down on his ankles, and glanced upwards.

Nothing.

Holding his pistol firmly in his hand, he took a breath, and then shot out into the open.

The tail of a shadow passed out of view up above.

A windowsill served as a step up. He stuffed his gun into the back of his trousers and lifted his foot on to the ledge, reaching up to some iron railings spiking out from the sides. Within a few seconds he was up on to the lower section of a sloping roof.

Away to the left, he heard the loosening and cracking sound of more tiles as feet scampered away over neighbouring houses. He stood up and started following, his ankles bending sharply as his shoes got stuck in the ruts.

As he moved slowly upwards, an earthen red landscape of rooftops came into view like an undulating patchwork, some flat, others cascading down to the street or to more patios like the one he had just climbed out of. Three or four houses further on, he spotted the *torre-miramar* rising up another four metres or so above the height of the surrounding buildings.

Mezquita was skipping along a ridgeway only a few yards distant. Seeing that Cámara had almost caught up with him, he sped across to a nearby terrace, gripping on to the railings and hauling himself up. Cámara made chase, feeling the roofs creak and bend under his feet as he charged across.

Mezquita had miscalculated, though: on the far side of the terrace was a steep drop to a courtyard patio. Cámara managed to reach the edge and lift himself over on to the flat roof before Mezquita was able to find a way off.

The two men faced each other. The kitchen knife that had moments ago plunged into Lucía's breast was flashing silver and red in Mezquita's hand. His face was stained with crimson droplets where the pulse of her severed artery had spat at him. There was a smell of petrol about him, no doubt from the fuel he had used to set La Mar on fire earlier, and his eyes had the dulled, black stare of a man divorced from any human spark. He had killed once that day, perhaps twice, and in the surging heat of his escape he was more than capable of killing a third time.

Cámara felt the icy rush of blood through his veins: this was what he wanted, this was what part of him was always seeking – a bloody fight. The gun was nestling in the small of his back, and he knew that faced with a man with a knife – a man taller and longer-limbed than he was – he should reach out and draw it on him. But there was a hesitation there: to fight this man and beat him, even though unarmed? A swaggering, animal arrogance overcame him for an instant: he could do this; he didn't need any gun.

But the momentary uncertainty had made him pause, and in that second Mezquita launched himself at him. Cámara took a step to the side as the blade came swooping forward in a vicious, rapid thrust. Mezquita was quick, lashing out in a series of wild swipes and cuts, aware himself that his strength lay in the weapon in his hand: Cámara was obviously strong; he had to wound or kill him at arm's length.

Cámara ducked and parried as best he could, slapping the knife away while trying to get a grip on Mezquita's wrist, but he had been backed up against the terrace railings and was in danger of getting cornered. Blood was beginning to flow from the cuts in his hands where he had caught the point of the blade, and still Mezquita kept coming at him. It was impossible to think of a counter-attack, of kicking his shins, or using his knee against his torso: all attention had to be focused on the knife, and not getting caught on the end of it.

Cámara's feet slipped and he fell on the ground. Mezquita tried again for a mortal thrust, but Cámara fended him off with his feet. It worked, for a second. Mezquita would take only a moment, however, to realise that Cámara's feet and legs could now be a new target. And it was only a matter of time before he stabbed him well enough to disable and then murder him.

Never taking his eyes off the knife, Cámara reached around him for something he could use against Mezquita. The gun was trapped between his back and the ground, but at least he might find a loose tile or some rusty wire lying around – something he could throw at him and win a precious second in which to draw his pistol.

What a stupid way this would be to die, he thought to himself. Why, people would ask themselves, if he had a gun, didn't he use it? Faced with an imminent end, he was no longer sure himself.

His hands and arms were wet with blood, and although he kicked out as hard as he could, his lower legs were now beginning to suffer from Mezquita's lashing out. No giving in, no sense that this fight was over, but he was losing, perhaps had already lost. Images began to flash through his mind and he pushed them away: no, these were not his final moments, he told himself, no reliving his life.

But one face kept repeating itself, forcing its way in.

Alicia.

Hot tears were squeezed from his eyes as the panic began to take hold. Mezquita was tiring, but his thrusts were getting stronger, harder. The floor was spattered now from the cuts in Cámara's calves and shins. Once he reached up to the thigh, and the femoral artery, it would be over.

BANG!

There was the crack of gunshot. Mezquita stopped and looked up from the panting Cámara lying at his feet. A voice called out.

'Police!'

It was Torres.

Mezquita pulled away as the sound of feet pounding over the tiles came from behind. Cámara tried to roll over and reach for his pistol, but his hands could hardly grip it as layers of shredded skin caught in the fabric of his clothes.

Another shot.

He looked up and saw the figure of Mezquita climbing over the railings and taking off once again over the rooftops.

Seconds later, Torres was beside him, pulling his shirt off and wrapping it around the wounds on Cámara's arms.

'Don't bother with me,' Cámara said. 'Get him!'

Torres paused for a second, seeking and finding the assurance in Cámara's eyes, then pulled himself over the railings and headed after Mezquita.

Cámara rolled on to his front, pulling at Torres's shirt with his teeth to tighten the pressure on his bleeding cuts. He felt thirsty and cold, unable even to stand up as he lay in a streaky pool of his own blood.

His pistol had fallen from the back of his belt and lay on the rooftop in front of him.

Mezquita raced away and was scattering roof tiles in his wake as he passed over first one, then another house. Torres chased after, pausing a couple of times to take aim with his gun, but unable to make the shot.

The *miramar* tower rose up from the third house along. Mezquita leapt towards it, stuffing the knife down the front of his trousers and catching hold of the bottom of a glassless window. Finding weather-worn holes in the brickwork, he began lifting himself up, his long arms and legs allowing him to scale the outside like a mountain goat.

Within a few seconds he was up on the top of the tower.

Behind, Torres halted again, holding his pistol to shoot.

'Stop!' he cried. 'Stop!'

Mezquita looked around at him, then back over at the sight of the bleeding Cámara lying on the terrace roof.

Cámara pulled the cloth from around his hand and picked up the gun.

Shooting straight is simple but not easy.

He's already dead, he thought.

The shot rang out as Mezquita fell forwards and off the tower.

The solid, muffled thud of his body hitting the tarmac resounded from the street.

Silence.

Then a scream.

THIRTY-TWO

A Few Days Later

Lucía lived.

Torres's intervention, thrusting his fingers into her wound and pressing on the artery, gave her enough time before medics could arrive and take over. She lost three litres of blood, but was saved by having a common blood type which made receiving a massive transfusion that much simpler.

Once she was stable, and could be interviewed by police officers, she confirmed that Mezquita had been the real father of the child she'd aborted back in 1977. Roures was the only other person who knew, and in all these years she'd never mentioned it to anyone until she received a phone call from Sofía Bodí, asking her to confirm what Roures had told her shortly before he was murdered. Even then she was reluctant to say anything, but her ex-husband's death had disturbed her, and in the end she had given in to Sofía's insistence.

Less than a week after being stabbed, she was able to leave hospital, and a brother and his wife came to look after her at home. In El Cabanyal she was received like a returning heroine. The neighbourhood was still going through difficult times and needed a cause for celebration.

Lying in hospital, Cámara saw pictures on the television of the large demonstration through the streets of the city in protest at Sofía's death. The charred corpse inside La Mar was identified as hers:

Mezquita had stabbed her in the abdomen repeatedly with one of Roures's knives.

Mezquita himself had died virtually on impact after falling from the *torre-miramar*. Cámara's shot had hit him in the lower back. The subsequent fall had almost killed him, while the knife thrust into the front of his trousers had been pushed deep into his groin, causing serious blood loss. He was dead before ambulance men could get to him.

There was no protest or march in his memory. Flores had already begun a Town Hall campaign to distance Emilia and her councillors from him in a swift and ugly damage-limitation operation: further allegations against him were brought out, including that Mezquita had taken kickbacks from construction companies for projects carried out in the city – although not, surprisingly, from Valconsa. The idea, however, was to show that the Town Hall was glad to have had the chance to distance itself from this one. The rest of them were entirely clean.

Meanwhile, members of Mezquita's church refused point blank to believe any of the story, insisting it was a conspiracy to bring the anti-abortion movement into disrepute. For his part the Pope didn't comment, but a Vatican official issued a bland statement lamenting recent events in Valencia, but affirming the Holy See's opposition to abortion and gay weddings as dangerous threats to the institution of marriage. Despite this, however, few churchgoers showed up for Mezquita's funeral, which was attended by his wife, a priest, and only a handful of acquaintances. Neither his sister, nor her husband, José Manuel Cuevas, was there.

Rafael Mezquita, the rapidly rising star, had turned out to be just a passing, brightly burning comet, now extinguished in the mother-waters of the horizon.

From his bed, unable to still his imagination, Cámara meditated on what the probable outcomes of the case were likely to be.

No firm link, he thought, would be established in the end between the Roures case and José Manuel Cuevas. Cuevas, the former *Guardia Civil* intelligence officer, would be able to throw up enough doubt in people's minds about how close he'd actually been to Mezquita. Valconsa would continue its position as the number-one construction firm in the Valencian region, principally engaged in public works, with Cuevas as its CEO for many years to come.

Corporal Navarro would get anything up to six years for his part in the kidnapping of Sofía Bodí. He'd be released after two and a half years, and probably get a job with a security firm.

Juan Antonio Guisado, Mezquita's driver and Navarro's former colleague, would also be condemned for the kidnapping, but would get a harsher sentence, perhaps ten years.

A *Guardia Civil* inquiry would be launched into Lázaro's investigation into *La Clínica Levantina de Salud Ginecológica*. It would conclude that Comandante Lázaro's conduct throughout had been justified and entirely honourable.

Frustrated in his job, and unhappy at the punishment he'd received for passing on confidential information to the *Policía Nacional*, Captain Herrero would leave the *Guardia Civil* shortly after the events of the Sofía Bodí case, and take a job in the port authority.

Javier Flores would return to his position as Mayoress Emilia Delgado's right-hand man in the Town Hall.

With Mezquita dead, Flores would ensure that the former councillor of *urbanismo* could now take the blame for the collapse of Cámara's block of flats. It had happened on his watch. No one else, either in Valconsa or the Town Hall, would ever be held responsible for the deaths of Susana and Tomás.

The members of *El Cabanyal, Sí* would continue their struggle to preserve their neighbourhood in the face of continued Town Hall attempts to pull a large part of it down.

Cámara's wounds were bad but not life-threatening. The cuts in his lower legs were healing rapidly; at worst, walking was slightly uncomfortable. For a while the doctors had feared for one of the tendons in his right hand: it had been cut, but thankfully not severed completely. However, it would take time for him to have full use of it again.

He smiled, thanked them and ignored their words, getting out of bed as soon as he could, putting his bloodstained clothes back on and insisting he be discharged. The duty doctor, happy to have one less patient to think about, obliged.

It was mid-morning, but he picked up some of the new clothes he still had sitting in a plastic bag in his office and went upstairs to let himself into Pardo's bathroom. The soap slipped from his grip as he struggled against the stiffness of the slowly scarring tissue on his palms and fingers.

Fresh towels had been laid out for him when he got out of the shower.

As he dried himself he was aware of a sense of finality. Not just from the case ending, but about his life here. He felt as certain as he could ever be that he would never stand in this bathroom again, never come back and see these green-tiled walls.

A smile formed, not on his face but in some deep part of his brain. His hunches, his intuition – they felt stronger than they had done for a long time.

As he walked towards his office, a hand reached out and grabbed his shoulder – tight, hard, unfriendly.

He knew, before turning round, who it was.

'You're up for a disciplinary.'

The blotches on Maldonado's face were rosy pink.

'That's . . . kind of you to tell me.'

'Don't think you can fucking slip your way out of this one!' Maldonado barked. 'If you'd stuck to the plan rather than going off on your own like that Sofía might be alive right now. We might have got to her.'

Cámara looked him in the eye. The allegation was absurd, but he could tell Maldonado was completely serious. His entire investigation had been ridiculed by what had eventually happened; he needed a *cabeza de turco* – a scapegoat to remove the tarnish that was in danger of sullying his reputation. Maldonado thought of only one thing: moving up. His concern for Sofía was perfunctory, not heartfelt. Police work per se meant nothing to him. A captured drug distributor did not represent an improvement in social conditions but merely another step up in his relentless, meaningless climb towards higher pay, higher status and greater authority.

Towards nothing, in other words.

Maldonado reached over and pushed him in the chest. Solid and heavy, Cámara barely moved, but the offence was clear.

'Did you hear me?' Maldonado said. 'She's dead now because of your fuck-ups. The diaries you didn't tell anyone about, pissing off interviewing people on your own, not reporting back to *me*.'

Cámara took a deep breath; he wasn't going to let this turn into another scrap, but already a reaction, a different reaction, was starting to take form inside him.

'And you know what?' Maldonado continued. 'Someone had a look around your office.'

He shook his head in mock dismay.

'An executive member of the *Policía Nacional* with drugs on his person? It beggars belief.'

Cámara turned to go, but Maldonado reached out and pulled him back.

'You know what I think?' he said. 'I think you've been stoned on duty, that's what. There's a woman dead out there that we could have saved but didn't because you were fucking doped out of your brain. Now, some people might take pity on you, and say it was because your little house fell on your head, and you were upset about your neighbours getting crushed to death, and so you needed an escape.'

Cámara felt a spasm of pain in his right arm as his fist clenched, cracking open the still-fresh wounds. A single punch in the solar plexus would bring this man to the floor. And perhaps ruin his hand for ever.

Was it worth it?

'But I think you're just a fucking crap policeman,' Maldonado was saying. 'And you need to get fucked in order to hide that from yourself.'

Blood was beginning to seep into the bandages in his hand. He paused for a moment, then slowly allowed his fingers to relax.

He stepped away, and Maldonado's hand fell from his shoulder.

'Maldonado,' he said. 'You may be right.'

Pardo wasn't in his office, and Cámara had to find him on the top floor.

'What the fuck do you want?' Pardo hissed as Cámara interrupted his meeting with command and pulled him out into the corridor.

'I quit,' Cámara said.

'You're on extended sick leave,' Pardo hit back without blinking.

'No,' Cámara insisted. 'I'm off, I'm leaving. I'm not doing this any more.'

Pardo took a step towards him, his nose almost touching Cámara's.

'You're depressed.'

'I'm not. I haven't felt so relieved in ages.'

'You've got serious physical injuries—'

'They're just superficial,' Cámara interrupted him.

'—and they've made you depressed. I've got a doctor's note to prove it.'

'Doctor? What doctor?'

'It doesn't matter,' Pardo said. 'It's a doctor's note and it clearly states that Chief Inspector Maximiliano Cámara Reyes has got a bad fucking case of the blues and needs to piss off and sort his fucking life out.'

Cámara sucked on his teeth.

'Besides, you shot someone, you killed Mezquita.'

'He would have fallen anyway.'

'Yeah? You just keep telling yourself that. The truth is you've had your baptism; you're more of a *Homicidios* detective than you've ever been. You've got a big sin of your own to hide now.'

Cámara didn't move.

'Right, I've got to get back inside there sharp and continue covering up for the best policeman in my squad,' Pardo signalled the meeting room behind him, 'or I'm going to get it in the arse. *¿Comprendes?*'

Cámara shrugged.

'Now I would give you a kiss goodbye, but I'm in a hurry, and someone might get the wrong idea. Fuck off. I don't want to see you here for a long time.'

Torres wasn't in the office. Cámara thought about phoning, but decided against it and scribbled a short note to drop on his desk. Nothing to explain: just an apology for leaving suddenly, and a promise to call some time soon. He thought for a moment about adding that he hoped things worked themselves out at home, but decided against it. Torres was anything but sentimental, and he wouldn't appreciate words like that from his superior officer.

It was still painful and difficult to hold a pen, but he took out a form and filled it in, detailing the events in El Cabanyal. Inspector Torres had showed bravery and sound judgement throughout, saving the lives of both the civilian Lucía Bautista and Chief Inspector Cámara of the *Grupo de Homicidios*. He thought for a moment: Torres had actually saved him twice that day: first from the fire at La Mar and then afterwards from Mezquita, but he decided that the decorations board would think he was taking the piss if he mentioned both. One was enough.

Torres was a good *poli*, one of the very best. He deserved that medal.

He got up to go, taking one last look around the room. All so familiar, yet he felt divorced from it in a curious way. Was it guilt? Did he feel sullied? Pardo was right – he'd killed for the first time. Yet he couldn't feel guilty about killing someone like Mezquita.

A red leather-bound book on top of a pile of papers stood out from the usual office shades of brown, grey and grubby white.

The last volume of Sofia's diary; it was still here. He'd never got a chance to ask her about why she'd written down all those names. He picked it up and went to find an envelope to place it in. The pages fell open as he held it in his hand, and he glanced down at the familiar neat handwriting.

She had suffered. She had suffered from the moment the Lázaro investigation had started. She would have suffered when she thought she was being arrested, and when she discovered the truth that she had actually been kidnapped.

He felt a knotted swelling in his throat as images of her chained up and silenced passed through his mind.

Was it too much to pray that her death had been quick?

He scribbled Ballester's name and address on the envelope. The pages were still open, and he glanced through till he found the last entry:

> *6 July: A bad day. CB says things can't get any worse.*
> *And I try to believe him.*

THIRTY-THREE

The train station was stuffy and noisy, groups of backpackers lying in piles in the middle of the floor as they sucked on plastic bottles of water and plaited each other's hair in the lull between connecting trains.

Cámara dragged a compact dark blue wheeled suitcase behind him as he stepped into the shade of the front porch and headed to the ticket office. Sunlight was reflecting off the shiny marble floor, lighting up the mosaic designs decorating the walls, showing bucolic scenes of Valencian farmers in traditional dress picking oranges from trees.

He took a number and waited his turn. A newspaper on the floor showed pictures of the riot that had taken place the day before: Emilia's bulldozers had moved back into El Cabanyal and were ripping down more fishermen's houses. Members of *El Cabanyal, Sí* had tried to stop them, tying themselves to the railings, but had been dragged away and beaten by members of the *Policía Local*. The violence wasn't only architectural, but physical.

'*Dígame.*' The woman behind the hard plastic screen barked her command through a microphone.

'A ticket to Madrid, please.'

'Single or return?'

'Single.'

He passed his bag through security, handed his ticket to a girl in a blue-and-white uniform, and found a space on the platform. From further up the track the white sleek form of the train was coming into view.

His mobile vibrated in his pocket. Lifting it out, he pressed the button. It was a text message from Hilario.

Dentro de la concha está la perla, aunque no puedas verla, he'd written. The pearl is in the shell, even though you can't see it.

Cámara smiled as he stepped on to the train. His home – his shell – had been smashed. Now, his grandfather was telling him, was his chance to pick up a pearl of freedom nestling in the rubble.

He placed his suitcase on the rack and sat down next to the smoked-glass window.

The route would take him through the high, flat, burnt fields of La Mancha. His territory, his home.

It was dark by the time they pulled into the capital. The air was dry and hotter than on the coast, but the relief from the stickiness of the sea air made it feel cooler.

The taxi dropped him outside the front door. He found the button for her flat, pressed it and waited. Would she be in?

A pause, then the intercom crackled.

'*¿Sí?*' came a woman's voice.

'Alicia. It's Max,' he said. 'There's something I want to tell you.'

ACKNOWLEDGEMENTS

Many thanks to my friends Rafa Campo of the *Policía Científica*, policeman-cum-novelist Inspector Sebastián Roa, and Inspector Esther Maldonado of the Valencia *Grupo de Homicidios*, for passing on details of how the Spanish National Police operates. Also to Fiona Wright for getting in touch and setting things in motion.

G. and V. gave me invaluable insights into the conditions faced by ordinary Spaniards in the years before the abortion laws were relaxed. Abortion is a delicate subject, and so I won't give their full names here, but I thank them for their candour and trust.

Thanks also to Alexandre Guerrero, Sandra Ferrandez and Gisela Dombek for their support, backup, ideas and good company.

My knowledge of the Cabanyal area was greatly enhanced by meeting Maribel Domenech, Rafa Brines and Rosanna Sagnelli. Many thanks to them for helping me get to know one of the most characteristic neighbourhoods in Valencia. Sadly, as I write this, the Town Hall still has plans to knock a large swathe through the *barrio*, as described in the book. A local pressure group, *Plataforma Salvem el Cabanyal*, is fighting the project. Their website is www.cabanyal.com.

Thanks again to everyone at Chatto and Vintage for their work on, and belief in, the Max Cámara series: Clara Farmer, Parisa Ebrahimi, Alison Hennessey, Bethan Jones, Vicki Watson, Jane Kirby, Monique Corless and Roger Bratchell. Mary Chamberlain is a genius who takes almost all of the pain away from copy editing. And very special thanks, as ever, to my editor Jenny Uglow, to whom I owe so much.

My agent, Peter Robinson, has been wonderful, and I thank him for his continued support and generosity. Thanks also to Alex Goodwin, for his patience and efficiency.

Lastly, my love and thanks to Salud, to Arturo, and to Gabriel, who was already on the way.